HAVE A TASTE FOR BRITISH MYSTERY? SAMPLE THESE GOODIES . . .

"The Crime of Miss Oyster Brown"
by Peter Lovesey
Two spinster sisters live a reclusive life. But when one of them goes missing, is the other one her killer? There is ample reason for suspicion. . . .

"Strychnine in the Soup" by P. G. Wodehouse
A swain in love, even if he is a small and bookish interior decorator, may be driven to desperate measures when a parent objects to the match. So young Cyril's pursuit of his lady may tempt him to blackmail . . . or worse. Much worse.

"The Borgia Heirloom" by Julian Symons
A young American writer visits a very old lady in a very large house with hopes of getting to the bottom of a dastardly unsolved murder . . . forty years old. We can only suggest he decline an invitation to stay for luncheon.

BUT WE INVITE YOU TO SEEK THE SATISFYING PLEASURES OF ALL THIRTEEN TALES OF— MURDER

MURDER AT TEATIME

Mysteries in the Classic Cozy
Tradition from *Ellery Queen's
Mystery Magazine* and *Alfred
Hitchcock's Mystery Magazine*

EDITED BY

Cynthia Manson

A SIGNET BOOK

SIGNET
Published by the Penguin Group
Penguin Books USA Inc., 375 Hudson Street,
New York, New York 10014, U.S.A.
Penguin Books Ltd, 27 Wrights Lane,
London W8 5TZ England
Penguin Books Australia Ltd, Ringwood,
Victoria, Australia
Penguin Books Canada Ltd, 10 Alcorn Avenue,
Toronto, Ontario, Canada M4V 3B2
Penguin Books (N.Z.) Ltd, 182-190 Wairau Road,
Auckland 10, New Zealand

Penguin Books Ltd, Registered Offices:
Harmondsworth, Middlesex, England

First published by Signet, an imprint of Dutton Signet,
a division of Penguin Books USA Inc.

First Printing, January, 1996
10 9 8 7 6 5 4 3 2 1

(The following page constitutes an extension of this copyright page.)

Contents

The Name on the Wrapper
by Margery Allingham   11

The Necklace of Pearls
by Dorothy L. Sayers   33

The Crime of Miss Oyster Brown
by Peter Lovesey   45

Strychnine in the Soup
by P. G. Wodehouse   64

Murder at Rokeby House
by C. M. Chan   87

The Borgia Heirloom
by Julian Symons   142

Dr. Hyde, Detective, and the White Pillars Murder
by G. K. Chesterton   148

Policeman's Holiday
by Michael Innes   164

The Ministering Angel
  by E. C. Bentley   170

Home Is Where the Heart Is
  by Nell Lamburn   188

The Wicked Ghost
  by Christianna Brand   204

The Gallowglass
  by David Braly   219

Fen Hall
  by Ruth Rendell   254

Introduction

In this third book in our series of mysteries in the "classic cozy tradition," the stories have a common bond, the locale of England. Through each of the stories the lifestyles of the British upper class are revealed. The classic symbols of such a life present themselves in most of the stories in this collection. These include the elegant country manor with its drawing rooms, gardens, and servants, and the lavish parties thrown by the lords or ladies of such estates. Yet lurking behind the hedges and walls of these palatial residences are well-bred men and women with the basest of criminal instincts, no different from those of the criminals on the outside.

Among our impressive lineup of authors is Dorothy L. Sayers, who chooses as her setting a Christmas party at a country house in Essex during which a theft occurs. Peter Lovesey weaves a wonderful tale of two spinster sisters, one of whom goes missing while the other comes under suspicion for her murder. In Michael Innes's story, his well-known series character Sir John Appleby investigates the theft of an El Greco painting from a wealthy lord. In Ruth Rendell's "Fen Hall," a suspicious accident takes place at a country house in the woods. Julian

Symons uses an American writer sent to interview a wealthy British heiress at her country manor as a catalyst for uncovering an old murder mystery. Margery Allingham's famous sleuth Mr. Albert Campion is on another intriguing case, and G. K. Chesterton's brilliant whodunit will leave his fans captivated. Another masterful writer, P. G. Wodehouse, writes a clever and amusing story that involves the courtship of a titled lady by an avid reader of mystery whose passion for such books is the key to his winning his lady's hand in marriage.

Without any further ado I leave you to the reading of this entertaining anthology of cozies and classic English mysteries. Cheerio!

—*Cynthia Manson*

The Name on the Wrapper
by Margery Allingham

Mr. Albert Campion was one of those useful if at times exasperating people who remain interested in the world in general at three o'clock on a chilly winter's morning. When he saw the overturned car, dark and unattended by the grass verge, therefore, he pulled up his own saloon and climbed out on to the road, whose frosty surface was glistening like a thousand diamonds.

His lean figure wrapped in a dark overcoat was rendered slightly top-heavy by the fact that he wore over it a small traveling rug arranged as a cape. This sartorial anachronism was not of his own devising. His dinner hostess, old Mrs. Laverock, was notorious both for her strong will and her fear of throat infections, and when Mr. Campion had at last detached himself from her husband's brandy and reminiscences she had appeared at the top of the Jacobean staircase, swaddled in pink velvet, with the rug in her arms.

"Either that young man wears this round his throat or he does not leave this house."

The edict went forth with more authority than ever her husband had been able to dispense from the bench, and Mr. Campion had gone out into the night for a fifty-mile run back to Piccadilly wearing the rug, with his silk hat perched precariously above it.

Now its folds, which reached his nose, prevented him from seeing that part of the ground which lay directly at his feet, so that he kicked the ring and sent it wheeling down the moonlit road before he saw it. The colored flash in the pale light caught his attention and he went after it. It lay in his hand a few minutes later, as unattractive a piece of jewellery as ever he had been called upon to consider. It was a circle of different-colored stones mounted on heavy gold, and was certainly unusual, if not particularly beautiful or valuable. He thrust it absently into his coat pocket before he resumed his investigation of the abandoned car.

He had just decided that the departed driver had been either drunk or certifiably insane in the moment of disaster when the swift crackle of bicycle wheels on the frost behind him made him swing round, and he found himself confronted by another caped figure who came to a wobbling and suspicious halt at his elbow.

"Now, now, there's no use you putting up a fight. I ain't alone, and if I were I'm more'n a match for you."

The effect of these two thundering lies, uttered in a pleasant country voice rendered unnaturally high by what was, no doubt, excusable nervousness, delighted Mr. Campion, but unfortunately the folds of his hostess's rug hid his disarming smile and the country policeman stood gripping his bicycle as if it were a weapon.

"You're caught!" he said, his East Anglian accent bringing the final word out in a roar of triumph not altogether justified. "Take off your mask."

"My what?" Mr. Campion's startled question was muffled by his drapery, and he pulled it down to let his chin out.

"That's right," said the constable with a return of confidence, as his prisoner appeared so tractable.

"Now, what have you been a-doing of? Answer up. It'll be best for you."

"My good oaf—" Mr. Campion's tone was forgiving "—you're making an ass of yourself, and I should hold that bicycle still if I were you or you'll get the back wheel between your legs and fall over it."

"Now then, no names, no names, if you please, sir." The Law was showing signs of disquiet again, but the bicycle was straightened hastily. "You'll have to come down to see the inspector."

Mr. Campion's astonishment began to grow visible and convincing, for, after all, the country bobby is not as a rule a night bird of prey.

"Look here," he said patiently, "this pathetic-looking mess here isn't *my* car."

"No, I know that's not." The triumphant note crept into the constable's voice again. "I seen the number as soon as I come up."

"Since you've observed so much," continued Mr. Campion politely, "would it be tactless to inquire if you've noticed that?"

He swung round as he spoke and pointed to his own car, standing like a silver ghost a few yards down the road.

"Eh?" The Law was evidently taken by surprise. "Oh, you ran into him, did you? Where is he?"

Campion sighed and embarked on the slow process of convincing his captor that the car ahead belonged to him, his licenses were in order, and that he was properly and expensively insured. He also gave his own name and address, Colonel Laverock's name and address, and the time at which he had left the house. By way of full measure he also delivered a short lecture on "Cars and How to Overturn Them," with special reference to the one on the verge, and was finally conducted to his own vehicle and grudgingly permitted to depart.

"I don't really know as how you oughtn't to have

come along to find the inspector," said the constable finally as he leaned on the low near-side door. "You
didn't ought to have been masked. I'll have to report it.
That rug might have been to protect your throat, but
then that might not."

"That cape of yours may be buttoned up against the
cold or it may be worn simply to disguise the fact that
your tunic is loosened at the throat," retorted Mr. Campion, and, letting in the clutch, he drove away, leaving
a startled countryman with the conviction that he had
actually encountered a man with X-ray eyes at last.

On the bypass Mr. Campion ran into a police cordon, and once again was subjected to a searching inquiry concerning his licenses. Having been, in his
opinion, held up quite long enough while the police
fooled about looking for stolen cars, he said nothing
about the overturned one but drove peacefully home to
his flat in Bottle Street and went to bed. His ridiculous
encounter with the excitable constable had driven all
recollection of the ring from his head and he thought
no more about it until it appeared on his breakfast table
the following morning.

His man had discovered it in the coat pocket and,
deducing the conventional worst, had set it out with an
air of commiseration not altogether tactful; anxious, no
doubt, that his employer should remember first thing
in the morning any lady who might have refused him
on the night before.

Campion put aside the *Times* with regret and took up
the ring. By morning light it was even less beautiful than
it had appeared under the moon. It was a woman's size
and was heavy in the baroque fashion that has returned after fifty or sixty years. Some of the stones, which ran all
the way round the hoop, were very good and some were
not; and as he sat looking at it his eyebrows rose. He was
still admiring it as a curio rather than a work of art when

his old friend Superintendent Stanislaus Oates rang up from Scotland Yard. He sounded heavily amused.

"So you've been running round the country in disguise, have you?" he said cheerfully. "Like to come in for a chat this morning?"

"Not particularly. What for?"

"I want an explanation for a telephoned report which has come in this morning. We've been called in by the Colnewych police on a very interesting little case. I'm going over the stuff now. I'll expect you in half an hour."

"All right." Mr. Campion did not sound enthusiastic. "Shall I wear my mask?"

"Come with your head in a bag, if you like," invited the superintendent vulgarly. "Keep your throat wrapped up. There's nothing like an old sock, they say. Place the toe upon the windpipe and . . ."

Mr. Campion rang off.

Half an hour later, however, he presented himself at the superintendent's office and sat, affable and exquisite, in the visitor's chair. Oates dismissed his secretary and leaned over the desk. His grey face, which was usually so lugubrious, had brightened considerably as Campion appeared and now he had some difficulty in hiding a grin of satisfaction.

"Driving round the country with a topper over your eyes and a blanket round your neck at three o'clock in the morning," he said. "You *must* have been lit. Still, I won't go into that. I'll be magnanimous. What do you know about this business?"

"I'm innocent," announced his visitor flatly. "Whatever it is, I haven't done it. I went to dinner with a wealthy and childless godparent. I mention this in case your mercenary soul may not be able to believe that any sober man will motor fifty miles into the wilds of East Anglia for a meal. When I left, my godparent's wife, who once had tonsillitis as a child and has never forgotten it, lent me a small rug. (It is sixty inches by sixty inches and is of a rather lurid tartan which I am not entitled to wear.) As she will tell you, if you ask her, she safety-pinned this firmly to the back of my neck. On my way home I passed a very interestingly overturned car, and while I was looking at it a large red-faced ape dressed up as a policeman attempted to arrest me. That's my story and I'm sticking to it."

"Then you don't know anything about the crime?" The superintendent was disappointed but unabashed. "I'll tell you. You never know, you might be useful."

"It has happened," murmured Mr. Campion.

"It's a case of robbery," went on Oates, ignoring the interruption. "A real big haul. The assessors are on to it now but, roughly speaking, it's in the neighborhood of twenty thousand pounds' worth of jewellery and little boxes."

"Little boxes?"

"Snuff boxes and patch boxes, enamel things covered with diamonds and what-not." Oates sounded contemptuous and Campion laughed.

"People of ostentatious tastes?" he ventured.

"No, it's a collection of antiques," said Oates seriously, and looked up to find Campion grinning. "You're a bit lah-di-blinking-dah today, aren't you?" he protested. "What is it? The effects of your night on the tiles? Look here, you pay attention, my lad. You were found nosing round the wreckage of a car thought to have been driven by thief or thieves, and the very least you can do is to try and make yourself useful. Last night there was a bit of a do at St. Bede's Priory, about five miles away from your godpapa's place. It was a largish show, and the place, which seems to be about as big as the British Museum and rather like it, was full to bursting."

Campion stared at him.

"You're talking about the Hunt Ball at old Allenbrough's private house, I take it?" he put it mildly.

"Then you do know about it?"

"I don't know about the robbery. I know about the ball. It's an annual affair. Old Porky Allenbrough's ball is almost an institution, like the Lord Mayor's Show— it's very like that in general effect, too, now I come to think of it. I used to attend regularly when I was young."

Oates sniffed.

"Well, anyway, there seem to have been close on five hundred people gathered together there," he said. "They were all over the house and grounds, cars going and coming all the time. A real party, the local super says it was. All we know is that about two o'clock, just when the crowd was thinning a bit, her ladyship goes up to her room and finds her jewellery gone and her famous collection of antiques pinched out of the glass-fronted cupboard in the boudoir next door to her bedroom.

"All the servants were downstairs watching the fun, of course, and hadn't seen a thing. The local police decided it must have been a professional job and they flung a cordon round the whole district. They figured that a crook had taken advantage of the general excitement to burgle the place in the ordinary way. They were very smart on the job, but they didn't lay hands on a single 'pro.' In fact, the only suspicious character who showed up during the whole of the evening was a lad in a top hat with a plaid blanket—"

"What about that overturned car?" interrupted his visitor.

"I'm coming to that," said Oates severely. "Wait a minute. That car belonged to a very respectable couple who went to the dance and stayed at it. They were just going to leave when the alarm was given and it was then they discovered the car had been stolen. The gardeners who were acting as car-park attendants didn't remember it going, but then, as they said, cars were moving in and out all the evening. People would drive

'em off a little way to sit out in. It was a real old mud-
dle by the sound of it. The super told me on the phone
that in his opinion every manservant on the place was
as tight as a lord the whole evening."

"And every lord as tight as a drum, no doubt,"
added Mr. Campion cheerfully. "Very likely. It sounds
like the good old days before the Conferences. I see.
Well, the suggestion is that the car was pinched by the
burglar, who used it to escape in. What did he arrive
in? A howdah?"

Oates sat back and scratched his chin.

"Yes," he said. "That's the trouble. The police are in
a bit of a difficulty. You see, her ladyship is howling
for the return of her valuables, but neither she nor her
husband will admit for an instant that one of their
guests might be the culprit. That was the awkward
thing at the time. A watch was kept on those guests
who left after the discovery of the theft, but no one
was searched, of course."

Mr. Campion was silent for a moment.

"These shows are done in parties," he remarked at
last. "People take a party to a ball like that. Porky and
his missis would invite a hundred friends or so and ask
them each to bring a party. It's a private affair, you see,
not an ordinary Hunt Ball. Allenbrough calls it the
Whippersfield Hunt Ball because he likes to see a pink
coat or two about. He's M.F.H. and can do what he
likes, and it's a wealthy hunt, anyway. Yes, I see the
trouble. I don't envy the local super if he has to go
round to all old Allenbrough's pals and say: 'Excuse
me, but did you include a professional jewel thief in
the party you took to the ball at St. Bede's on the
twenty-third last?' "

"I know. That's what it amounts to." Oates was
gloomy. "Got any ideas? You're our Society expert."

"Am I? Well, in that capacity let me advise you that
such a course would provoke endless correspondence

both to the Chief Constable and the heavier daily Press. You're sure this was a professional job?"

"Yes. The jewellery was in a wall safe which had been very neatly cracked and the show cupboard had been opened by an expert. Also there were no finger-prints."

"No trademarks, either, I expect?"

"No, it was a simple job for a 'pro.' It didn't call for anything sensational. It was simply far too neat for an amateur, that's all. We're rounding up all the likelies, of course, but with such a field to choose from, the right man may easily slip the stuff before we can get round to him."

Mr. Campion rose.

"You have all my sympathy. It's not what you your-self would call a picnic, is it? Still, I'll ferret round a bit and let you have any great thoughts that may come to me. By the way, what do you think of that?"

He crossed the room as he spoke and laid the many-stoned ring on the desk.

"Not very much," said Oates, turning it over with a dubious forefinger. "Where did you get it?"

"I picked it up in the street," said Mr. Campion truthfully. "I ought to take it to a police station, but I don't think I will. I'd rather like to give it back to the owner myself."

"Do what you like with it, my lad." Oates was mildly exasperated. "Keep your mind on the important jewellery, because now Scotland Yard has taken over the case it means the Metropolitan area pays for the inquiry; don't forget that."

Campion was still looking at the ring.

"Anyway, I showed it to you," he said, and wandered towards the door.

"Don't waste your time over trifles," Oates called after him. "You can have that ring. If anybody asks you, say I said you could."

* * *

It would have appeared that Mr. Campion took the superintendent's final offer seriously, for he replaced the trinket carefully in his waistcoat pocket before turning into the nearest telephone booth, where he rang up that unfailing source of Society gossip, old Lady Laradine. After listening to her for a full two minutes, while she asked after every relative he had in the world, he put the question he had in mind.

"Who is Gina Gray? I've heard the name, but I can't place her. Gray. Gray with an A."

"My dear boy! So pretty! Just the girl for you. Oh no, perhaps not. I've just remembered she's engaged. Announced last month. Still, she's very charming." The old voice, which was strong enough to penetrate any first-night babel in London, rattled on, and Campion felt for another twopence.

"I know," he shouted. "I know she's lovely, or at least I guessed she was. But who, *who* is she? Also, of course, where?"

"What? Oh, *where* is she? With her aunt, of course. She's spending the winter there. She's too young, Albert. Straight down from the shires. The father owns a row of Welsh mountains or something equally romantic."

"Who?" bellowed Mr. Campion through the din, "Who, my good gramophone, is the aunt?"

"What did you call me, Albert?" The famous voice was dangerously soft.

"Gramophone," said Mr. Campion, who was a great believer in the truth when the worst had come to the worst.

"Oh, I thought you said . . . never mind." Lady Laradine, who had several grandchildren and regarded each new arrival as a personal insult, was mollified. "I do talk very fast, I know, especially on the phone. It's my exuberant spirit. You want to know who the aunt is. Why, Dora Carrington. You know her."

"I do," said Campion with relief. "I didn't realize she had a niece."

"Oh, but she has; just out of the nest. Presented last year. A sweetly pretty child. Such a pity she's engaged. Tell me, have you any information about Wivenhoe's son? No? Then what about the Pritchards?"

She went on and on with the relentless energy of the very bored, and it was not until Mr. Campion ran out of coppers that the monologue came to an end.

It was late in the morning, therefore, when Mr. Campion presented himself at the charming Lowndes Square house which Dora Carrington had made her London home.

Miss Gina Gray only decided to see him after a considerable pause, during which, he felt, old Pollard, the butler, must have worked hard vouching for his desirability.

She came into the lounge at last, looking much as he had thought she might, very young and startled, with frank, miserable eyes, but dark, curling hair instead of the sleek blonde he had somehow expected.

He introduced himself apologetically.

"It's rather odd turning up like this out of the blue," he said, "but you'll have to forgive me. Perhaps you could think of me as a sort of long-lost elderly relative. I might have been your uncle, of course, if Dora had taken it into her head to marry me instead of Tubby, not that the idea ever occurred to either of us at the time, of course. Don't get that into your head. I only say it might have happened so that you'll see the sort of reliable bird I am."

He paused. The alarm had died out of her eyes and she even looked wanly amused. He was relieved. Idiotic conversation, although invaluable, was not a luxury which he often permitted himself now that the thirty-five-year-old landmark was passed.

"It's very nice of you to come," she said in a polite, small voice. "What can I do?"

"Nothing. I came to return something I think you've lost, that's all." He fished in his pocket and drew out the ring. "That's yours, isn't it?" he said gently.

He had expected some reaction, but not that it would be so violent. She stood trembling before him, every tinge of color draining out of her face.

"Where did you get it?" she whispered, and then, pulling herself together with a desperate courage which he rather admired, she shook her head. "It's not mine. I've never seen it before. I don't know who you are either, and I—I don't want to. Please go away."

"Oh, Gina Gray!" said Mr. Campion. "Gina Gray, don't be silly. I'm the original old gentleman with the kind heart. Don't deny the irrefutable."

"It's not mine." To his horror he saw tears in her eyes. "It's not mine. It's not. It's not. Go away."

She turned and made for the door, her slender, brown-suited figure looking very small and fugitive as she ran.

Mr. Campion was still debating his next move when Dora came in, a vision of fox-furs and smiles.

"My dear!" she said. "You haven't been to see us for years and years and now you turn up when I'm due out to lunch in fifteen minutes. Where have you been?"

"About," said Mr. Campion truthfully, reflecting that it was all wrong that the people one never had time to visit were always one's oldest and closest friends.

They drank a cocktail together and were still reminiscing happily when Dora's luncheon escort arrived. In the end Mr. Campion showed his hostess out of her own house and was standing rather forlornly on the pavement, waving after her departing car, when he observed a familiar figure stumping dejectedly down the steps which he had so recently descended himself.

"Jonathan!" he said. "What are you doing here?"

Mr. Jonathan Peters started violently, as if he had

been caught sleep-walking, and looked up with only a
faint smile on his gloomy young face.

"Hallo, Campion," he said. "I didn't see you. I've
been kicking my heels in the breakfast room. Hell!
Let's go and have a drink."

In the end, after some half-hearted bickering, they
went along to that home from home, the Junior Greys,
and Mr. Campion, who, in company with the rest of
the world, considered himself to be the best listener on
earth, persuaded his young acquaintance to unburden
himself.

Jonathan was a younger brother of the two Peterses
who had been Campion's Cambridge companions, and
in the ordinary way the ten years' difference in their
ages would have raised an insurmountable barrier between them; but at the moment Jonathan was a man
with a sorrow.

"It's Gina," he said. "We're engaged, you know."

"Really?" Mr. Campion was interested. "What's the
row?"

"Oh, I suppose it'll be all right in the end." The
young man sounded wistful and only partially convinced. "I mean, I think she'll come round. Anyway, I
hope so. What annoys me is that I'm the one with the
grievance, and yet here I am dithering around as
though it were all my fault." He frowned and shook his
head over the unreasonableness of life in general and
love in particular.

"You were at Porky Allenbrough's show last night, I
suppose?" Mr. Campion put the question innocently
and was rewarded.

"Yes, we both were. I didn't see you there. There
was a tremendous crush and it might have been a really
good bust if it hadn't been for one thing and another.
I've got a genuine grouch, you know." Mr. Peters'
young face was very earnest, and under the influence

of half a pint of excellent Chablis he came out with the
full story.

As far as Mr. Campion could make out from his
somewhat disjointed account the history was a simple
one. Miss Gina Gray, while enjoying the London season, had yet not wished to give up all strenuous physical exercise and so had formed the habit of hunting
with the Whippersfield five or six times a month. On
these occasions she had been entertained by a relation
of Dora Carrington's husband who lived in the district
and had very kindly stabled her horses for her. Her
custom had been to run down by car early in the morning, returning to London either at night or on the following day.

In view of all this hospitality, it had been arranged
that she should go to the Priory Ball with her host and
his party, while Jonathan should attend with another
group of people from a different house. The arrangement between the couple had been, therefore, that,
while Gina should arrive at the ball with her own
crowd, Jonathan should have the privilege of driving
her back before joining his own host and hostess.

"It was a bit thick," he concluded resentfully. "Gina
turned up with a crowd of people I didn't know, including a lad whom nobody seemed to have seen before. She danced with him most of the evening and
finally he drove her home himself. He left me a message to say so, the little toot. I felt fed up and I imagine I may have got pretty tight, but anyway, when I
arrived at the town house this morning ready to forgive
and forget like a hero, she wouldn't even see me."

"Infuriating," agreed Mr. Campion, his eyes thoughtful.
"Did you find out who this interloping tick happened to
be?"

Jonathan shrugged his shoulders.

"I did hear his name ... Robertson, or something.
Apparently he's been hunting fairly regularly this sea-

son and he came along with Gina's lot. That's all I
know."

"What did he look like?"

Jonathan screwed up his eyes in an effort of recollection.

"An ugly blighter," he said at last. "Ordinary height,
I think. I don't remember much about him except that
I disliked his face."

It was not a very helpful description, but Mr. Campion sat pondering over it for some time after the de-
spondent Jonathan had wandered off to keep an
afternoon appointment.

Suddenly he sat up, a new expression on his lean,
good-humored face.

"Rocks," he said under his breath. "Rocks Denver . . ."
and he made for the nearest telephone.

It was nine o'clock that evening when Superintendent Oates came striding into his office and, flinging
his hat upon the desk, turned to survey the elegant,
dinner-jacketed visitor who had been patiently
awaiting his arrival for the best part of half an hour.

"Got him," he said briefly. "The lads shadowed him
to Peachy Dale's club in Rosebery Avenue, and then,
of course, we knew we were safe. Peachy may be a
rotten fence, but he's the only man in London who
would have handled those snuff boxes, now I come to
think of it. It was a lovely cop. We gave him time to
get settled and then closed in on all five entrances.
There he was with the stuff in a satchel. It was beautiful. I've never seen a man so astounded in my life."

He paused and a reminiscent smile floated over his
sad face.

"A little work of art, that's what that arrest was, a
little work of art."

"That's fine, then," said his visitor, rising. "I think
I'll drift."

"No, you don't, my lad." The superintendent was

firm. "You don't do conjuring tricks under my nose without an explanation. You come across."

Mr. Campion sighed.

"My dear good Enthusiast, what more can you possibly want?" he protested. "You've got the man and you've got the swag. That's enough for a conviction—and Porky's blessing."

"Very likely. but what about my dignity?" Oates was severe. "It may be enough for the Bench, but it's not enough for me. Who do you think you are, the Home Office?"

"Heaven forbid," said Mr. Campion piously. "I thought you might express your ingratitude in this revolting way. Look here, if I explain, my witness doesn't go into Court. Is that a bet?"

The superintendent held out his hand.

"May I be struck pink," he said sincerely. "I mean it."

Since he knew from experience that this was an oath that Oates held peculiarly sacred, Mr. Campion relented.

"Give me twenty minutes," he said. "I'll go and fetch her."

Oates groaned. "Another woman!" he exploded. "You find 'em, don't you? All right, I'll wait."

Miss Gina Gray looked so genuinely pathetic as she came into the office clinging to Mr. Campion's arm a little over half an hour later that Oates, who had an unexpected weakness for youth and beauty, was inclined to be mollified. Campion observed the first signs of his heavily avuncular mood with relief.

"It's perfectly all right," he said to the girl at his side. "I've given you my word you'll be kept clean out of it. This solemn-looking person will be struck a fine hunting pink if he attempts to make me break it. That's written in the unchanging stars. Isn't that so, superintendent?"

Oates regarded him with fishy eyes.

"You go and put on your mask," he said. "Now, what is all this? What's been going on?"

Gina Gray required a little gentle pumping, but beneath Campion's expert treatment she began to relax, and within ten minutes she was pouring out her story with all the energy of injured innocence behind it.

"I met the man I knew as Tony Roberts—you say his real name is Rocks Denver—in the hunting-field," she said. "He always seemed to be out when I was, and he talked to me as people do out hunting. I didn't know him, he wasn't a friend, but I got used to him being about. He rode very well and he helped me out of a mess once or twice. You know that sort of acquaintance, don't you?"

Oates nodded and shook his head. He was smiling.

"We do," he said. "And then what?"

"Then nothing," declared Miss Gray innocently. "Nothing at all until last night. We were all getting ready to go to the Priory in three or four cars when he phoned me at Major Carrington's, where I was staying, and said his car had broken down in the village and he'd got to leave it and would it be awful cheek of him to ask if one of us would give him a lift to the hall. I said of course, naturally, and when we met him trudging along, rather disconsolate in full kit, we stopped and picked him up."

Oates glanced at Campion triumphantly.

"So that's how he got in?" he said. "Neat, eh? I see, Miss Gray. And then when you got your acquaintance to the party you didn't like to leave him cold. Is that how it was?"

The girl blushed and her dark eyes were very frank.

"Well, he *was* rather out of everything and he *did* dance very well," she admitted apologetically. "He hadn't talked much about himself, and it was only then I realized he didn't live near and didn't know everybody else. His—his manners were all right."

Oates laughed. "Oh yes, Rocky's very presentable,"

he agreed. "He's one of the lads who let his old school down, I'm afraid. Well, and then what?"

She hesitated and turned to Campion.

"I've been so incredibly silly," she murmured. It was a direct appeal, and the superintendent was not unchivalrous.

"There's nothing new in that, miss," he observed kindly. "We all make errors of judgment at times. You missed him for a bit, I suppose?"

"Yes, I danced with several people and I'd half forgotten him when he turned up at my elbow with a raincoat over his arm. He took me out on the terrace and put it over my shoulders and said—oh, a lot of silly things about being there alone without a soul to speak to. He said he'd found one man he knew, but that he was wrapped up with some woman or other, and suggested that we borrow this friend's car and go for a run round. It was getting rather late and I was livid with Jonathan anyway, so I said all right."

"Why were you livid with Jonathan?" Campion put the question curiously and Miss Gray met his eyes.

"He got jealous as soon as we arrived and drowned his sorrows rather too soon."

"I see." Campion smiled as he began to understand Mr. Peters' astonishing magnanimity, which had hitherto seemed somewhat too saintly to be strictly in character.

"Well then . . ." Oates went back to the main story ". . . off you went in the car. You drove around for quite a while."

Gina took a deep breath.

"Yes," she said steadily. "We drove around for a bit, but not very far. The car wasn't his, you see, and he had trouble with it. It started all right, but it conked out down the lane and he was fooling about with it for a long time. He got so frightfully angry that I began to feel—well, rather uncomfortable. Also I was cold. He had taken the raincoat off my shoulders and flung it in the back seat, and I remembered that it was heavy and warm, so I turned to get it. Just then he closed the bonnet and came back. He snatched the coat and swore at me, and I began to get thoroughly frightened. I tried to persuade him to take me back, but he just drove on down the lane towards the main road. It was then that we passed the three policemen on motorcycles racing towards the Priory. That seemed to unnerve him completely and he turned off towards Major Carrington's house, with the car limping and misfiring all the time. I didn't know what to do. I was far too frightened to make a row, you see, because I was a guest at the major's, and—well, there was Jonathan and Aunt Dora to consider and—oh, you do understand, don't you?"

"I think so," said Campion gravely. "When did you take off your ring?"

She gaped at him.

"Why, at that moment," she said. "How did you know? It's a stupid trick I have when I'm nervous. It was rather loose, and I pulled it off and started to play with it. He looked down and saw me with it and seemed to lose his head. He snatched it out of my hand and demanded to know where I'd got it, and then, when he saw it clearly by the dashboard light, he suddenly pitched it out of the window in disgust. It was so utterly unexpected that I forgot where I was and made a leap for it across him. Then—then I'm afraid the car turned over."

"Well, well," said Oates inadequately. "And so there you were, so to speak."

She nodded gravely. "I was so frightened," she said. "Fortunately we were quite near the house, but my dress was spoilt and I was shaken and bruised, and I just set off across the fields and let myself in by the stable gate. He came after me, and we had a dreadful sort of row in whispers, out in the drive. He wanted me to put him up for the night, and didn't seem to realize that I was a visitor and couldn't dream of doing such a thing. In the end I showed him where the saddle room was, off the stable yard. There was a stove there and some rugs and things. Then I sneaked up to my room and went to bed. This morning I pretended that I'd had a headache and got somebody to give me a lift home. He'd gone by then, of course."

"Of course he had. Hopped on one of those country buses before the servants stirred," Oates put in with satisfaction. "He relied on you to hold your tongue for your own sake."

"There wasn't much else he could do in the circumstances," observed Campion mildly. "Once he had the howling misfortune to pick a sick car all his original plans went to pieces. He used Miss Gray to get the stuff safely out of the house in the usual false pocket of the raincoat. Then his idea must have been to drive her a mile or two down the road and strand her, while he toddled off to Town alone. The breakdown delayed him and, once he saw the police were about, he knew the cordon would go round and that he was trapped, so he had to think out other tactics. That exercise seems to have unnerved him entirely. I can understand him wanting to get into the house. After all, it'd be a first-class hiding-place in the circumstances. Yes, well, that's fairly clear now, I hope, superintendent. Here's your ring, Miss Gray."

As Gina put out her hand for the trinket her eyes grew puzzled.

"You're a very frightening person," she said. "How on earth did you know it was mine?"

"Quite." Oates was frankly suspicious. "If you've never met this young lady before, I don't see how you guessed it belonged to her."

Campion stood regarding the girl with genuine surprise.

"My dear child," he said, "surely you know yourself? Who had this ring made for you?"

"No one. It was left to me. My father's sister died about six months ago and told me in a letter always to wear it for luck. It doesn't seem to have brought me much."

For a moment Campion seemed completely bewildered. After a while, however, he laughed.

"Your father's sister? Were you named after her?"

"Yes, I was." Miss Gray's dark eyes were widening visibly. "How do you know all this? You're frightening."

Campion took the ring between his thumb and forefinger and turned it slowly round, while the stones winked and glittered in the hard electric light.

"It's such a simple trick I hardly like to explain and spoil the effect," he said. "About fifty years ago it was a fairly common conceit to give young ladies rings like this. You see, I knew this was Gina Gray's ring because it had her name on the wrapper, as it were. Look, start at the little gold star and what have you? Garnet, Indicolite—that's an indigo variety of tourmaline, superintendent—Nephrite, Amethyst, then another smaller gold star and Garnet again, Rose Quartz, Agate, and finally Yellow Sapphire. There you are. I thought you must know. G.I.N.A. G.R.A.Y., all done according to the best sentimental jewellery tradition. As soon as I came to consider the ring in cold blood it was obvious. Look at it, Oates. What man in his senses would put that collection of stones together if he didn't mean something by them?"

The superintendent did not answer immediately. He sat turning the ring round and round with an expression of grudging astonishment on his grey face. When at last he did look up he expressed himself unexpectedly.

"Fancy that," he said. "Dear me."

When Miss Gray had departed in a taxicab, which, on Mr. Campion's suggestion, a patient and sober Jonathan had kept ticking up outside on the Embankment during the whole of the short interview, he was more explicit.

"She had her name in it," he said after a moment or two of purely decorative imagery. "She had her dear little name on it! Very smart of you, Mr. Campion. Don't let it go to your head. I don't know if I'm quite satisfied yet. Who put you on to Rocky? Why Rocky? Why not any other of the fifty first-class jewel thieves in London?"

Campion grinned. It was not often that the superintendent condescended to ask straight questions and he felt justifiably gratified by the phenomenon.

"You said he was a 'pro,' " he explained. "That was the first step. Then young Jonathan Peters told me Gina had met the fellow hunting regularly, and so, putting two and two together, I arrived at Rocky. Rocky is an anachronism in the underworld; he can ride. How many jewel thieves do you know who can ride well enough to turn up at a hunt, pay their caps, and not make an exhibition of themselves? Hunting over strange country isn't trotting round the Row, you know."

Oates shook his head sadly.

"You depress me," he said. "First you think of the obvious and then you go and say it, and then you're proved right. It's very irritating. The ring was a new one on me, though. D'you know, I wouldn't mind giving my wife one of those. It's a pretty idea. She'd like it. Besides," he added seriously, "it might come in useful some time. You never know."

In the end Campion sat down and worked it out for him.

The Necklace of Pearls
by Dorothy L. Sayers

Sir Septimus Shale was accustomed to assert his authority once in the year and once only. He allowed his young and fashionable wife to fill his house with diagrammatic furniture made of steel; to collect advanced artists and anti-grammatical poets; to believe in cocktails and relativity and to dress as extravagantly as she pleased; but he did insist on an old-fashioned Christmas. He was a simple-hearted man, who really liked plum pudding and cracker mottoes, and he could not get it out of his head that other people, "at bottom," enjoyed these things also. At Christmas, therefore, he firmly retired to his country house in Essex, called in the servants to hang holly and mistletoe upon the cubist electric fittings; loaded the steel sideboard with delicacies from Fortnum & Mason; hung up stockings at the heads of the polished walnut bedsteads; and even, on this occasion only, had the electric radiators removed from the modernist grates and installed wood fires and a Yule log. He then gathered his family and friends about him, filled them with as much Dickensian good fare as he could persuade them to swallow, and, after their Christmas dinner, set them down to play "Charades" and "Clumps" and "Animal, Vegetable, and Mineral" in the drawing-room, concluding these diversions by "Hide and Seek" in the dark all over the house. Because Sir Septimus was a very rich man, his guests fell in with this invariable program, and if they were bored, they did not tell him so.

Another charming and traditional custom which he followed was that of presenting to his daughter Margharita a pearl on each successive birthday—this anniversary happening to coincide with Christmas Eve. The pearls now numbered twenty, and the collection was beginning to enjoy a certain celebrity, and had been photographed in the Society papers. Though not sensationally large—each one being about the size of a marrowfat pea—the pearls were of very great value. They were of exquisite color and perfect shape and matched to a hair's-weight. On this particular Christmas Eve the presentation of the twenty-first pearl had been the occasion of a very special ceremony. There was a dance and there were speeches. On the Christmas night following, the more restricted family party took place, with the turkey and the Victorian games. There were eleven guests, in addition to Sir Septimus and Lady Shale and their daughter, nearly all related or connected to them in some way: John Shale, a brother, with his wife and their son and daughter, Henry and Betty; Betty's fiancé, Oswald Truegood, a young man with parliamentary ambitions; George Comphrey, a cousin of Lady Shale's, aged about thirty and known as a man-about-town; Lavinia Prescott, asked on George's account; Joyce Trivett, asked on Henry Shale's account; Richard and Beryl Dennison, distant relations of Lady Shale, who lived a gay and expensive life in town on nobody precisely knew what resources; and Lord Peter Wimsey, asked, in a touching spirit of unreasonable hope, on Margharita's account. There were also, of course, William Norgate, secretary to Sir Septimus, and Miss Tomkins, secretary to Lady Shale. Dinner was over—a seemingly endless succession of soup, fish, turkey, roast beef, plum pudding, mince pies, crystallized fruit, nuts, and five kinds of wine, presided over by Sir Septimus, all smiles, by Lady Shale, all mocking deprecation, and by Margharita, pretty and bored, with the necklace of twenty-one pearls gleaming softly on her slender throat. Gorged and dyspeptic and longing only for the horizontal position, the company had been shepherded into the drawing-room and set to play "Musical Chairs" (Miss Tomkins at the piano), "Hunt the Slipper" (slipper provided by Miss Tomkins), and "Dumb Crambo" (costumes by Miss Tomkins and Mr. William Norgate). The back drawing-room (for Sir Septimus clung to these old-fashioned names) provided an admirable dressing-room, being screened by folding doors from the large drawing-room in which the audience sat on aluminum chairs, scrabbling uneasy toes on a floor of black glass under the tremendous illumination of electricity reflected from a brass ceiling.

It was William Norgate who, after taking the temperature of the meeting, suggested to Lady Shale that they should play something less athletic. Lady Shale agreed and, as usual, suggested bridge. Sir Septimus, as usual, blew the suggestion aside.

"Bridge? Nonsense! Nonsense! Play bridge every day of your lives. This is Christmas time. Something we can all play together. How about 'Animal, Vegetable, and Mineral'?"

This intellectual pastime was a favorite with Sir Septimus; he was rather good at putting pregnant questions. After a brief discussion it became evident that this game was an inevitable part of the program. The party settled down to it, Sir Septimus undertaking to "go out" first and set the thing going.

Presently they had guessed among other things Miss Tomkins's mother's photograph, a gramaphone record of "I Want To Be Happy" (much scientific research into the exact composition of records, settled by Wil-

liam Norgate out of the *Encyclopoedia Britannica*), the
smallest stickleback in the stream at the bottom of the
garden, the new planet Pluto, the scarf worn by Mrs.
Dennison (very confusing, because it was not silk,
which would be animal, or artificial silk, which would
be vegetable, but made of spun glass—mineral, a very
clever choice of subject), and had failed to guess the
Prime Minister's wireless speech—which was voted
not fair, since nobody could decide whether it was animal by nature or a kind of gas. It was decided that
they should do one more word and then go on to "Hide
and Seek." Oswald Truegood had retired into the back
room and shut the door behind him while the party discussed the next subject of examination, when suddenly
Sir Septimus broke in on the argument by calling to his
daughter:

"Hullo, Margy! What have you done with your
necklace?"

"I took it off, Dad, because I thought it might get
broken in 'Dumb Crambo.' It's over here on this table.
No, it isn't. Did you take it, Mother?"

"No, I didn't. If I'd seen it, I should have. You are
a careless child."

"I believe you've got it yourself, Dad. You're teasing."

Sir Septimus denied the accusation with some energy. Everybody got up and began to hunt about. There
were not many places in that bare and polished room
where a necklace could be hidden. After ten minutes'
fruitless investigation Richard Dennison, who had
been seated next to the table where the pearls had been
placed, began to look rather uncomfortable.

At this moment Oswald Truegood put his head
through the folding-doors and asked whether they
hadn't settled on something by now.

This directed the attention of the searchers to the inner room. Margharita must have been mistaken. She
had taken it in there, and it had got mixed up with the

dressing-up clothes somehow. The room was ransacked. Everything was lifted up and shaken. The thing began to look serious. After half an hour of desperate energy it became apparent that the pearls were nowhere to be found.

"They must be somewhere in these two rooms, you know," said Wimsey. "The back drawing-room has no door and nobody could have gone out of the front drawing-room without being seen. Unless the windows—"

No. The windows were all guarded on the outside by heavy shutters which it needed two footmen to take down and replace. The pearls had not gone out that way. In fact, the mere suggestion that they had left the drawing-room at all was disagreeable. Because—because—

It was William Norgate, efficient as ever, who boldly faced the issue.

"I think, Sir Septimus, it would be a relief to the minds of everybody present if we could all be searched."

Sir Septimus was horrified, but the guests, having found a leader, backed up Norgate. The door was locked, and the search was conducted—the ladies in the inner room and the men in the outer.

Nothing resulted from it except some very interesting information about the belongings habitually carried about by the average man and woman. It was natural that Lord Peter Wimsey should possess a pair of forceps, a pocket lens, and a small folding foot-rule—was he not a Sherlock Holmes in high life? But that Oswald Truegood should have two liver-pills in a screw of paper and Henry Shale a pocket edition of *The Odes of Horace* was unexpected. Why did John Shale distend the pockets of his dress-suit with a stump of red sealing-wax, an ugly little mascot, and a five-shilling piece? George Comphrey had a pair of folding scissors, and three wrapped lumps of sugar, of the sort served in restaurants and dining-cars—evidence of a not uncommon form of kleptomania; but that the tidy and exact Norgate should burden himself with a reel of white cotton, three separate lengths of string, and twelve safety-pins on a card seemed really remarkable till one remembered that he had superintended all the Christmas decorations. Richard Dennison, amid some confusion and laughter, was found to cherish a lady's garter, a powder-compact and half a potato; the last-named, he said, was a prophylactic against rheumatism (to which he was subject), while the other objects belonged to his wife. On the ladies' side, the more striking exhibits were a little book on palmistry, three invisible hair-pins, and a baby's photograph (Miss Tomkins); a Chinese trick cigarette-case with a secret compartment (Beryl Dennison); a *very* private letter and an outfit for mending stocking-runs (Lavinia Prescott); and a pair of eyebrow tweezers and a small packet of white powder, said to be for headaches (Betty Shale). An agitating moment followed the production from Joyce Trivett's handbag of a small string of pearls—but it was promptly remembered that these had come out of one of the crackers at dinner-time, and they were, in fact, synthetic. In short, the search was unproductive of anything beyond a general shame-facedness and the discomfort always produced by undressing and re-dressing in a hurry at the wrong time of the day.

It was then that somebody, very grudgingly and haltingly, mentioned the horrid word *Police*. Sir Septimus, naturally, was appalled by the idea. It was disgusting. He would not allow it. The pearls must be somewhere. They must search the rooms again. Could not Lord Peter Wimsey, with his experience of—er—mysterious happenings, do something to assist them?

"Eh?" said his lordship. "Oh, by Jove, yes—by all means, certainly. That is to say, provided nobody supposes—eh, what? I mean to say, you don't know that I'm not a suspicious character, do you, what?"

Lady Shale interposed with authority.

"We don't think *anybody* ought to be suspected," she said, "but, if we did, we'd know it couldn't be you. You know *far* too much about crimes to want to commit one."

"All right," said Wimsey. "But after the way the place has been gone over—" He shrugged his shoulders.

"Yes, I'm afraid you won't be able to find any footprints," said Margharita. "But we may have overlooked something."

Wimsey nodded.

"I'll try. Do you all mind sitting down on your chairs in the outer room and staying there. All except one of you—I'd better have a witness to anything I do or find. Sir Septimus—you'd be the best person, I think."

He shepherded them to their places and began a slow circuit of the two rooms, exploring every surface, gazing up to the polished brazen ceiling and crawling on hands and knees in the approved fashion across the black and shining desert of the floors. Sir Septimus followed, staring when Wimsey stared, bending with his hands upon his knees when Wimsey crawled, and puffing at intervals with astonishment and chagrin.

They reached the inner drawing-room, and here the dressing-up clothes were again minutely examined, but without result. Finally, Wimsey lay down flat on his stomach to squint under a steel cabinet which was one of the very few pieces of furniture which possessed short legs. Something about it seemed to catch his attention. He rolled up his sleeve and plunged his arm into the cavity, kicked convulsively in the effort to reach farther than was humanly possible, pulled out from his pocket and extended his folding foot-rule, fished with it under the cabinet, and eventually succeeded in extracting what he sought.

It was a very minute object—in fact, a pin. Not an ordinary pin, but one resembling those used by ento-

mologists to impale extremely small moths on the
setting-board. It was about three-quarters of an inch in
length, as fine as a very fine needle, with a sharp point
and a small head.

"Bless my soul!" said Sir Septimus. "What's that?"

"Does anybody here happen to collect moths or bee-
tles or anything?" asked Wimsey.

"I'm pretty sure they don't," replied Sir Septimus.
"I'll ask them."

"Don't do that." Wimsey bent his head and stared at
the floor, from which his own face stared back at him.

"I see," said Wimsey presently. "That's how it was
done. All right, Sir Septimus. I know where the pearls
are, but I don't know who took them. Perhaps it would
be as well—for everybody's satisfaction—just to find
out. In the meantime they are perfectly safe. Don't tell
anyone that we've found this pin or that we've discovered anything. Send all these people to bed. Lock the
drawing-room door and keep the key, and we'll get our
man—or woman—by breakfast-time."

Lord Peter Wimsey kept careful watch that night
upon the drawing-room door. Nobody, however, came
near it. Either the thief suspected a trap or he felt con-
fident that any time would do to recover the pearls.
Wimsey, however, did not feel that he was wasting his
time. He was making a list of people who had been left
alone in the back drawing-room during the playing of
"Animal, Vegetable, or Mineral." The list ran as follows:

Sir Septimus Shale
Lavinia Prescott
William Norgate
Joyce Trivett and Henry Shale (together, because
    they had claimed to be incapable of guessing any-
    thing unaided)
Mrs. Dennison

Betty Shale
George Comphrey
Richard Dennison
Miss Tomkins
Oswald Truegood

He also made out a list of the persons to whom pearls might be useful or desirable. Unfortunately, this list agreed in almost all respects with the first (always excepting Sir Septimus) and so was not very helpful. The two secretaries had both come well recommended, but that was exactly what they would have done had they come with ulterior designs; the Dennisons were notorious livers from hand to mouth; Betty Shale carried mysterious white powders in her handbag, and was known to be in with a rather rapid set in town; Henry was a harmless dilettante, but Joyce Trivett could twist him round her little finger and was what Jane Austen liked to call "expensive and dissipated"; Comphrey speculated; Oswald Truegood was rather frequently present at Epsom and Newmarket—the search for motives was only too fatally easy.

When the second housemaid and the under-footman appeared in the passage with household implements, Wimsey abandoned his vigil, but he was down early to breakfast.

The party assembled gradually, but, as though by common consent, nothing was said about pearls until after breakfast, when Oswald Truegood took the bull by the horns.

"Well, now!" said he. "How's the detective getting along? Got your man, Wimsey?"

"Not yet," said Wimsey easily.

Sir Septimus, looking at Wimsey as though for his cue, cleared his throat and dashed into speech.

"All very tiresome," he said, "all very unpleasant. Hr'rm. Nothing for it but the police, I'm afraid. Just at Christmas, too. Hr'rm. Spoiled the party. Can't stand seeing all this stuff about the place." He waved his hand towards the festoons of evergreens and colored paper that adorned the walls. "Take it all down, eh, what? No heart in it. Hr'rm. Burn the lot."

"Oh, leave it, Uncle," said Henry Shale. "You're bothering too much about the pearls."

"Shall I ring for James?" suggested William Norgate.

"No," interrupted Comphrey, "let's do it ourselves. It'll give us something to do and take our minds off our troubles."

"That's right," said Sir Septimus. "Start right away."

He savagely hauled a great branch of holly down from the mantelpiece and flung it, crackling, into the fire.

"That's the stuff," said Richard Dennison. "Make a good old blaze!" He leaped up from the table and snatched the mistletoe from the chandelier. "Here goes! One more kiss for somebody before it's too late."

"Isn't it unlucky to take it down before the New Year?" suggested Miss Tomkins.

"Unlucky be hanged! We'll have it all down. Off the stairs and out of the drawing-room too. Somebody go and collect it."

"Isn't the drawing-room locked?" asked Oswald.

"No. Lord Peter says the pearls aren't there, wherever else they are, so it's unlocked. That's right, isn't it, Wimsey?"

"Quite right. The pearls were taken out of these rooms. I can't yet tell you how, but I'm positive of it."

"Oh, well," said Comphrey, "in that case, have at it! Come along, Lavinia—you and Dennison do the drawing-room and I'll do the back room. We'll have a race."

Oswald and Margharita were already pulling the holly and ivy from the staircase, amid peals of laughter. The party dispersed. Wimsey went quietly upstairs and into the drawing-room, where the work of demolition was taking place at a great rate, George having bet the other two ten shillings to a tanner that they would not finish their part of the job before he finished his.

"You mustn't help," said Lavinia, laughing to Wimsey. "It wouldn't be fair."

Wimsey said nothing, but waited till the room was clear. Then he followed them down again to the hall, where the fire was sending up a great roaring and spluttering, suggestive of Guy Fawkes night. He whispered to Sir Septimus, who went forward and touched George Comphrey on the shoulder.

"Lord Peter wants to say something to you, my boy," he said.

Comphrey started, and went with him a little reluctantly, as it seemed. He was not looking very well.

"Mr. Comphrey," said Wimsey, "I fancy these are some of your property." He held out the palm of his hand, in which rested twenty-two fine, small-headed pins.

"Ingenious," said Wimsey, "but something less ingenious would have served his turn better. It was very unlucky, Sir Septimus, that you should have mentioned the pearls when you did. Of course, he hoped that the loss wouldn't be discovered till we'd chucked guessing games and taken to 'Hide and Seek.' Then the pearls might have been anywhere in the house, we shouldn't have locked the drawing-room door, and he could have recovered them at his leisure. He had had this possibility in his mind when he came here, obviously, and that was why he brought the pins, and Miss Shale's taking off the necklace to play 'Dumb Crambo' gave him his opportunity.

"He had spent Christmas here before, and knew perfectly well that 'Animal, Vegetable, and Mineral' would form part of the entertainment. He had only to gather up the necklace from the table when it came to his turn to retire, and he knew he could count on at least five minutes by himself while we were all arguing about the choice of a word. He had only to snip the pearls from the string with his pocket-scissors, burn the string in the grate, and fasten the pearls to the mistletoe with the fine pins. The mistletoe was hung on the chandelier, pretty high—it's a lofty room—but he could easily reach it by standing on the glass table, which wouldn't show footmarks, and it was almost certain that nobody would think of examining the mistletoe for extra berries. I shouldn't have thought of it myself if I hadn't found that pin which he had dropped. That gave me the idea that the pearls had been separated, and the rest was easy. I took the pearls off the mistletoe last night—the clasp was there, too, pinned among the holly-leaves. Here they are. Comphrey must have got a nasty shock this morning. I knew he was our man when he suggested that the guests should tackle the decorations themselves and that he should do the back drawing-room—but I wish I had seen his face when he came to the mistletoe and found the pearls gone."

"But you never even looked at the mistletoe when you found the pin."

"I saw it reflected in the black glass floor, and it struck me then how much the mistletoe berries looked like pearls."

The Crime of Miss Oyster Brown
by Peter Lovesey

Miss Oyster Brown, a devout member of the Church of England, joined passionately each Sunday in every prayer of the Morning Service—except for the general Confession, when, in all honesty, she found it difficult to class herself as a lost sheep. She was willing to believe that everyone else in church had erred and strayed. In certain cases she knew exactly how, and with whom, and she would say a prayer for them. On her own account, however, she could seldom think of anything to confess. She tried strenuously, more strenuously—dare I say it?—than you or me to lead an untainted life. She managed conspicuously well. Very occasionally, as the rest of congregation joined in the Confession, she would own up to some trifling sin.

You may imagine what a fall from grace it was when this virtuous woman committed not merely a sin, but a crime. She lived more than half her life before it happened.

She resided in a Berkshire town with her twin sister Pearl, who was a mere three minutes her senior. Oyster and Pearl—a flamboyance in forenames that owed something to the fact that their parents had been plain John and Mary Brown. Up to the moment of birth the

Browns had been led to expect one child, who, if female, was to be named Pearl. In the turmoil created by a second, unscheduled, daughter, John Brown jokingly suggested naming her Oyster. Mary, bosky from morphine, seized on the name as an inspiration, a delight to the ear when said in front of dreary old Brown.

Of course the charm was never so apparent to the twins, who got to dread being introduced to people. Even in infancy, they were aware that their parents' friends found the names amusing. At school they were taunted as much by the teachers as the children. The names never ceased to amuse. Fifty years on, things were still said just out of earshot and laced with pretended sympathy. "Here come Pearl and Oyster, poor old ducks. Fancy being stuck with names like that."

No wonder they faced the world defiantly. In middle age, they were a formidable duo, stalwarts of the choir, the Bible-reading Circle, the Townswomen's Guild, and the Magistrates' Bench. Neither sister had married. They lived together in Lime Tree Avenue, in the mock-Tudor house where they were born. They were not short of money.

There are certain things people always want to know about twins, the more so in mystery stories. I can reassure the wary reader that Oyster and Pearl were not identical. Oyster was an inch taller, more sturdy in build than her sister and slower of speech. They dressed individually, Oyster as a rule in tweed skirts and check blouses that she made herself, always from the same Butterick pattern; Pearl in a variety of mail-order suits in pastel blues and greens. No one confused them.

As for that other question so often asked about twins, neither sister could be characterized as "dominant." Each possessed a forceful personality by any standard. To avoid disputes they had established a household routine, a division of the duties that worked pretty harmoniously, all things considered. Oyster did most of the cooking and the gardening, for example, and Pearl attended to the housework and paid the bills when they became due. They both enjoyed shopping, so they shared it. They did the church flowers together when their turn came, and they always ran the bottle stall at the church fete. Five vicars had held the living at St. Saviour's in the twins' time as worshipers there. Each new incumbent was advised by his predecessor that Pearl and Oyster were the mainstays of the parish. Better to fall foul of the diocesan bishop himself than the Brown twins.

All of this was observed from a distance, for no one, not even a vicar making his social rounds, was allowed inside the house in Lime Tree Avenue. The twins didn't entertain, and that was final. They were polite to their neighbors without once inviting them in. When one twin was ill, the other would transport her to the surgery in a state of high fever rather than call the doctor on a visit.

It followed that people's knowledge of Pearl and Oyster was limited. No one could doubt that they lived an orderly existence; there were no complaints about undue noise or unwashed windows or neglected paintwork. The hedge was trimmed and the garden mown. But what really bubbled and boiled behind the regularly washed net curtains—the secret passion that was to have such a dire result—was unsuspected until Oyster committed her crime.

She acted out of desperation. On the last Saturday in July, 1990, her well ordered life suffered a seismic shock. She was parted from her twin sister. The parting was sudden, traumatic, and had to be shrouded in secrecy. The prospect of anyone finding out what had occurred was unthinkable.

So for the first time in her life Oyster had no Pearl to change the light bulbs, pay the bills, and check that all the doors were locked. Oyster—let it be understood—was not incapable or dim-witted. Bereft as she was, she managed tolerably well until the Friday afternoon, when she had a letter to post, a letter of surpassing importance, capable—God willing—of easing her desolation. She had agonized over it for hours. Now it was crucial that the letter caught the last post of the day. Saturday would be too late. She went to the drawer where Pearl always kept the postage stamps and—calamity—not one was left.

Stamps had always been Pearl's responsibility. To be fair, the error was Oyster's; she had written more letters than usual and gone through the supply. She should have called at the Post Office when she was doing the shopping.

It was too late. There wasn't time to get there before the last post at 5:15. She tried to remain calm and consider her options. It was out of the question to ask a neighbor for a stamp; she and Pearl had made it a point of honor never to be beholden to anyone else. Neither could she countenance the disgrace of despatching the letter without a stamp in the hope that it would get by, or the recipient would pay the amount due.

This left one remedy, and it was criminal.

Behind one of the Staffordshire dogs on the mantelpiece was a bank statement. She had put it there for the time being because she had been too busy to check where Pearl normally stored such things. The significant point for Oyster at this minute was not the statement, but the envelope containing it. More precisely, the top right-hand corner of the envelope, because the first-class stamp had somehow escaped being cancelled.

Temptation stirred and uncoiled itself.

Oyster had never in her life steamed an unfranked stamp from an envelope and used it again. Nor, to her knowledge, had Pearl. Stamp collectors sometimes removed used specimens for their collections, but what Oyster was contemplating could in no way be confused with philately. It was against the law. Defrauding the Post Office. A crime.

There was under twenty minutes before the last collection.

I couldn't, she told herself. *I'm on the Parochial Church Council. I'm on the Bench.*

Temptation reminded her that she was due for a cup of tea in any case. She filled the kettle and pressed the switch. While waiting, watching the first wisp of steam rise from the spout, she weighed the necessity of posting the letter against the wickedness of reusing a stamp. It wasn't the most heinous of crimes, Temptation whispered. And once Oyster began to think about the chances of getting away with it, she was lost. The kettle sang, the steam gushed, and she snatched up the envelope and jammed it against the spout. Merely, Temptation reassured her, to satisfy her curiosity as to whether stamps could be separated from envelopes by this method.

Those who believe in retribution will not be in the least surprised that the steam was deflected by the surface of the envelope and scalded three of Oyster's fingers quite severely. She cried out in pain and dropped the envelope. She ran the cold tap and plunged her hand under it. Then she wrapped the sore fingers in a piece of kitchen towel.

Her first action after that was to turn off the kettle. Her second was to pick up the envelope and test the corner of the stamp with the tip of her fingernail. It still adhered to some extent, but with extreme care she was able to ease it free, consoled that her discomfort had not been entirely without result. The minor accident failed to deter her from the crime. On the contrary, it acted like a prod from Old Nick.

There was a bottle of gum in the writing desk and she applied some to the back of the stamp, taking care not to use too much, which might have oozed out at the edges and discolored the envelope. When she had positioned the stamp neatly on her letter, it would have passed the most rigorous inspection. She felt a wicked frisson of satisfaction at having committed an undetectable crime. Just in time, she remembered the post and had to hurry to catch it.

There we leave Miss Oyster Brown to come to terms with her conscience for a couple of days.

We meet her again on the Monday morning in the local chemist's shop. The owner and pharmacist was John Trigger, whom the Brown twins had known for getting on for thirty years, a decent, obliging man with a huge moustache who took a personal interest in his customers. In the face of strong competition from a national chain of pharmacists, John Trigger had persevered with his old-fashioned service from behind a counter, believing that some customers still preferred it to filling a wire basket themselves. But to stay in business, he had been forced to diversify by offering some electrical goods.

When Oyster Brown came in and showed him three badly scalded fingers out in blisters, Trigger was sympathetic as well as willing to suggest a remedy. Understandably, he inquired how Oyster had come by such a painful injury. She was expecting the question and had her answer ready, adhering to the truth as closely as a God-fearing woman should.

"An accident with the kettle."

Trigger looked genuinely alarmed. "An electric kettle? Not the one you bought here last year?"

"I didn't," said Oyster at once.

"Must have been your sister. A Steamquick. Is that what you've got?"

"Er, yes."

"If there's a fault—"

"I'm not here to complain, Mr. Trigger. So you think this ointment will do the trick?"

"I'm sure of it. Apply it evenly, and don't attempt to

pierce the blisters, will you?" John Trigger's conscience was troubling him. "This is quite a nasty scalding, Miss Brown. Where exactly did the steam come from?"

"The kettle."

"I know that. I mean was it the spout?"

"It really doesn't matter," said Oyster sharply. "It's done."

"The lid, then? Sometimes if you're holding the handle you get a rush of steam from that little slot in the lid. I expect it was that."

"I couldn't say," Oyster fudged, in the hope that it would satisfy Mr. Trigger.

It did not. "The reason I asked is that there may be a design fault."

"The fault was mine, I'm quite sure."

"Perhaps I ought to mention it to the manufacturers."

"Absolutely not," Oyster said in alarm. "I was careless, that's all. And now, if you'll excuse me—" She started backing away and then Mr. Trigger ambushed her with another question.

"What does your sister say about it?"

"My sister?" From the way she spoke, she might never have had one.

"Miss Pearl."

"Oh, nothing. We haven't discussed it," Oyster truthfully stated.

"But she must have noticed your fingers."

"Er, no. How much is the ointment?"

Trigger told her and she dropped the money on the counter and almost rushed from the shop. He stared after her, bewildered.

The next time Oyster Brown was passing, Trigger took the trouble to go to the door of his shop and inquire whether the hand was any better. Clearly she wasn't overjoyed to see him. She assured him without much gratitude that the ointment was working. "It was nothing. It's going to clear up in a couple of days."

"May I see?"

She held out her hand.

Trigger agreed that it was definitely on the mend. "Keep it dry, if you possibly can. Who does the washing up?"

"What do you mean?"

"You or your sister? It's well known that you divide the chores between you. If it's your job, I'm sure Miss Pearl won't mind taking over for a few days. If I see her, I'll suggest it myself."

Oyster reddened and said nothing.

"I was going to remark that I haven't seen her for a week or so," Trigger went on. "She isn't unwell, I hope?"

"No," said Oyster. "Not unwell."

Sensing correctly that this was not an avenue of conversation to venture along at this time, he said instead, "The Steamquick rep was in yesterday afternoon, so I mentioned what happened with your kettle."

She was outraged. "You had no business!"

"Pardon me, Miss Brown, but it *is* my business. You were badly scalded. I can't have my customers being injured by the products I sell. The rep was very concerned, as I am. He asked if you would be so good as to bring the kettle in next time you come so that he can check if there's a fault."

"Absolutely not," said Oyster. "I told you I haven't the slightest intention of complaining."

Trigger tried to be reasonable. "It isn't just your kettle. I've sold the same model to other customers."

"Then they'll complain if they get hurt."

"What if their children get hurt?"

She had no answer.

"If it's inconvenient to bring it in, perhaps I could call at your house."

"No," she said at once.

"I can bring a replacement. In fact, Miss Brown, I'm more than a little concerned about this whole episode. I'd like you to have another kettle with my compliments. A different model. Frankly, the modern trend is for jug kettles that couldn't possible scald you as yours did. If you'll kindly step into the shop, I'll give you one now to take home."

The offer didn't appeal to Oyster Brown in the least. "For the last time, Mr. Trigger," she said in a tight, clipped voice, "I don't require another kettle." With that, she walked away up the high street.

Trigger, from the motives he had mentioned, was not content to leave the matter there. He wasn't a churchgoer, but he believed in conducting his life on humanitarian principles. On this issue, he was resolved to be just as stubborn as she. He went back into the shop and straight to the phone. While Oyster Brown was out of the house, he would speak to Pearl Brown, the sister, and see if he could get better cooperation from her.

Nobody answered the phone.

At lunchtime, he called in to see Ted Collins, who ran the garden shop next door, and asked if he had seen anything of Pearl Brown lately.

"I had Oyster in this morning," Collins told him.

"But you haven't see Pearl?"

"Not in my shop. Oyster does all the gardening, you know. They divide the work."

"I know."

"I can't think what came over her today. Do you know what she bought? Six bottles of Rapidrot."

"What's that?"

"It's a new product. An activator for composting. You dilute it and water your compost heap and it speeds up the process. They're doing a special promotion to launch it. Six bottles are far too much, and I tried to tell her, but she wouldn't be told."

"Those two often buy in bulk," said Trigger. "I've

sold Pearl a dozen tubes of toothpaste at a go, and they must be awash with Dettol."

"They won't use six bottle of Rapidrot in twenty years," Collins pointed out. "It's concentrated stuff, and it won't keep all that well. It's sure to solidify after a time. I told her one's plenty to be going on with. She's wasted her money, obstinate old bird. I don't know what Pearl would say. Is she ill, do you think?"

"I've no idea," said Trigger, although in reality an idea was beginning to form in his brain. A disturbing idea. "Do they get on all right with each other? Daft question," he said before Collins could answer it. "They're twins. They've spent all their lives in each other's company."

For the present he dismissed the thought and gave his attention to the matter of the electric kettles. He'd already withdrawn the Steamquick kettles from sale. He got on the phone to Steamquick and had an acrimonious conversation with some little Hitler from their public-relations department who insisted that thousands of the kettles had been sold and the design was faultless.

"The lady's injury isn't imagined, I can tell you," Trigger insisted.

"She must have been careless. Anyone can hurt themselves if they're not careful. People are far too ready to put the blame on the manufacturer."

"People, as you put it, are your livelihood."

There was a heavy sigh. "Send us the offending kettle, and we'll test it."

"That isn't so simple."

"Have you offered to replace it?"

The man's whole tone was so condescending that Trigger had an impulse to frighten him rigid. "She won't let the kettle out of her possession. I think she may be keeping it as evidence."

"Evidence?" There was a pause while the implication dawned. "Blimey."

On his end of the phone, Trigger permitted himself to grin.

"You mean she might take us to court over this?"

"I didn't say that."

"Ah."

"But she does know the law. She's a magistrate."

An audible gasp followed, then: "Listen, Mr., er—"

"Trigger."

"Mr. Trigger. I think we'd better send someone to meet this lady and deal with the matter personally. Yes, that's what we'll do."

Trigger worked late that evening, stocktaking. He left the shop about 10:30. Out of curiosity he took a route home via Lime Tree Avenue and stopped the car opposite the Brown sisters' house and wound down the car window. There were lights upstairs and presently someone drew a curtain. It looked like Oyster Brown.

"Keeping an eye on your customers, Mr. Trigger?" a voice close to him said.

He turned guiltily. A woman's face was six inches from his. He recognized one of his customers, Mrs. Wingate. She said, "She's done that every night this week."

"Oh?"

"Something fishy's going on in there," she said. "I walk my little dog along the verge about this time every night. I live just opposite them, on the side, with the wrought-iron gates. That's Pearl's bedroom at the front. I haven't seen Pearl for a week, but every night Oyster draws the curtains and leaves the light on for half an hour. What's going on, I'd like to know. If Pearl is ill, they ought to call a doctor. They won't, you know."

"That's Pearl's bedroom, you say, with the light on?"

"Yes, I often see her looking out. Not lately."

"And now Oyster switches on the light and draws the curtains?"

"And pulls them back at seven in the morning. I don't know what *you* think, Mr. Trigger, but it looks to me as if she wants everyone to think Pearl's in there, when it's obvious she isn't."

"Why is it obvious?"

"All the windows are closed. Pearl always opens the top window wide, winter and summer."

"That is odd, now you mention it."

"I'll tell you one thing," said Mrs. Wingate, regardless that she had told him several things already, "whatever game she's up to, we won't find out. Nobody ever sets foot inside that house except the twins themselves."

At home and in bed that night, Trigger was troubled by a gruesome idea, one that he'd tried repeatedly to suppress. Suppose the worst had happened a week ago in the house in Lime Tree Avenue, his thinking ran. Suppose Pearl Brown had suffered a heart attack and died. After so many years of living in that house as if it were a fortress, was Oyster capable of dealing with the aftermath of death, calling in the doctor and the undertaker? In her shocked state, mightn't she decide that anything was preferable to having the house invaded, even if the alternative was disposing of the body herself?

How would a middle-aged woman dispose of a body? Oyster didn't drive a car. It wouldn't be easy to bury it in the garden, nor hygienic to keep it in a cupboard in the house. But if there was one thing every well bred English lady knew about, it was gardening.

Oyster was the gardener.

In time, everything rots in a compost heap. If you want to accelerate the process, you buy a preparation like Rapidrot.

Oyster Brown had purchased six bottles of the stuff.

And every night she drew the curtains in her sister's bedroom to give the impression that she was there.

He shuddered.

In the fresh light of morning, John Trigger told himself that his morbid imaginings couldn't be true. They were the delusions of a tired brain. He decided to do nothing about them.

Just after 11:30, a short fat man in a dark suit arrived in the shop and announced himself as the Area Manager of Steamquick. His voice was suspiciously like the one Trigger had found so irritating when he had phoned their head office. "I'm here about this allegedly faulty kettle," he announced.

"Miss Brown's?"

"I'm sure there's nothing wrong at all, but we're a responsible firm. We take every complaint seriously."

"You want to see the kettle? You'll be lucky."

The Steamquick man sounded smug. "That's all right. I telephoned Miss Brown this morning and offered to go to the house. She wasn't at all keen on that idea, but I was very firm with the lady and she compromised. We're meeting here at noon. She's agreed to bring the kettle for me to inspect. I don't know why you found her so intractable."

"High noon, eh? Do you want to use my office?"

Trigger had come to a rapid decision. If Oyster was on her way to the shop, he was going out. He had two capable assistants.

This was a heaven-sent opportunity to lay his macabre theory to rest. While Oyster was away from the house in Lime Tree Avenue, he would drive there and let himself into the back garden. Mrs. Wingate or any other curious neighbor watching from behind the lace curtains would have to assume he was trying to deliver something. He kept his white coat on, to reinforce the idea that he was on official business.

Quite probably, he told himself, the compost heap

will turn out to be no bigger than a cowpat. The day was sunny and he felt positively cheerful as he turned up the avenue. He checked his watch. Oyster would be making mincemeat of the Steamquick man about now. It would take her twenty minutes, at least, to walk back.

He stopped the car and got out. Nobody was about, but just in case he was being observed he walked boldly up the path to the front door and rang the bell. No one came.

Without appearing in the least furtive, he stepped around the side of the house. The back garden was in a beautiful state. Wide, well stocked, and immaculately weeded borders enclosed a finely trimmed lawn, yellow roses on a trellis, and a kitchen garden beyond. Trigger took it in admiringly, and then remembered why he was there. His throat went dry. At the far end, beyond the kitchen garden, slightly obscured by some runner beans on poles, was the compost heap—as long as a coffin and more than twice as high.

The flesh on his arms prickled.

The compost heap was covered with black-plastic bin liners weighted with stones. They lay across the top, but the sides were exposed. A layer of fresh green garden refuse, perhaps half a meter in depth, was on the top. The lower part graduated in color from a dull yellow to earth-brown. Obvious care had been taken to conserve the shape, to keep the pressure even and assist the composting process.

Trigger wasn't much of a gardener. He didn't have the time for it. He did the minimum and got rid of his garden rubbish with bonfires. Compost heaps were outside his experience, except that as a scientist he understood the principle by which they generated heat in a confined space. Once, years ago, an uncle of his had demonstrated this by pushing a bamboo cane into his heap from the top. A wisp of steam had issued from the hole as he withdrew the cane. Recalling it now, Trigger felt a wave of nausea.

He hadn't the stomach for this.

He knew now that he wasn't going to be able to walk up the garden and probe the compost heap. Disgusted with himself for being so squeamish, he turned to leave, and happened to notice that the kitchen window was ajar, which was odd considering that Oyster wasn't at home. Out of interest, he tried the door handle. The door was unlocked.

He said, "Anyone there?" and got no answer.

From the doorway he could see a number of unopened letters on the kitchen table. After the humiliation of turning his back on the compost heap, this was like a challenge, a chance to regain some self-respect. This, at least, he was capable of doing. He stepped inside and picked up the letters. There were five, all addressed to Miss P. Brown. The postmarks dated from the beginning of the previous week.

Quite clearly, Pearl had not been around to open her letters.

Then his attention was taken by an extraordinary lineup along a shelf. He counted fifteen packets of cornflakes, all open, and recalled his conversation with Ted Collins about the sisters buying in bulk. If Collins had wanted convincing, there was ample evidence here; seven bottles of decaffeinated coffee, nine jars of the same brand of marmalade, and a tall stack of boxes of paper tissues. Eccentric housekeeping, to say the least. Perhaps, he reflected, it meant that the buying of six bottles of Rapidrot had not, after all, been so sinister.

But now that he was in the house, he wasn't going to leave without seeking an answer to the main mystery, the disappearance of Pearl. His mouth was no longer dry and the gooseflesh had gone from his arms. He made up his mind to go upstairs and look into the front bedroom.

On the other side of the kitchen door, more extravagance was revealed. The passage from the kitchen to the stairway was lined on either side with sets of goods that must have overflowed from the kitchen. Numerous tins of cocoa, packets of sugar, pots of jam, gravy powder, and other grocery items were stored as if for a siege, stacked along the skirting boards in groups of at least half a dozen. Trigger began seriously to fear for the mental health of the twins. Nobody had suspected anything like this behind the closed doors. The stacks extended halfway upstairs.

As he stepped upward, obliged to tread close to the banister, he was gripped by the sense of alienation that must have led to hoarding on such a scale. The staid faces that the sisters presented to the world gave no intimation of this strange compulsion. What was the mentality of people who behaved as weirdly as this?

An appalling possibility crept into Trigger's mind. Maybe the strain of so many years of appearing outwardly normal had finally caused Oyster to snap. What if the eccentricity so apparent all around him now were not so harmless as it first appeared? No one could know what resentments, what jealousies lurked in this house, what mean-minded cruelties the sisters may have inflicted on each other. What if Oyster had fallen out with her sister and attacked her? She was a sturdy woman, physically capable of killing.

If she'd murdered Pearl, the compost-heap method of disposal would certainly commend itself.

Come now, he told himself, this is all speculation.

He reached the top stair and discovered that the stockpiling had extended to the landing. Toothpaste, talcum powder, shampoos, and soap were stacked up in profusion. All the doors were closed. It wouldn't have surprised him if when he opened one he was knee-deep in toilet rolls.

First he had to orientate himself. He decided that the

front bedroom was to his right. He opened it cautiously and stepped in.

What happened next was swift and devastating. John Trigger heard a piercing scream. He had a sense of movement to his left and a glimpse of a figure in white. Something crashed against his head with a mighty thump, causing him to pitch forward.

About four, when the Brown twins generally stopped for tea, Oyster filled the new kettle that the Steam-quick Area Manager had exchanged for the other one. She plugged it in. It was the newfangled jug type and she wasn't really certain if she was going to like it, but she certainly needed the cup of tea.

"I know it was wrong," she said, "and I'm going to pray for forgiveness, but I didn't expect that steaming a stamp off a letter would lead to this. I suppose it's a judgment."

"Whatever made you do such a wicked thing?" her sister Pearl asked, as she put out the cups and saucers.

"The letter had to catch the post. It was the last possible day for the Kellogg's Cornflakes competition, and I'd thought of such a wonderful slogan. The prize was a fortnight in Venice."

Pearl clicked her tongue in disapproval. "Just because I won the Birds Eye trip to the Bahamas, it didn't mean *you* were going to be lucky. We tried for twenty years and only ever won consolation prizes."

"It isn't really gambling, is it?" said Oyster. "It isn't like betting."

"It's all right in the Lord's eyes," Pearl told her. "It's a harmless pastime. Unfortunately, we both know that people in the church won't take a charitable view. They wouldn't expect us to devote so much of our time and money to competitions. That's why we have to be careful. You didn't tell anyone I was away?"

"Of course not. Nobody knows. For all they know, you were ill, if anyone noticed at all. I drew the curtains in your bedroom every night to make it look as if you were here."

"Thank you. You know I'd do the same for you."

"I *might* win," said Oyster. "Someone always does. I put in fifteen entries altogether, and the last one was a late inspiration."

"And as a result we have fifteen packets of corn-flakes with the tops cut off," said Pearl. "They take up a lot of room."

"So do your frozen peas. I had to throw two packets away to make some room in the freezer. Anyway, I felt entitled to try. It wasn't much fun being here alone, thinking of you sunning yourself in the West Indies. To tell you the truth, I didn't really think you'd go and leave me here. It was a shock."

Oyster carefully poured some hot water into the tea-pot to warm it. "If you want to know, I've also entered the Rapidrot Trip of a Lifetime competition. A week in San Francisco followed by a week in Sydney. I bought six bottles to have a fighting chance."

"What's Rapidrot?"

"Something for the garden." She spooned in some tea and poured on the hot water. "You must be exhausted. Did you get any sleep on the plane?"

"Hardly any," said Pearl. "That's why I went straight to bed when I got in this morning." She poured milk into the teacups. "The next thing I knew was the doorbell going. I ignored it, naturally. It was one of the nastiest shocks I ever had, hearing the footsteps coming up the stairs. I could tell it wasn't you. I'm just thankful that I had the candlestick to defend myself with."

"Is there any sign of life yet?"

"Well, he's breathing, but he hasn't opened his eyes, if that's what you mean. Funny, I would never have thought Mr. Trigger was dangerous to women."

Oyster poured the tea. "What are we going to do if

he doesn't recover? We can't have people coming into the house." Even as she was speaking, she put down the teapot and glanced out of the kitchen window toward the end of the garden. She had the answer herself.

Strychnine in the Soup
by P. G. Wodehouse

From the moment the Draught Stout entered the bar parlor of *The Angler's Rest,* it had been obvious that he was not his usual cheery self. His face was drawn and twisted, and he sat with bowed head in a distant corner by the window, contributing nothing to the conversation which, with Mr. Mulliner as its center, was in progress around the fire.

From time to time he heaved a hollow sigh.

A sympathetic Lemon and Angostura, putting down his glass, went across and laid a kindly hand on the sufferer's shoulder.

"What is it, old man?" he asked. "Lost a friend?"

"Worse," said the Draught Stout. "A mystery novel. Got halfway through it on the journey down here, and left it on the train."

"My nephew Cyril, the interior decorator," said Mr. Mulliner, "once did the very same thing. These mental lapses are not infrequent."

"And now," proceeded the Draught Stout, "I'm going to have a sleepless night, wondering who poisoned Sir Geoffrey Tuttle, Bart."

"The bart. was poisoned, was he?"

"You never said a truer word. Personally, I think it

was the vicar who did him in. He was known to be interested in strange poisons."

Mr. Mulliner smiled indulgently.

"It was not the vicar," he said. "I happen to have read *The Murglow Manor Mystery*. The guilty man was the plumber."

"What plumber?"

"The one who comes in Chapter Two to mend the shower bath. Sir Geoffrey had wronged his aunt in the year '96, so he fastened a snake in the nozzle of the shower bath with glue; and when Sir Geoffrey turned on the stream the hot water melted the glue. This released the snake, which dropped through one of the holes, bit the baronet in the leg, and disappeared down the waste pipe."

"But that can't be right," said the Draught Stout. "Between Chapter Two and the murder there was an interval of several days."

"The plumber forgot his snake and had to go back for it," explained Mr. Mulliner. "I trust this revelation will prove sedative."

"I feel a new man," said the Draught Stout. "I'd have lain awake worrying about that murder all night."

"I suppose you would. My nephew Cyril was just the same. Nothing in this modern life of ours," said Mr. Mulliner, taking a sip of his hot Scotch and lemon, "is more remarkable than the way in which the mystery novel has gripped the public. Your true enthusiast, deprived of his favorite reading, will stop at nothing in order to get it. He is like a victim of the drug habit when withheld from cocaine. My nephew Cyril—"

"Amazing the things people will leave in trains," said a Small Lager. "Bags . . . umbrellas . . . even stuffed chimpanzees, occasionally, I've been told. I heard a story the other day . . ."

My nephew Cyril (said Mr. Mulliner) had a greater passion for mystery stories than anyone I have ever met. I attribute this to the fact that, like so many interior decorators, he was a fragile, delicate young fellow, extraordinarily vulnerable to any ailment that happened to be going the rounds. Every time he caught mumps or influenza or German measles or the like, he occupied the period of convalescence in reading mystery stories. And, as the appetite grows by what it feeds on, he had become, at the time at which this narrative opens, a confirmed addict. Not only did he devour every volume of this type on which he could lay his hands, but he was also to be found at any theatre which was offering the kind of drama where skinny arms come unexpectedly out of the chiffonier and the audience feels a mild surprise if the lights stay on for ten consecutive minutes.

And it was during a performance of *The Grey Vampire* at the St. James's that he found himself sitting next to Amelia Bassett, the girl whom he was to love with all the stored-up fervor of a man who hitherto had been inclined rather to edge away when in the presence of the other sex.

He did not know her name was Amelia Bassett. He had never seen her before. All he knew was that at last he had met his fate, and for the whole of the first act he was pondering the problem of how he was to make her acquaintance.

It was as the lights went up for the first intermission that he was aroused from his thoughts by a sharp pain in the right leg. He was just wondering whether it was gout or sciatica when, glancing down, he perceived that what had happened was that his neighbor, absorbed by the drama, had absent-mindedly collected a handful of his flesh and was twisting it in an ecstasy of excitement.

It seemed to Cyril a good *point d'appui.*

"Excuse me," he said.

The girl turned. Her eyes were glowing, and the tip of her nose still quivered.

"I beg your pardon?"

"My leg," said Cyril. "Might I have it back, if you've finished with it?"

The girl looked down. She started visibly.

"I'm awfully sorry," she gasped.

"Not at all," said Cyril. "Only too glad to have been of assistance."

"I got carried away."

"You are evidently fond of mystery plays."

"I love them."

"So do I. And mystery novels?"

"Oh, yes!"

"Have you read *Blood on the Banisters*?"

"Oh, yes! I thought it was better than *Severed Throats!*"

"So did I," said Cyril. "Much better. Brighter murders, subtler detectives, crisper clues . . . better in every way."

The two twin souls gazed into each other's eyes. There is no surer foundation for a beautiful friendship that a mutual taste in literature.

"My name is Amelia Bassett," said the girl.

"Mine is Cyril Mulliner. Bassett?" He frowned thoughtfully. "The name seems familiar."

"Perhaps you have heard of my mother. Lady Bassett. She's rather a well-known big game hunter and explorer. She tramps through jungles and things. She's gone out to the lobby for a smoke. By the way"—she hesitated—"if she finds us talking, will you remember that we met at the Polterwoods'?"

"I quite understand."

"You see, Mother doesn't like people who talk to me without a formal introduction. And when Mother doesn't like anyone, she is so apt to hit him over the head with some hard instrument."

"I see," said Cyril. "Like the Human Ape in *Gore by the Gallon.*"

"Exactly. Tell me," said the girl, changing the sub-

ject, "if you were a millionaire, would you rather be
stabbed in the back with a paperknife or found dead
without a mark on you, staring with blank eyes at some
appalling sight?"

Cyril was about to reply when, looking past her, he
found himself virtually in the latter position. A woman
of extraordinary formidableness had lowered herself
into the seat beyond and was scrutinizing him keenly
through a tortoise-shell lorgnette. She reminded Cyril
of Wallace Beery.

"Friend of yours, Amelia?" she said.

"This is Mr. Mulliner, Mother. We met at the Polterwoods.' "

"Ah?" said Lady Bassett.

She inspected Cyril through her lorgnette.

"Mr. Mulliner," she said, "is a little like the chief of
the lower Isisi—though, of course, he was darker and
had a ring through his nose. A dear, good fellow," she
continued reminiscently, "but inclined to become familiar under the influence of trade gin. I shot him in
the leg."

"Er—why?" asked Cyril.

"He was not behaving like a gentleman," said Lady
Bassett primly.

"After taking your treatment," said Cyril, awed, "I'll
bet he could have written a Book of Etiquette."

"I believe he did," said Lady Bassett carelessly.
"You must come and call on us some afternoon, Mr.
Mulliner. I am in the telephone book. If you are interested in man-eating pumas, I can show you some nice
heads."

The curtain rose on Act Two, and Cyril returned to
his thoughts. Love, he felt joyously, had come into his
life at last. But then so, he had to admit, had Lady
Bassett. There is, he reflected, always something. . . .

I will pass lightly over the period of Cyril's wooing.
Suffice it to say that his progress was rapid. From the

moment he told Amelia he had once met Dorothy L. Sayers, he never looked back. And one afternoon, calling and finding that Lady Bassett was away in the country, he took the girl's hand in his and told his love.

For a while all was well. Amelia's reactions proved satisfactory to a degree. She checked up enthusiastically on his proposition. Falling into his arms, she admitted specifically that he was her Dream Man.

Then came the jarring note.

"But it's no use," she said, her lovely eyes filling with tears. "Mother will never give her consent."

"Why not?" said Cyril, stunned. "What is it she objects to about me?"

"I don't know. But she generally alludes to you as 'that pipsqueak.' "

"Pipsqueak?" said Cyril. "What *is* a pipsqueak?"

"I'm not quite sure, but it's something Mother doesn't like very much. It's a pity she ever found out that you are an interior decorator."

"An honorable profession," said Cyril, a little stiffly.

"I know; but what she admires are men who have to do with the great open spaces."

"Well, I also design ornamental gardens."

"Yes," said the girl doubtfully, "but still—"

"And, dash it," said Cyril indignantly, "this isn't the Victorian Age. All that business of Mother's Consent went out twenty years ago."

"Yes, but no one told Mother."

"It's preposterous!" cried Cyril. "I never heard such rot. Let's just slip off and get married quietly and send her a picture postcard from Venice or somewhere, with a cross and a 'This is our room. Wish you were with us' on it."

The girl shuddered.

"She would be with us," she said. "You don't know Mother. The moment she got that picture postcard, she would come over to wherever we were and put you across her knee and spank you with a hairbrush. I don't think I could ever feel the same towards you if I saw you lying across Mother's knee, being spanked with a hairbrush. It would spoil the honeymoon."

Cyril frowned. But a man who has spent most of his life trying out a series of patent medicines is always an optimist.

"There is only one thing to be done," he said. "I shall see your mother and try to make her listen to reason. Where is she now?"

"She left this morning for a visit to the Winghams in Sussex."

"Excellent! I know the Winghams. In fact, I have a standing invitation to go and stay with them whenever I like. I'll send them a wire and push down this evening. I will oil up to your mother sedulously and try to correct her present unfavorable impression of me. Then, choosing the moment, I will shoot her the news. It may work. It may not work. But at any rate I consider it a fair sporting venture."

"But you are so diffident, Cyril. So shrinking. So retiring and shy. How can you carry through such a task?"

"Love will nerve me."

"Enough, do you think? Remember what Mother is. Wouldn't a good, strong drink be more help?"

Cyril looked doubtful.

"My doctor has always forbidden me alcoholic stimulants. He says they increase the blood pressure."

"Well, when you meet Mother, you will need all the blood pressure you can get. I really do advise you to fuel up a little before you see her."

"Yes," agreed Cyril, nodding thoughtfully. "I think you're right. It shall be as you say. Goodbye, my angel one."

"Goodbye, Cyril, darling. You will think of me every minute while you're gone?"

"Every single minute. Well, practically every single minute. You see, I have just got Horatio Slingsby's lat-

est book, *Strychnine in the Soup,* and I shall be dipping
into that from time to time. But all the rest of the
while ... Have you read it, by the way?"

"Not yet. I had a copy, but Mother took it with her."

"Ah? Well, if I am to catch a train that will get me
to Barkley for dinner, I must be going. Goodbye,
sweetheart, and never forget that Gilbert Glendale in
The Missing Toe won the girl he loved in spite of being
up against two mysterious stranglers and the entire
Black Mustache gang."

He kissed her fondly, and went off to pack.

Barkley Towers, the country seat of Sir Mortimer
and Lady Wingham, was two hours from London by
rail. Thinking of Amelia and reading the opening chap-
ters of Horatio Slingsby's powerful story, Cyril found
the journey passing rapidly. In fact, so preoccupied
was he that it was only as the train started to draw out
of Barkley Regis station that he realized where he was.
He managed to hurl himself onto the platform just in
time.

As he had taken the five-seven express, stopping
only at Gluebury Perveril, he arrived at Barkley Towers at an hour which enabled him not only to be on
hand for dinner but also to take part in the life-giving
distribution of cocktails which preceded the meal.

The house party, he perceived on entering the
drawing-room, was a small one. Besides Lady Bassett
and himself, the only visitors were a nondescript couple of the name of Simpson, and a tall, bronzed, handsome man with flashing eyes who, his hostess
informed him in a whispered aside, was Lester
Mapledurham (pronounced Mum). the explorer and
big-game hunter.

Perhaps it was the oppressive sensation of being in
the same room with two explorers and big-game hunters that brought home to Cyril the need for following
Amelia's advice as quickly as possible. But probably

the mere sight of Lady Bassett alone would have been enough to make him break a life-long abstinence. To her normal resemblance to Wallace Beery she appeared now to have added a distinct suggestion of Victor McLaglen, and the spectacle was sufficient to send Cyril leaping toward the cocktail tray.

After three rapid glasses he felt a better and a braver man. And so lavishly did he irrigate the ensuing dinner with hock, sherry, champagne, old brandy, and port that at the conclusion of the meal he was pleased to find that his diffidence had completely vanished. He rose from the table feeling equal to asking a dozen Lady Bassetts for their consent to marry a dozen daughters.

In fact, as he confided to the butler, prodding him genially in the ribs as he spoke, if Lady Bassett attempted to put on any dog with *him*, he would know what to do about it. He made no threats, he explained to the butler; he simply stated that he would know what to do about it. The butler said, "Very good, sir. Thank you, sir," and the incident closed.

It had been Cyril's intention—feeling, as he did, in this singularly uplifted and dominant frame of mind—to get hold of Amelia's mother and start oiling up to her immediately after dinner. But, what with falling into a doze in the smoking room and then getting into an argument on theology with one of the underfootmen whom he met in the hall, he did not reach the drawing-room until nearly half-past ten. And he was annoyed, on walking in with a merry cry of "Lady Bassett! Call for Lady Bassett!" on his lips, to discover that she had retired to her room.

Had Cyril's mood been even slightly less elevated, this news might have acted as a check on his enthusiasm. So generous, however, had been Sir Mortimer's hospitality that he merely nodded eleven times, to indicate comprehension, and then, having ascertained that

his quarry was roosting in the Blue Room, sped thither
with a brief "Tally-ho!"

Arriving at the Blue Room, he banged heartily on
the door and breezed in. He found Lady Bassett
propped up with pillows. She was smoking a cigar and
reading a book. And that book, Cyril saw with intense
surprise and resentment, was none other than Horatio
Slingsby's *Strychnine in the Soup*.

The spectacle brought him to an abrupt halt.

"Well, I'm dashed!" he cried. "Well, I'm blowed!
What do you mean by pinching my book?"

Lady Bassett had lowered her cigar. She now raised
her eyebrows.

"What are you doing in my room, Mr. Mulliner?"

"It's a little hard," said Cyril, trembling with self-
pity. "I go to enormous expense to buy detective stories, and no sooner is my back turned than people rush
about the place sneaking them."

"This book belongs to my daughter Amelia."

"Good old Amelia!" said Cyril cordially. "One of
the best."

"I borrowed it to read on the train. Now will you
kindly tell me what you are doing in my room, Mr.
Mulliner?"

Cyril smote his forehead.

"Of course. I remember now. It all comes back to
me. She told me you had taken it. And, what's more,
I've suddenly recollected something which clears you
completely. I was hustled and bustled at the end of the
journey. I sprang to my feet, hurled bags onto the
platform—in a word, lost my head. And, like a chump,
I went and left my copy of *Strychnine in the Soup* in
the train. Well, I can only apologize."

"You can not only apologize. You can also tell me
what you are doing in my room."

"What I am doing in your room?"

"Exactly."

"Ah!" said Cyril, sitting down on the bed. "You may well ask."

"I *have* asked. Three times."

Cyril closed his eyes. For some reason, his mind seemed cloudy and not at its best.

"If you are proposing to go to sleep here, Mr. Mulliner," said Lady Bassett, "tell me, and I shall know what to do about it."

The phrase touched a chord in Cyril's memory. He recollected now his reasons for being where he was. Opening his eyes, he fixed them on her.

"Lady Bassett," he said, "you are, I believe, an explorer."

"I am."

"In the course of your explorations, you have wandered through many a jungle in many a distant land?"

"I have."

"Tell me, Lady Bassett," said Cyril keenly, "while making a pest of yourself to the denizens of those jungles, did you notice one thing? I allude to the fact that Love is everywhere—aye, even in the jungle. Love, independent of bounds and frontiers, of nationality and species, works its spell on every living thing. So that, no matter whether an individual be a Congo native, an American song writer, a jaguar, an armadillo, a bespoke tailor, or a tsetse-tsetse fly, he will infallibly seek his mate. So why shouldn't an interior decorator and designer of ornamental gardens? I put this to you, Lady Bassett."

"Mr. Mulliner," said his roommate, "you are blotto!"

Cyril waved his hand in a spacious gesture, and fell off the bed.

"Blotto I may be," he said, resuming his seat, "but, none the less, argue as you will, you can't get away from the fact that I love your daughter Amelia."

"What did you say?" cried Lady Bassett.

"When?" said Cyril absently, for he had fallen into a daydream and, as far as the intervening blankets would permit, was playing This Little Pig Went to Market with his companion's toes.

"Did I hear you say . . . my daughter Amelia?"

"Gray-eyed girl, medium height, sort of browny red hair," said Cyril, to assist her memory. "Dash it, you *must* know Amelia. She goes everywhere. And let me tell you something, Mrs.—I've forgotten your name. We're going to be married, if I can obtain her foul mother's consent. Speaking as an old friend, what would you say the chances were?"

"Extremely slight."

"Eh?"

"Seeing that I am Amelia's mother . . ."

Cyril blinked, genuinely surprised.

"Why, so you are! I didn't recognize you. Have you been there all the time?"

"I have."

Suddenly Cyril's gaze hardened. He drew himself up stiffly.

"What are you doing in my bed?" he demanded.

"This is not your bed."

"Then whose is it?"

"Mine."

Cyril shrugged his shoulders helplessly.

"Well, it all looks very funny to me," he said. "I suppose I must believe your story, but, I repeat, I consider the whole thing odd, and I propose to institute very strict inquiries. I may tell you that I happen to know the ringleaders. I wish you a very hearty good night."

It was perhaps an hour later that Cyril, who had been walking on the terrace in deep thought, repaired once more to the Blue Room in quest of information. Running the details of the recent interview over in his head, he had suddenly discovered that there was a point which had not been satisfactorily cleared up.

"I say," he said.

Lady Bassett looked up from her book, plainly annoyed.

"Have you no bedroom of your own, Mr. Mulliner?"

"Oh, yes," said Cyril. "They've bedded me out in the Moat Room. But there was something I wanted you to tell me."

"Well?"

"Did you say I might or mightn't?"

"Might or mightn't what?"

"Marry Amelia?"

"No. You may not."

"No?"

"No!"

"Oh!" said Cyril. "Well, pip-pip once more."

It was a moody Cyril Mulliner who withdrew to the Moat Room. He now realized the position of affairs. The mother of the girl he loved refused to accept him as an eligible suitor. A dickens of a situation to be in, felt Cyril, somberly unshoeing himself.

Then he brightened a little. His life, he reflected, might be wrecked, but he still had two-thirds of *Strychnine in the Soup* to read.

At the moment when the train reached Barkley Regis station, Cyril had just got to the bit where Detective-Inspector Mould looks through the half-open cellar door and, drawing in his breath with a sharp hissing sound, recoils in horror. It was obviously going to be good. He was just about to proceed to the dressing-table where, he presumed, the footman had placed the book on unpacking his bag, when an icy stream seemed to flow down the center of his spine, and the room and its contents danced before him.

Once more he had remembered that he had left the volume in the train.

He uttered an animal cry and tottered to a chair.

The subject of bereavement is one that has often been treated powerfully by poets, who have run the

whole gamut of the emotions while laying bare for us
the agony of those who have lost parents, wives, children, gazelles, money, fame, dogs, cats, doves, sweet-
hearts, horses, and even collar studs. But no poet has
yet treated of the most poignant bereavement of all—
that of a man halfway through a detective story who
finds himself at bedtime without the book.

Cyril did not care to think of the night that lay before him. Already his brain was lashing itself from side
to side like a wounded snake as it sought for some explanation of Inspector Mould's strange behavior. Horatio Slingsby was an author who could be relied on to
keep faith with his public. He was not the sort of man
to fob the reader off in the next chapter with the statement that what had made Inspector Mould look horrified was the fact that he had suddenly remembered that
he had forgotten all about the letter his wife had given
him to post. If looking through cellar doors disturbed a
Slingsby detective, it was because a dismembered
corpse lay there, or at least a severed hand.

A soft moan, as of something in torment, escaped
Cyril. What to do? What to do? Even a makeshift sub-
stitute for *Strychnine in the Soup* was beyond his
reach. He knew so well what he would find if he went
to the library in search of something to read. Sir
Mortimer Wingham was heavy and country-squirish.
His wife affected strange religions. Their literature was
in keeping with their tastes. In the library there would
be books on Ba-ha-ism, volumes in old leather of the
Rural Encyclopaedia, My Two Years in Sunny Ceylon,
by the Rev. Orlo Waterbury ... but of anything that
would interest Scotland Yard, of anything with a bit of
blood in it and a corpse or two into which a fellow
could get his teeth, not a trace.

What, then, coming right back to it, to do?

And suddenly, as if in answer to the question, came
the solution. Electrified, he saw the way out.

The hour was now well advanced. By this time Lady

Bassett must surely be asleep. *Strychnine in the Soup* would be lying on the table beside her bed. All he had to do was to creep in and grab it.

The more he considered the idea, the better it looked. It was not as if he did not know the way to Lady Bassett's room or the topography of it when he got there. It seemed to him as if most of his later life had been spent in Lady Bassett's room. He could find his way about it with his eyes shut.

He hesitated no longer. Donning a dressing-gown, he left his room and hurried along the passage.

Pushing open the door of the Blue Room and closing it softly behind him, Cyril stood for a moment full of all those emotions which come to a man revisiting some long-familiar spot. There the dear old room was, just the same as ever. How it all came back to him! The place was in darkness, but that did not deter him. He knew where the bed-table was, and he made for it with stealthy steps.

In the manner in which Cyril Mulliner advanced towards the bed-table there was much which would have reminded Lady Bassett, had she been an eye-witness, of the furtive prowl of the Lesser Iguanodon tracking its prey. In only one respect did Cyril and this creature of the wild differ in their technique. Iguanodons—and this applies not only to the Lesser but to the Larger Iguanodon—seldom, if ever, trip over cords on the floor and bring the lamps to which they are attached crashing to the ground like a ton of bricks.

Cyril did. Scarcely had he snatched up the book and placed it in the pocket of his dressing-gown, when his foot became entangled in the trailing cord and the lamp on the table leaped nimbly into the air and, to the accompaniment of a sound not unlike that made by a hundred plates coming apart simultaneously in the hands of a hundred scullery maids, nose-dived to the floor and became a total loss.

At the same moment, Lady Bassett, who had been

chasing a bat out of the window, stepped in from the balcony and switched on the lights.

To say that Cyril Mulliner was taken aback would be to understate the facts. Nothing like this recent misadventure had happened to him since his eleventh year, when, going surreptitiously to his mother's cupboard for jam, he had jerked three shelves down on his head, containing milk, butter, homemade preserves, pickles, cheese, eggs, cakes, and potted meat. His feelings on the present occasion closely paralleled that boyhood thrill.

Lady Bassett also appeared somewhat discomposed.

"You!" she said.

Cyril nodded, endeavoring the while to smile in a reassuring manner.

"Hullo!" he said.

His hostess's manner was now one of unmistakable displeasure.

"Am I not to have a moment of privacy, Mr. Mulliner?" she asked severely. "I am, I trust, a broad-minded woman, but I cannot approve of this idea of communal bedrooms."

Cyril made an effort to be conciliatory.

"I do keep coming in, don't I?" he said.

"You do," agreed Lady Bassett. "Sir Mortimer informed me, on learning that I had been given this room, that it was supposed to be haunted. Had I known that it was haunted by you, Mr. Mulliner, I should have packed up and gone to the local inn."

Cyril bowed his head. The censure, he could not but feel, was deserved.

"I admit," he said, "that my conduct has been open to criticism. In extenuation, I can but plead my great love. This is no idle social call, Lady Bassett. I looked in because I wished to take up again this matter of my marrying your daughter Amelia. You say I can't. Why can't I? Answer me that, Lady Bassett."

I have other views for Amelia," said Lady Bassett

stiffly. "When my daughter gets married it will not be to a spineless, invertebrate product of our modern hothouse civilization, but to a strong, upstanding, keen-eyed, two-fisted he-man of the open spaces. I have no wish to hurt your feelings, Mr. Mulliner," she continued, more kindly, "but you must admit that you are, when all is said and done, a pipsqueak."

"I deny it," cried Cyril warmly. "I don't even know what a pipsqueak is."

"A pipsqueak is a man who has never seen the sun rise beyond the reaches of the Lower Zambezi; who would not know what to do if faced by a charging rhinoceros. What, pray, would you do if faced by a charging rhinoceros, Mr. Mulliner?"

"I am not likely," said Cyril, "to move in the same social circles as charging rhinoceri."

"Or take another simple case, such as happens every day. Suppose you are crossing a rude bridge over a stream in Equatorial Africa. You have been thinking of a hundred trifles and are in a reverie. From this you wake to discover that in the branches overhead a python is extending its fangs towards you. At the same time, you observe that at one end of the bridge is a crouching puma; at the other are two head hunters—call them Pat and Mike—with poisoned blowpipes to their lips. Below, half-hidden in the stream, is an alligator. What would you do?"

Cyril weighed the point.

"I should feel embarrassed," he had to admit. "I shouldn't know where to look."

Lady Bassett laughed an amused, scornful little laugh.

"Precisely. Such a situation would not, however, disturb Lester Mapledurham."

"Lester Mapledurham!"

"The man who is to marry my daughter Amelia. He asked me for her hand shortly after dinner."

Cyril reeled. The blow, falling so suddenly and unexpectedly, had made him feel boneless. And yet, he felt, he might have expected this. These explorers and big-game hunters stick together.

"In a situation such as I have outlined, Lester Mapledurham would simply drop from the bridge, wait till the alligator made its rush, insert a stout stick between its jaws, and then hit it in the eye with a spear, being careful to avoid its lashing tail. He would then drift downstream and land at some safer spot. That is the type of man I wish for a son-in-law."

Cyril left the room without a word. Not even the fact that he now had *Strychnine in the Soup* in his possession could cheer his mood of unrelieved blackness. Back in his room, he tossed the book moodily onto the bed and began to pace the floor. And he had scarcely completed two laps when the door opened.

For an instant, when he heard the click of the latch, Cyril supposed that his visitor must be Lady Bassett, who, having put two and two together on discovering her loss, had come to demand her property back. And he cursed the rashness which had led him to fling it so carelessly upon the bed, in full view.

But it was not Lady Bassett. The intruder was Lester Mapledurham. Clad in a suit of pajamas which in their general color scheme reminded Cyril of a boudoir he had recently decorated for a society poetess, he stood with folded arms, his keen eyes fixed menacingly on the young man.

"Give me those jewels!" said Lester Mapledurham.

Cyril was at a loss.

"Jewels?"

"Jewels!"

"What jewels?"

Lester Mapledurham tossed his head impatiently.

"I don't know what jewels. They may be the Wingham Pearls or the Bassett Diamonds or the Simpson Sapphires. I'm not sure which room it was I saw you coming out of."

Cyril began to understand.

"Oh, did you see me coming out of a room?"

"I did. I heard a crash and, when I looked out, you were hurrying along the corridor."

"I can explain everything," said Cyril. "I had just been having a chat with Lady Bassett on a personal matter. Nothing to do with diamonds."

"You sure?" said Mapledurham.

"Oh, rather," said Cyril. "We talked about rhinoceri and pythons and her daughter Amelia and alligators and all that sort of thing, and then I came away."

Lester Mapledurham seemed only half-convinced.

"H'm!" he said. "Well, if anything is missing in the morning, I shall know what to do about it." His eye fell on the bed. "Hullo!" he went on, with sudden animation. "Slingsby's latest? Well, well! I've been wanting to get hold of this. I hear it's good. The Leeds *Mercury* says: 'These gripping pages . . .' "

He turned to the door, and with a hideous pang of agony Cyril perceived that it was plainly his intention to take the book with him. It was swinging lightly from a bronzed hand about the size of a medium ham.

"Here!" he cried, vehemently.

Lester Mapledurham turned.

"Well?"

"Oh, nothing," said Cyril. "Just good night."

He flung himself face downwards on the bed as the door closed, cursing himself for the craven cowardice which had kept him from snatching the book from the explorer. There had been a moment when he had almost nerved himself to the deed, but it was followed by another moment in which he had caught the other's eye. And it was as if he had found himself exchanging glances with Lady Bassett's charging rhinoceros.

And now, thanks to this pusillanimity, he was once more *Strychnine in the Soup*-less.

How long Cyril lay there, a prey to the gloomiest thoughts, he could not have said. He was aroused from his meditations by the sound of the door opening again.

Lady Bassett stood before him. It was plain that she was deeply moved. In addition to resembling Wallace Beery and Victor McLaglen, she now had a distinct look of George Bancroft.

She pointed a quivering finger at Cyril.

"You hound!" she cried. "Give me that book!"

Cyril maintained his poise with a strong effort.

"What book?"

"The book you sneaked out of my room."

"Has someone sneaked a book out of your room?" Cyril struck his forehead. "Great heavens!" he cried.

"Mr. Mulliner," said Lady Bassett coldly, "more book and less gibbering!"

Cyril raised a hand.

"I know who's got your book. Lester Mapledurham!"

"Don't be absurd."

"He has, I tell you. As I was on my way to your room just now, I saw him coming out, carrying something in a furtive manner. I remember wondering a bit at the time. He's in the Clock Room. If we pop along there now, we shall just catch him red-handed."

Lady Bassett reflected.

"It is impossible," she said at length. "He is incapable of such an act. Lester Mapledurham is a man who once killed a lion with a sardine opener."

"The very worst sort," said Cyril. "Ask anyone."

"And he is engaged to my daughter." Lady Bassett paused. "Well, he won't be long, if I find that what you say is true. Come, Mr. Mulliner!"

Together the two passed down the silent passage. At the door of the Clock Room they paused. A light streamed from beneath it. Cyril pointed silently to this sinister evidence of reading in bed, and noted that his companion stiffened and said something to herself in an undertone in what appeared to be some sort of native dialect.

The next moment she had flung the door open and, with a spring like that of a crouching zebu, had leaped to the bed and wrenched the book from Lester Mapledurham's hands.

"So!" said Lady Bassett.

"So!" said Cyril, feeling that he could not do better than follow the lead of such a woman.

"Hullo!" said Lester Mapledurham. "Something the matter?"

"So it was you who stole my book!"

"Your book?" said Lester Mapledurham. "I borrowed this from Mr. Mulliner there."

"A likely story!" said Cyril. "Lady Bassett is aware that I left my copy of *Strychnine in the Soup* in the train."

"Certainly," said Lady Bassett. "It's no use talking, young man, I have caught you with the goods. And let me tell you one thing that may be of interest. If you think that, after a dastardly act like this, you are going to marry Amelia, forget it!"

"Wipe it right out of your mind," said Cyril.

"But listen——"

"I will not listen. Come, Mr. Mulliner."

She left the room, followed by Cyril.

"A merciful escape," said Cyril.

"For whom?"

"For Amelia. My gosh, think of her tied to a man like that. Must be a relief to you to feel that she's going to marry a respectable interior decorator."

Lady Bassett halted. They were standing outside the Moat Room now. She looked at Cyril, her eyebrows raised.

"Are you under the impression, Mr. Mulliner," she said, "that, on the strength of what has happened, I intend to accept you as a son-in-law?"

"Don't you?"

"Certainly not."

Something inside Cyril seemed to snap. Recklessness descended upon him. He became for a space a thing of courage and fire, like the African leopard in the mating season.

"Oh!" he said.

And, deftly whisking *Strychnine in the Soup* from his companion's hand, he darted into his room, banged the door, and bolted it.

"Mr. Mulliner!"

It was Lady Bassett's voice, coming pleadingly through the woodwork. It was plain that she was shaken to the core, and Cyril smiled sardonically. He was in a position to dictate terms.

"Give me that book!"

"Certainly not," said Cyril. "I intend to read it myself. I hear good reports of it on every side. The Peebles *Intelligencer* says: 'Vigorous and absorbing.' "

A low wail from the other side of the door answered him.

"Of course," said Cyril, suggestively, "if it were my future mother-in-law who was speaking, her word would naturally be law."

There was a silence outside.

"Very well," said Lady Bassett.

"I may marry Amelia?"

"You may."

Cyril unbolted the door.

"Come—Mother," he said, in a soft, kindly voice. "We will read it together, down in the library."

Lady Bassett was still shaken.

"I hope I have acted for the best," she said.

"You have," said Cyril.

"You will make Amelia a good husband?"

"Grade A," Cyril assured her.

"Well, even if you don't," said Lady Bassett resignedly, "I can't go to bed without that book. I had just got to the bit where Inspector Mould is trapped in the underground den of the Faceless Fiend."

Cyril quivered.

"*Is* there a Faceless Fiend?" he cried.

"There are two Faceless Fiends," said Lady Bassett.

"My gosh!" said Cyril. "Let's hurry."

Murder at Rokeby House
by C. M. Chan

"That's torn it," said Carrie Prendergast, slamming down the phone receiver.

Phillip Bethancourt, startled, looked round from where he sat in the window seat, smoking a leisurely cigarette and looking out on a perfect spring day. Beyond the window, a small knot of day-trippers were gathering on the terrace in preparation for the five o'clock tour of Rokeby House, one of the finest late Georgian manor houses in Norfolk. Bethancourt had been idly watching them assemble with an air of superiority, since he was not a tourist but a guest. Rokeby House was presently owned by his old school chum, Arnold Prendergast. The death of Arnold's father two years ago and the resultant taxes were what had impelled Arnold to open the house to the public. The family had rallied round, moving en masse into the west wing and denuding their own rooms in order to cram all the family treasures into the rooms to be displayed. Since the family had been living on the estate for almost three hundred years and had been eagerly collecting and furnishing for most of that time, the treasures made quite an impressive show. Only a very few pieces had been sold off to help with the death duties.

"And where," wailed Carrie, addressing herself to the ceiling, "is Arnold? It's really too bad of him to go off like this."

Bethancourt considered her. She was Arnold's sister, and until their meeting last night, Bethancourt had not seen her since she was twelve. She was twenty now, and he was much impressed with how she had grown.

"There didn't seem," he ventured, "to be anyone else available to pick your uncle up at the station."

"Well, he should have been back by now," said Carrie unforgivingly.

Bethancourt privately thought this unlikely. The station was at least half an hour's drive away, and Arnold had left only twenty minutes ago.

"Mother's gone off to that nursery," continued Carrie, ticking off her family on her fingers, "Miss Chisleton's in bed with a cold, Eric and Beryl are walking the dogs, I don't know where Tom is, and now this. What a day."

"May I be of some help?" asked Bethancourt politely.

Carrie eyed him calculatingly. "Of course!" she exclaimed. "Why didn't I think of it before? You can give the tour."

Bethancourt was considerably taken aback. "No, I can't," he said.

"Of course you can," she retorted. "I've simply got to go. That was Dr. Colton on the phone—Aunt Alice has fallen and broken something, and you know how flustered she gets."

"But I don't know anything about the house," protested Bethancourt while Carrie snatched up her purse.

"You know enough not to mix up Canaletto with Scott," she replied. "Here." She grabbed a brochure from the desk and thrust it at him. "There's a floor plan on the back—make sure you don't take them into any of the private rooms. Oh Lord! All the cars are out. I'll have to borrow yours."

With great reluctance, Bethancourt handed over the keys to his Jaguar.

"Thanks," said Carrie, beaming a megawatt smile at him briefly. "Don't worry. You'll do fine."

She was gone. Bethancourt looked down at the large Borzoi hound who was curled up by the empty fireplace.

"I think we're in trouble, Cerberus," he said.

The dog, hearing his name, thumped his tail sympathetically on the stone hearth. Bethancourt, turning his attention to the brochure, was relieved to see that it mentioned the highlights of each room. Still, since the tourists were also in possession of the brochure, it was incumbent upon him as the guide to come up with other points of interest. He checked his watch. It was already two minutes past five.

"You had better stay here, Cerberus," he said. With a sigh, he rose and went to meet his doom, brochure in hand.

As the height of the season was still more than a month away, only a handful of tourists were waiting. There were an older American couple, a pair of newlyweds from London on their honeymoon, two middle-aged sisters from Kent who had really come to see the gardens and were only taking the house tour because it was included in the price of admission, and a young, dark-haired man who looked like a motor mechanic and who volunteered nothing about himself.

Bethancourt started off well enough, leading them into the oak paneled hall and giving them a little speech about when and by whom the house was built and setting them to admire the parquet floor and the Adam staircase. But by the time they reached the drawing room, he was beginning to feel unequal to his task. He knew enough about art and antiques to place things in their proper period and even to assign them to

the appropriate artists, but he had no idea how they had
come to be in the family's possession. He easily recognized the portraits of Arnold's parents, but he didn't
know where Arnold's portrait (if there was one) was
hung, nor did he have a clue as to who all the other
portraits represented. He knew that Allenby was the
founder's name and that Prendergast was the result of
a generation of daughters, but he was astonished to
discover that there had been a previous change of
name in the mid-nineteenth century.

He felt that to simply tell the tourists he didn't know
the answers to their questions was inappropriate, since
they had already paid for the answers. Throwing cau-
tion to the winds, he began to embroider, and then to
make up history out of whole cloth. By the time they
reached the dining room, the home of several more
portraits and the family plate, he was enjoying himself
immensely, having made up a family history so scan-
dalous that, had it been true, it is doubtful the Prendergasts would have survived in their present respectable
incarnation.

Having described how Hepplewhite had remained to
design the dining room furniture after the second
Allenby daughter (portrait over the mantel) had jilted
him, Bethancourt consulted the floor plan and shepherded his group toward the billiard room.

"This is the last room on the ground floor," he announced as he swung the door open. "It also holds the
gun collect—"

He was cut short by a scream from the female half
of the honeymoon couple and startled cries from the
rest. Bethancourt himself had frozen, his hand still on
the doorknob, his gaze riveted on the billiard table.

Sprawled across it was the body of a young man
with his head battered in, his glazed eyes staring
blankly at the door, his cheek nestled in a pool of
blood that had turned the green baize black.

Swiftly Bethancourt pushed the others back and shut the door. He found that everyone was staring at him.

"I think," he said, rather shaken, "we should all go back to the office while I telephone for the police."

The next forty-five minutes were extremely awkward. The office was a small room off the main hall, and there were not enough seats for everyone. The American woman was afraid of large dogs and let out a shriek upon seeing Cerberus that very nearly outdid the newlywed's scream over the body. Recklessly, Bethancourt pulled two of the Bradshaw tapestry armchairs in from the hall and stationed his dog outside the door. It was then that he realized the motor mechanic was missing. Swearing under his breath, he rang the police, somewhat hampered in his description of events by the fact that the others were hanging on his every word. He rang off and announced that they would have to await the arrival of the authorities. The Americans turned out to be mystery fans, and wild horses wouldn't have dragged them away, but they wanted to know when Scotland Yard would arrive and seemed affronted when Bethancourt told them it would only be the Norfolk C.I.D. Everyone else wanted to leave. Bethancourt had to make it clear that this was not on, at which point the newlywed wife started crying. The Kentish sisters suggested that they could wait in the garden and turned sullen when Bethancourt wouldn't let them. It would all have been easier if he could have offered them refreshment, but he didn't dare leave them on their own for long enough to fetch it.

Carrie and her aunt arrived back before the police. Carrie, having settled her aunt in the sitting room, looked harassed as she answered Bethancourt's summons. He broke the news as gently as he could, stepping out into the hall and closing the office door behind him for privacy. Cerberus looked up at them hopefully.

"My God," she said, stunned. She pushed her hair off her forehead, her eyes worried. "You say you don't know him, Phillip?" she asked anxiously.

"I didn't recognize him," said Bethancourt. "My first guess is that he might be one of the tourists."

Carrie's relief showed as irritation. "Then why the hell couldn't they murder him at *their* house?"

"I'm having to keep the others bottled up till the police arrive," said Bethancourt, ignoring this. "They're getting very fractious—" a vast understatement "—so do you think you could oblige with a brew up?"

"Oh, you poor thing," she said, laying a hand on his arm. "You must have been having a dreadful time. Of course I'll get the tea—and a bottle, too, I should think. I'll just have a look in the billiard room on my way."

"Don't touch anything," said Bethancourt uneasily. "And don't go in—just look from the door."

"I'll be good," she promised. "I just want to make sure it's nobody to do with us. After all, you don't know Alcock's help in the garden or the boy who brings up the groceries."

Bethancourt was still not entirely reassured, and he remained in the hall, watching her as she went toward the billiard room. But she was back in a moment, her face very white, her blue eyes wide with shock.

"Not a very pleasant sight, is he?" said Bethancourt sympathetically.

She sank down on one of the Bradshaw chairs. "It's Len," she said blankly.

Bethancourt was startled. "Len?" he repeated. "Who's Len?"

"Leonard Camden," she said carefully. "My fiancé."

Bethancourt, who hadn't known she was engaged, stared at her, at a loss for words.

* * *

"I'm sorry you've got let in for all this, Phillip."

Arnold Prendergast was still in his twenties, but he looked older. After his father's death, worry lines had seemed to appear on his face overnight, and although lately Bethancourt had thought he was looking less anxious, the news of the murder had brought back all the original lines and more.

He was slouched now on the chintz sofa in the private sitting room, the posture contrasting oddly with the impeccable three-piece suit he had taken to wearing on tourist days. There was a glass of whisky on the end table at his side, but he had barely touched it.

It was very late. The police had finally left a half hour ago, and the rest of the family had retired to bed, still in shock and exhausted by the endless questioning.

"It's no trouble for me," said Bethancourt, polishing his glasses with his handkerchief. "You know what a murder fan I am. I'm only sorry that it turned out to be Carrie's fiancé instead of some nice, anonymous stranger."

Arnold frowned. "I'm not," he said abruptly. "And I rather doubt anyone else is. Even Carrie."

Bethancourt replaced his glasses on his nose and raised an eyebrow. He had already noticed that Carrie was suffering more from shock than from grief and that the other members of the family—whom he had always found to be kindly people—seemed more worried than regretful.

"Len wasn't generally well-liked, then?" he asked.

"That's putting it mildly," answered Arnold. "Mother nearly had a fit. She absolutely forbade Carrie to marry him, but of course that did more harm than good. It only put Carrie's back up. She can be very headstrong, you know."

"But what was so awful about him?"

"Well," Arnold ran his hand through his hair, "it's hard to say, really."

"Common?" suggested Bethancourt.

"Oh, very. But I don't expect that would have mattered to anyone. No, it was more that he was, well, sly. Secretive, and rather cold, as if he were always looking for some sort of angle."

"So why did Carrie want to marry this complete wart?"

Arnold looked surprised. "He was rich," he answered simply. "Carrie was trying to do her bit for the old homestead. I suppose," he added reflectively, "that was Mother's real objection. She wouldn't have cared how awful he was if Carrie really loved him. But the rest of us couldn't stick him. We were all dreading the day they actually got married and he moved in."

It was Bethancourt's turn to be surprised. "They were going to live at Rokeby?"

"Well, of course, old chap. Len's money wouldn't do us much good if he was spending it elsewhere, would it?" Arnold hesitated. "I rather think he was hinting that I should move out of the master suite and let them have it. He was that sort."

Bethancourt ignored this last comment. "You don't think Len had made a will, do you?" he asked uneasily.

"A will?" Arnold looked puzzled. "Well, I shouldn't have thought so. He didn't seem to me to be the kind of person who thought much about the future. Why?"

"Oh, no reason," said Bethancourt vaguely. He busied himself with lighting a cigarette. "Look here, Arnold," he said in a moment, "all this is damned awkward. I think perhaps I'd better take myself off tomorrow morning—the others won't want an outsider looking on while the police push all their little secrets out into the light of day."

"No, don't go," began Arnold, and then he stopped and reddened. "I'm sorry," he said. "I can see you'd rather be out of it."

"It's not that," answered Bethancourt, examining the glowing tip of his cigarette with great care. "Aside from considerations of delicacy, I'm afraid I don't really approve of hitting people over the head and killing them. Especially not when it leaves the rest of your family under suspicion. I'm on the wrong side here, Arnold."

"But that's just it," burst out his friend. "We can't live forever wondering which of us did the man in. Much as I loathe the thought of seeing one of my family in the dock, it would be better than watching us all disintegrate into separate islands because we can't trust each other any more. And Rokeby needs us all—I couldn't carry on here if I had to hire people to do all the things the family does now." He shook his head.

"Well, if that's how you feel about it," said Bethancourt, "I'll stay on till Monday as we'd planned as long as no one else objects. But feel free to give me the heave-ho if you think it's better."

"Thank you, Phillip," said Arnold. "I just hope it's all cleared up quickly."

"Take heart," said Bethancourt. "The police are very good at their job."

Detective Chief Inspector Sam Kennick sat in his office at C.I.D. headquarters in Norwich and stared down at the photographs of Leonard Camden's body. Kennick was a small, thin man with a quiet demeanor and brown eyes that missed nothing. He was, indeed, very good at his job, but he was not feeling very clever as he focused tired eyes on the photographs. Camden had apparently been leaning over the billiard table to make a shot when someone had come up behind him and hit him on the head with a rifle butt. The assailant had struck him again, pretty well crushing the left side of the skull, then dropped the rifle on the floor and left, presumably by the small back door at the end of the hall next to the billiard room. It had been open, although all the Prendergasts agreed it ought to have been locked. However, they had also agreed that it was frequently overlooked. This had occurred no more than an hour or two before his body was found at five thirty.

Since Camden had been shooting pool, Kennick had surmised that his murderer must have been his playing partner, but that idea had been scotched by the Prendergasts, who all said Camden had a habit of going off alone to shoot practice shots, since none of them were very good players.

Kennick's gaze turned to the statements he and his sergeant had spent the evening taking from the Prendergasts. The two scions of the family lived at Rokeby House with Mrs. Emily Prendergast: her son Arnold, who had inherited the estate, and her daughter Carrie. They were joined by James, the late owner's brother, and his family, which included his wife Alice, and two sons, Eric and Thomas. In addition there was Eric's wife Beryl. On one thing they were all agreed: no one had expected Leonard Camden at Rokeby this weekend. Since his engagement to Carrie Prendergast two months before, he had often spent weekends in Norfolk, but no arrangement had been made for this weekend, and when Carrie had spoken to him by phone on Thursday, he had made no mention of plans to leave London. Indeed, he had asked her to come up to town, but she had refused, since her brother had invited a houseguest and she had wanted to take over the house tours Arnold usually gave.

Kennick shook his head. He didn't like this case, and even less was he going to like the sort of headlines that were sure to appear tomorrow when the press discovered a man had been murdered on an antique billiard table in a historic home and that the members of one of the most respectable families in Norfolk were the prime suspects. Thank God that Arnold Prendergast, the present head of the family, appeared to be out of it. He had had tea at three thirty with his sister Carrie; his houseguest, Phillip Bethancourt; his aunt, Alice Prendergast; her son Eric; and Eric's wife, Lady Beryl. Thomas, Alice's second son, had come in late from giving the three o'clock house tour.

After tea, Arnold and Bethancourt had gone out to look at a summerhouse on the property that Arnold hoped to restore. At about four forty they had returned to the garage, where Arnold had taken out a car to go pick up his uncle, James Prendergast, at the train station. Bethancourt had seen him go and had then returned to the house, where he wound up giving the five o'clock tour.

Several people had seen Arnold arrive at the station, had seen him waiting in his Rover in the car park, and had seen him drive off with his uncle after the London train had come in. Arnold's time seemed well-accounted for.

His uncle was a different matter. At first Kennick had been relieved to discover that James Prendergast had taken the nine oh-six A.M. train to London, stayed there all day, and not returned until five eleven. Unfortunately, he hadn't. His son Thomas had dropped him off that morning, but the stationmaster was quite sure he hadn't seen Mr. James Prendergast all day. The ticket collector was equally certain James had not gotten off the five eleven from London that afternoon. There was nothing for it but for Kennick to return to Rokeby tomorrow, call James a liar, and demand to know where he had been. Kennick wasn't looking forward to it. The Prendergasts were well-known and well-liked in the district, but if any of them could be accused of high-handedness, it was James.

Unlike her husband's, Alice Prendergast's alibi checked out. After tea, she and her daughter-in-law, Lady Beryl, had cleared up, and Alice had taken a car into the village to do some shopping. Coming out of the post office, she had slipped and fractured her ankle and had had to be taken round to Dr. Colton's surgery.

Mrs. Emily Prendergast, Arnold's mother, had left after lunch to drive to a nursery halfway across Norfolk where they had some new breed of tea rose she was interested in. Mrs. Emily was known to be both delightfully charming and absolutely scatty; the drive had taken her nearly twice the time needed because she had gotten lost, but the nursery owner confirmed that she had arrived shortly before three and left not long past three thirty. Anyone else would have been back at Rokeby by four thirty at the latest, but Mrs. Emily had not arrived until after six. She had, she said, stopped for tea at a delightful little place in an unnamed village, and had afterwards lost her way again and ended up by a lovely field where she had stopped to pick wildflowers. Getting lost was to Mrs. Emily a regular feature of any trip she took, and she enjoyed it as much as any other part of a journey.

Kennick did not seriously think Mrs. Emily could have murdered anyone, but it was a fact that her time was not accounted for. He would have to try to find that cafe.

The rest of the family had no alibis at all.

Thomas Prendergast, who was trained in estate management, had taken himself off after tea to the manager's office above the stables and had remained working there alone until he returned to the house at six.

Eric and his wife, Lady Beryl, had gone to walk the dogs. This was an activity the family took in turns to do on days when the estate was open to the public. The Prendergasts had quickly found that some people found it necessary to investigate forbidden paths and to try to get into parts of the house not on the tour. The dogs had turned up quite a few of these miscreants over the years, but none had been found today. In order to cover as much ground as possible, Eric and Beryl had split up, meeting each other at the gates at about five thirty. Both explained that they had lingered over their task because it had been such a fine day. Either, reflected Kennick, could have seen Camden arriving, followed him back to the house, and killed him.

And then there was Carrie Prendergast, his prime suspect. Kennick sighed heavily and took a gulp of coffee without noticing it had grown cold. Carrie had left tea early, five minutes or so after Thomas had come in, so as not to leave the tour office empty for too long. The family had been taking turns at keeping the place staffed all day, doing double duty to make up for the lack of their usual office volunteer, Miss Chisleton, who was in bed with a cold.

So from about three fifty until Bethancourt had gone to the office at about four fifty-five, Carrie's time was unaccounted for. She had had the closest relationship with the dead man, and they had only her word that Camden hadn't meant to come to Rokeby this weekend. And she had certainly not appeared grief stricken at the demise of her intended.

The trouble was, neither had the rest of the family. They had been shocked, yes; unhappy, no.

With some relief, Kennick turned to the rest of the statements collected and the wonderfully mysterious young man who had departed so precipitously. The police hadn't managed to pick him up and probably wouldn't; the only thing that made it even remotely possible was that one of the other tourists had noticed his car and part of the registration plate number. This Bethancourt had the impression the stranger might have been a motor mechanic, and after some reflection had finally brought out of his memory the fact that the man's hands and fingernails were stained with oil.

Phillip Bethancourt himself did not seem a very likely suspect. He had been at school with Arnold Prendergast, but had not been to visit Rokeby in almost eighteen months, contenting himself with putting Arnold up at his flat in London on the latter's rare visits. So he was not very involved with the family. On the other hand, it had taken him fifteen minutes to make the five minute walk from the garage to the house, and it was possible he had known Camden in London.

Then there was Richard Alcock, the gardener. He claimed to be in his nineties, but the Prendergasts as-

sured Kennick he couldn't possibly be more than
eighty and was more likely seventy-five. In any case,
he had lost most of his teeth and had not bothered today with the dentures provided him by the National
Health. It was therefore almost impossible to make out
anything he said. The general gist of his information
was that he had stayed in the garden keeping a watch-
ful eye on the tourists and making certain they didn't
pick the flowers. The tourists had attested to seeing
him from time to time, usually glaring at them from a
distance, but these sporadic appearances by no means
gave him an alibi. Still, he had barely seemed to know
who Leonard Camden was. The name made no impression on him whatever, and it was not until the victim
was referred to as "Miss Carrie's fiancé" that Alcock
seemed to understand who they were talking about. He
had then expressed sympathy for Miss Carrie but had
little more to say.

The tourists had been principally outraged at being
interrogated, with the exception of the Americans, who
had wanted to know when Scotland Yard was coming.
They were Dick and Betty MacDonald, and Kennick
was inclined to exonerate them. Their passports
showed that they had been in the country only a few
days, and their plane tickets announced that they meant
to leave on Monday. They had never been in England
before and knew no one here; they were just a couple
of happy tourists who had retired early and were enjoying a bit of travel with the fruits of their labors.

Norah and Sarah Elkston were extremely sorry they
had decided to take in the house at all, since they were
principally interested in the garden, and they repeated
this sentiment firmly over and over again as if a lack
of interest in the house would absolve them of murder.
Kennick had already checked them out by a phone call
to the constable of their village in Kent, where the
Misses Elkston were well-known. They lived, according to the constable, very carefully within their some-

what slender means, devoting their time to their garden, which was deservedly famous in the village. The constable could not recall their ever going to London or to Norfolk before this, although they usually managed a short trip once a year to view other gardens. Last year's trip had been to Somerset, if he remembered correctly. The only visitor he ever recalled their having was a niece who lived in Canterbury.

Rick and Barbara Morris, the newlyweds, were harder to check out. Kennick's sergeant had managed to contact their landlady, who had confirmed that they had taken her first floor flat, but that had been only a fortnight ago. She understood that they had gotten married last weekend and although they had moved in a few belongings the week before, they had only stayed the Saturday night before leaving on Sunday for their honeymoon.

This was fine as far as it went, but that wasn't very far and Kennick knew he was going to have to do some very tedious work to try to make sure they hadn't known the dead man.

Unless he could solve the case before that became necessary.

Kennick sighed again. He knew perfectly well one of the Prendergasts had probably murdered Camden, but he was having a great deal of trouble believing it of them. He was from that part of Norfolk himself, and although he had no personal connection with the family, he had known of them all his life and had always heard them spoken of as decent Christian people—the sort who were the backbone of England. He was going to have to screw his courage to the sticking point and try to erase this bias from his mind.

A knock on the door heralded the arrival of Kennick's sergeant, Brown, who unexpectedly introduced a second man into the office.

"This is Wilson, sir, from Traffic Division."

"Ah yes." Kennick tried to look as if he were not utterly bewildered by the appearance of Traffic Division.

"Wilson thinks he may have your mystery tourist," said Brown.

"Yes, sir," said Wilson. "I pulled over a dark blue Cortina with a London number at five fifty this afternoon. Had her up to eighty, he did."

"Does the description fit?" asked Kennick eagerly.

"Yes, sir." Wilson nodded. "Dark-haired man in his early twenties, skinny. He seemed quite nervous, but a lot of people are when they're caught speeding like that. I've written down the information from his license for you. His name's Joe Crowley."

"Good work, Wilson," said Kennick, taking the proffered paper. "This is going to help our case no end. I hope to God," he added, after a highly gratified Wilson had left, "this really is the man. No matter whom we identify as the murderer, any barrister could get him off so long as there's an unknown man in the picture. We'll have to get that Bethancourt chap to identify him. How have you been coming along, Brown?"

"I've hit a snag, sir," answered Brown, seating himself on the other side of the desk and producing his notebook. "That brokerage firm where Miss Prendergast said Camden worked? Well, I got hold of the director, and he's never heard of Leonard Camden. Said he was quite sure they'd never employed anyone by that name."

Kennick was frowning. "That opens a whole new can of worms," he said. "Did Carrie Prendergast lie, or was she lied to?"

"I think perhaps she was lied to, sir," offered Brown. "I noticed that Camden's driver's license was only issued six weeks ago, and that made me curious. So I rang up his landlord, who said Camden's only lived in that flat for just over two months."

"I see. Well, it looks rather as if Camden was somebody else before he decided to marry Carrie Prendergast." Kennick turned back to her statement. "She says she met him in a nightclub about four months ago."

Brown coughed diffidently. "If they got engaged two months ago, she must have visited his previous address."

"I expect so," agreed Kennick. "We'll ask her tomorrow." He sighed. He really wasn't looking forward to returning to Rokeby. "Let's call it a night," he said. "We'll have a full day tomorrow, and we'd better start early."

"Yes, sir," said Brown, with relief. He had none of his superior's prejudices concerning the Prendergasts, but he was at least as tired as the chief inspector and had been thinking of his bed for the last two hours. He was glad Kennick hadn't decided to pull an all-nighter.

It was rather difficult, Bethancourt found, to have a group of one's friends suspected of murder. In previous cases he had always attached himself to his friend, Detective Sergeant Jack Gibbons of New Scotland Yard, and so had come to the investigation and those involved with a refreshing lack of prejudice. In theory, having his friends as the chief suspects should have given him additional insight, but he did not find it so in practice. He knew nothing about any of these people that would lead him to believe one of them was capable of murder.

So he sat at breakfast that Sunday morning thinking about blackmail. It was a grey, misty day, holding the promise of rain, and the Prendergast family had taken this as an excuse not to go to church. They were all very subdued and rather unhappy-looking, all except Arnold's mother, who was chatting comfortably about the roses she had seen yesterday. Uncle James had excused himself to take tea up to his wife, who was lying in her room with her ankle propped up. Eric, the eldest of the children and a rather stodgy personality, had barricaded himself behind the Sunday *Times* while his wife Beryl replied with a divided attention to Emily's rose conversation. Carrie had come down rather late and sat hunched over her coffee at the opposite end of the table from her mother. Tom had tried to interest her in the crossword but had given up the attempt, and Arnold was eating briskly, keeping his eyes on his plate.

Bethancourt, who never ate much breakfast, was sipping coffee and considering which of them was most likely to be blackmailed. He could not believe any of them would have killed Camden simply to prevent Carrie from marrying him. By all accounts, Camden had been an unscrupulous sort, not the kind of man who would be above blackmail. If he had dug up something nasty about one of the Prendergasts, said Prendergast might have killed him rather than pay up.

This theory, to Bethancourt's mind, favored Thomas Prendergast, the younger of James and Alice's sons. He gazed pensively at the young man, who was buttering a piece of toast. Tom was two years Bethancourt's junior. He had foregone a university education in favor of studying estate management and had made quite a success of it. He was Bethancourt's prime candidate for blackmail because of his position as manager of the Rokeby estate. If he was taking a little personal profit off the meager estate income and Camden had found out about it, it would provide not only excellent blackmail material but also the means of paying it. The problem with blackmailing any other member of the family was that they had nothing to pay with.

Of course, reflected Bethancourt, Camden might not have known that. If Carrie was marrying the man for his money, she might not have revealed the full glory of the Prendergast penury. In which case, the blackmailed Prendergast would have no choice but to murder, since they could not possibly pay up.

"Well," said Beryl, glancing out the window, "at least there won't be many tourists if it comes on to rain."

Her husband snorted into his paper. "You must be joking," he said. "They'll be out in droves to see—well, you know how people are," he ended lamely, glancing at Carrie.

"There won't be any tourists," said Arnold firmly. "I'm not opening the estate."

"Quite right, dear," said his mother. "We can't have people tramping about when there's been a death in the house."

"I'll make up a sign after breakfast," said Tom, "and put it up on the gate."

"I'll give you a hand," offered Beryl. "I think there's some of that blue paint left."

Carrie rose. "I'll do kitchen duty, since Aunt Alice is laid up," she said, and began to gather up empty plates.

"Oh," said Beryl, "I didn't mean to leave you with that. I can perfectly well—"

"No," said Carrie, a little desperately, "really, I'd rather."

"Well, if you're sure," said Beryl, eyeing her doubtfully.

"Quite," answered Carrie and escaped into the kitchen.

"It will be better for her to have something to do," Emily told Beryl. "It's all extremely unfortunate, but I suppose we must be grateful she hadn't already married him."

"I suppose so," said Beryl, who was not at all sure what Emily meant by the remark. She drained her coffee cup. "I'd better go look for that paint."

Tom left with her, and in another moment Eric took his paper off to the library. Arnold was trying to dissuade his mother from buying expensive rosebushes. Unobtrusively Bethancourt rose, collected some cups and saucers, and went into the kitchen.

The stone-flagged kitchen was enormous, an odd contrast between eighteenth century solidity and modern convenience. Carrie had left the dishes in the sink and was sitting by the huge fireplace, staring blankly at

the cold ashes. She looked round at the noise
Bethancourt made in setting down the crockery.

"Oh," she said. "It's you, Phillip."

"Yes," admitted Bethancourt, "it is. I came out to
help."

"Thanks," she answered listlessly, "but I don't need
help."

"Don't you?" he asked, lighting a cigarette and strolling
over to lean against the fireplace. "If I were in your position, I imagine I should be looking for help anywhere I
could find it."

"Oh God," she moaned, putting her head in her hands.
"I've really mucked up this time. Mother warned me not
to get engaged to him. Why on earth couldn't I have listened to her?"

"He wasn't blackmailing you into marriage, then?"

Her head came up, a look of honest puzzlement on
her face. "Blackmail?" she asked. "Whatever do you
mean?"

"Never mind," said Bethancourt. "If he wasn't,
that's one thing in your favor. Where did you meet
him, anyway?"

"At a nightclub. The Red Parrot."

Bethancourt raised an eyebrow. "Not the most sa-
vory of places," he remarked.

"Oh, it's all right," she said dully. "Not as bad as everyone seems to think."

Bethancourt eyed her carefully. He had the best of
reasons for thinking the Red Parrot a den of iniquity;
he had been there. However, he supposed it was possible, if one was a little naive and largely unobservant,
not to notice what was going on in the dark corners of
the place. "Do you go there often?" he asked.

She shook her head. "Only the once, actually. Len
said he didn't like it." She looked up at him. "If this is
your idea of helping me, I can't say I think much of it.
You're worse than the police with all these questions."

"It might end up helping, you know," he said persuasively. "You don't really mind, do you?"

His wheedling tone won a small smile from her. "You're a dear, Phillip," she said. "Why couldn't I have picked you to marry?"

"I have no idea," replied Bethancourt. "I seem to have the chief qualification: money."

"That's mean," she said, stung.

For a moment he thought she wouldn't answer. Then she sighed and said, "I suppose it *was* the money. It all seemed so perfect at first. I'd never met anyone quite like Len before. He was terribly romantic and mysterious, and in the beginning we just had such a good time together. He had simply pots of money. And then he was so enthusiastic about Rokeby."

"Really? Did you tell him that you were all broke because of Rokeby?"

"Yes—well, not in so many words. But I explained how we all had to pitch in to keep the old place going, and he seemed to really like the idea of settling in here and doing our bit. It seemed perfect. Only lately ..." Her voice trailed off.

"He didn't seem so keen?" asked Bethancourt.

"No, no. It wasn't him." She looked down at her hands.

"Perhaps," suggested Bethancourt, "in all this whirlwind of perfection, you hadn't stopped to consider what living with Len would really be like?"

She nodded, still studying her hands. "I was a bloody fool," she said in a low voice. "Mother tried to tell me."

"Oh well," said Bethancourt cheerfully, "that's why we're young, so we can be foolish. Everyone says so. And it doesn't always turn out as badly as this. But I understood from Arnold that the engagement was still on."

"Oh, it was," she agreed. "I was having doubts, but

I'd made such a to-do about it I didn't quite see how to break it off."

"Difficult," said Bethancourt. "I can see that. How did Len come by his money, by the way?"

Carrie shrugged. "I never really asked. He was a stockbroker, so I supposed he had inherited a bit and run it up on the exchange."

"His parents were dead, then?"

"Yes, and he hadn't any other relatives, so he was quite ready to adopt us." She sighed gloomily. "If only we'd been ready to adopt him. God, Phillip, I still can't believe one of them would kill him. And it's all my fault."

"Nonsense," said Bethancourt briskly. "No matter how objectionable Len was, that's no excuse for murdering the fellow. Carrie, can you think of any reason he would have shown up here unexpectedly?"

"I suppose he must have gotten bored in town and decided to surprise me. He was impulsive like that. I told him on Thursday that you were coming and that I'd be doing Arnold's tours, so I wouldn't have a lot of time. Really, I just didn't want to see him this weekend."

"He might have sensed that," said Bethancourt, "and decided he'd better come along and take you out to a romantic dinner or something. It's what I might do if I thought my girlfriend was going off me."

"Did you and Marla have another row?" asked Arnold from the doorway.

"No, no," said Bethancourt. "Carrie and I were just speculating about why Len would show up so abruptly."

"He must have come up after tea while everyone was out," said Arnold. "We found his bag upstairs in the room he usually had. Anyway, Chief Inspector Kennick is back, and he wants to see you two as soon as he's finished with Uncle James."

"James?" asked Bethancourt, raising an eyebrow.

"Yes, he wouldn't explain what it was about. I was to ask you both not to run off until he was done."

"We will hold ourselves in readiness," said Bethancourt.

Chief Inspector Kennick did not feel that he was having a very successful day. James Prendergast had maintained that both stationmaster and ticket collector were senile, and that he had most certainly gone to London and returned on the trains he had described. This was a blatant lie, but no appeal had shaken him, and it was clearly going to be up to Kennick to discover what James had been doing.

On the brighter side, Bethancourt had identified Joe Crowley with ease and certainty as the young man who had taken the tour of Rokeby House yesterday, but they had got no further with Crowley after that. He insisted he had left simply because he didn't want to be involved, but Kennick was sure he was lying. Crowley had been scared out of his wits from the moment he saw them, but nothing would shake him from his story: he did not know Leonard Camden. It had been a beautiful day, so he had decided to take a drive to see Rokeby House. He liked looking at historic houses.

"I fancy them myself," Kennick had said pleasantly. "Hampton Court—now, that's a showplace."

Crowley had agreed vaguely that it was.

"I always liked those crystal chandeliers in the front hall," Kennick had gone on. "Very spectacular, I always think."

Crowley had mumbled agreement.

Only there were no crystal chandeliers in the hall at Hampton Court. Crowley had clearly never been there, and Kennick was willing to bet he had never been to a historic house in his life before yesterday.

He had warned Crowley not to absent himself, that they would have further questions, but once again Kennick was clearly going to have to dig up some answers himself before he would have any questions that would open Crowley's mouth. However, at least Crowley was hiding something. Maybe the Prendergasts were innocent after all.

Kennick and his sergeant had proceeded to Camden's flat in Chelsea where they had spent several hours looking through his things. For all their time, they had turned up only one interesting piece of information: Camden's account at the nearest Barclay's Bank had been opened just over two months ago. Since that time, there had been several deposits—some extremely large—but none of a regular sum consistent with a paycheck.

They had stopped for a late lunch and now were on their way to Camden's previous address in Kensington, which Carrie Prendergast had readily supplied that morning. It was a large, modern block of flats, the type of place where no one knew his neighbor. However, the caretaker, who had the basement flat, proved to be available, if not very happy to have his Sunday dinner interrupted.

"It won't take long," said Kennick apologetically. "We'd just like to ask you one or two questions about an ex-tenant here. Leonard Camden was his name. He lived in flat 2B," he added as the caretaker's face remained blank, "and he only moved a couple of months ago."

"He wasn't in 2B," said the caretaker firmly. "A man named Crowley's got that flat and has had it for years."

Kennick gaped. "Joe Crowley?" he asked.

"No, not Joe." The caretaker rubbed his chin. "Lee, no, Les. That's it. Les Crowley. I haven't seen him about lately in any case. He keeps himself to himself."

The caretaker had nothing more to say. He did not remember Carrie, and he would not open up the flat unless they had a search warrant. He didn't think Mr.

Crowley was a motor mechanic, but he really didn't know anything about him.

"What about the keys, sir?" asked Sergeant Brown eagerly as they made their way back to the car.

"Keys?"

"The ones in Camden's flat. Remember, I said they must be a neighbors."

"You're right," said Kennick. "They could be the keys to this place. Let's run back and get them."

Bethancourt had spent the drive to London trying to find out why Kennick had wanted to talk to James again, and why he would be interested in Camden's previous address. Kennick, however, refused to say anything beyond commenting, in reference to the second question, that Carrie didn't seem to know much about her fiancé. Which, Bethancourt reflected, was true enough.

He had been hustled away by Sergeant Brown as soon as he had identified Joe Crowley, who, he was gratified to learn, actually was a mechanic. He had been about to return to Norfolk when it occurred to him that he could at least find out if Leonard Camden had a police record. He sought out his friend, Detective Sergeant Jack Gibbons.

Despite its being Sunday, Gibbons was in his office at Scotland Yard. This was because of two unidentified corpses who had been pulled from the Thames early that morning. Gibbons was now involved in the thankless task of looking through the missing persons file in an attempt to find out who they had been. He was in no mood to be bothered by an unrelated murder already in the capable hands of the Norfolk constabulary.

"Maybe one of the tourists did it," he said after Bethancourt had finished describing the crime and its deleterious effect on the Prendergasts.

"It would be nice to think so," said Bethancourt. "I

must say that chap Crowley looked awfully guilty when he saw me today. Still," he sighed, "it isn't likely, is it? The Prendergasts already knew Camden and loathed him—it seems a bit of a stretch to go looking for suspects elsewhere."

"Well, you never know," said Gibbons cheerfully, his eyes still glued to his computer screen.

"And I'm worried about Arnold's uncle," continued Bethancourt. "I thought he was safely out of it, being in London all day, but I think Kennick must suspect he met with Camden here, or maybe even returned with him."

"Could be," agreed Gibbons, scrolling down his list.

"What," asked Bethancourt peevishly, "*are* you looking at? Anybody would think you didn't care about my murder."

"Missing persons. We've got two unidentified bodies in the morgue."

"Two?" asked Bethancourt, his interest piqued. "Did they come together or separately?"

"Together," replied Gibbons. "It's a long story, but basically because of some shenanigans on the river last night, the police sent down divers at dawn this morning. I don't know if they found what they were looking for, but they did find two bodies neatly weighed down with cinderblocks. One man, one woman, both stark naked and both middle-aged."

"Drowned?" asked Bethancourt, rather horrified.

"No," answered Gibbons, hitting the scroll key again. "They had been quite professionally garrotted. They'd been in the water about a week," he added.

"Oh." Bethancourt considered. "I wonder why they were stripped," he mused.

"Probably because they didn't buy their clothes at Marks and Sparks like everybody else," answered Gibbons. He shot a glance at his friend. "Look at yourself, for instance. If you were murdered, we could probably trace you through your clothes in a few hours. Particularly that shirt."

"What's wrong with it?" asked Bethancourt defensively, looking down at his chest.

"Nothing's *wrong* with it," retorted Gibbons, "but it's custom-made, isn't it?"

"I see your point," admitted Bethancourt. "Well, to get back to my case, what I want to know is whether Leonard Camden had a police record."

"Why didn't you say so in the first place?" asked Gibbons. "There was no need to go on for half an hour if that was all you wanted."

"I don't think finding naked bodies in the Thames agrees with you, Jack," said Bethancourt. "I've never seen you so irritable."

Gibbons did not reply. He had moved to a second computer and was typing rapidly. "There," he said, resuming his seat.

"It only says 'Searching,' " said Bethancourt, bending over to peer at the screen.

"It'll either come up with him in a minute or it won't," said Gibbons, turning back to his own machine. "Keep an eye on it."

Bethancourt waited. In a moment the computer informed him that the subject had not been found.

"Damn," he said, disappointed. "He's not here."

"It only means he's never been caught," said Gibbons kindly. "And if you really think blackmail's his game, well, it's not too likely he'd be in our files."

"I suppose so," said Bethancourt. "Well, I must get back to Norfolk. Thanks, Jack."

Gibbons waved a hand. "Ring me and let me know how it works out," he said.

In the end, Gibbons was destined to find that out for himself.

The keys from the desk in Leonard Camden's Chelsea flat fit the locks of Les Crowley's flat in Kensing-

ton. Jubilant, Kennick and Brown let themselves in and
then looked about them in surprise.

The flat had already been searched.

Moreover, from the telltale traces of black finger-
print powder, it was evident who the previous searchers had been.

"Well, sergeant," said Kennick, "we're here—we
might as well have a look. But then we'd better run
Les Crowley's name through the computer and ring the
chief constable."

They found nothing in the flat to connect Les
Crowley with Leonard Camden until Kennick discovered a wallet in a dresser drawer. It contained the usual
things, all with Crowley's name and the Kensington
address, including a driver's license. The picture on it
was that of Leonard Camden.

In the morning, the chief constable lost no time in
ringing Scotland Yard, who had issued a warrant a
week ago for Les Crowley's arrest on charges of cocaine dealing and who had obtained a search warrant
for his Kensington flat.

When Detective Superintendent Wallace Carmichael
of Scotland Yard was given the case, he took one look
at the name of the man who had found the body and
demanded that Jack Gibbons be taken off the river
murders and assigned to the Rokeby case.

"Did you know," he thundered when Gibbons appeared, "that your friend Bethancourt is now *finding*
bodies?"

"He did mention it, sir," replied Gibbons, who was
very tired of missing persons reports and rather relieved to be reassigned.

Carmichael snorted. "Well, you can tell me what he
said later—we've got to see Chief Superintendent
Hoving now."

"Hoving?" asked Gibbons, falling into step beside
his superior. "Isn't he in Narcotics?"

"That's right. They're the ones who searched Crowley's flat."

"Crowley, sir?"

"The dead man, Gibbons," said Carmichael with a withering glance in his sergeant's direction.

Gibbons scratched his head. "I admit I wasn't paying a lot of attention to Bethancourt," he said, "but I'm quite sure the body he found was named Leonard Camden."

"So it was," agreed Carmichael without breaking stride. "That was the alias Crowley was using. Hurry up, lad. We can't keep Hoving waiting."

Gibbons followed, a little bewildered, wondering how a drug dealer with a double identity had ended up murdered in one of England's historic houses. At least, he thought, things were looking up for the Prendergast family.

The Prendergasts would have been relieved to hear it. Upon returning to Rokeby on Sunday afternoon, Bethancourt found Carrie and Eric having a tremendous row in the garden in which accusations and insults were flung heatedly, as if they were stones. It was the more absurd since most of the faults mentioned seemed to stem from childhood injustices. The arrival of Bethancourt, an outsider, put an abrupt end to the argument, but they were still smoldering as they parted and there was no denying that some unfortunate things had been said that were bound to come home to roost later.

After dinner that evening, James, fortified by one too many brandies, attempted to explain to his sister-in-law where she had gone wrong in rearing her children, implying that the said child-rearing methods had clearly molded her offspring into reckless adults who unerringly chose potential murder victims as spouses. Anyone else would have laughed off the extreme absurdity of these charges, but Emily, known for her intuition rather than her logic, saw nothing but the antagonism behind them and replied in kind. The argument became more heated, with James's accusations growing increasingly wilder while Emily's grew more pointed. Arnold and Tom, who had heard raised voices and were coming in to play peacemakers, unfortunately arrived just as Emily dredged up an ancient indiscretion of James's, long ago forgiven and forgotten, which the younger members of the family knew nothing about. Arnold and Tom were horrified; James, embarrassed by their presence, was reduced to roaring like a lion, while Emily turned to her son and demanded that he eject James from the house. It was with some difficulty that the combatants were separated, and it took the rest of the night to calm them down to the point where apologies were offered.

This incident sent Carrie into a black depression, and she spent an hour sobbing on Bethancourt's shoulder while he attempted to alleviate her guilt. He partly succeeded and was rewarded later that night by the appearance of Carrie in his bedroom. Whether this was meant as some bizarre gesture of thanks or whether she was simply searching for further distraction, Bethancourt had no idea, but whatever her motives, he wanted no part of it. He had to say so rather firmly, especially since her idea of seduction appeared to rely on the pouncing method, leaving very little room for conversation. He was afraid he had offended her, but even if only her pride had been hurt, he knew the morning was sure to be awkward.

He was quite right. Carrie refused to so much as glance in his direction at breakfast, a meal which the entire family gulped down in record time, deserting the dining room as quickly as possible. Carrie was one of the first to flee. Bethancourt swallowed some coffee and went in pursuit of her.

He found her giving the dogs their morning run, and

he and Cerberus joined her, although she clearly did not want his company.

"I can take him along with the others," she said, still not meeting his eyes. "You don't have to stick around."

"I want to," he said. "It's a lovely morning for a walk."

"Henry!" she called out sharply. "Leave it!"

"Besides," he continued, "I think we ought to talk."

"Really, I don't want to," she said coolly. "Henry, I said leave it!"

Clearly, he had offended her more than he thought. Taking a deep breath, he launched into a lengthy and tedious speech about how his moral code wouldn't let him take advantage of a lady in a distressed frame of mind, not to mention his desire to remain faithful to his current girlfriend. By the end of it, she had broken down enough to vent her own feelings and was viewing him in a somewhat friendlier light. It took another hour of conversation to convince her that she hadn't really wanted him at all and that he had merely anticipated her true desires and therefore spared her the awkwardness of an involvement she would have regretted. Bethancourt was quite proud of this effort and was only sorry he couldn't share it with anyone.

Having settled Carrie, he turned to the gardens in search of Alcock, who had been the only person in a position to witness Camden's arrival at the house. Luckily the old gardener had put his teeth in that morning, and he also remembered Bethancourt as a boy. As a longtime friend of the family, Bethancourt could be trusted, and Alcock seemed almost eager to answer his questions. Unfortunately, he had noticed nothing.

"I was watching them tourists," he said. "You have to watch 'em every minute, you know. If I didn't, there wouldn't be a bud nor a flower left. You turn your back for a second, and they've got half the garden in bouquets. I keep telling Mr. Arnold I could use some help, but all he did was post those signs." Alcock snorted, showing his opinion of signs. "That don't do any good—it only puts ideas in their heads. And if they're not picking the flowers, they're wandering off the paths, trampling over things, or getting into the kitchen garden. I don't let 'em in there, and don't you think it."

Bethancourt assured him that such a thought had never entered his head and had he happened to see Miss Carrie's fiancé arriving?

"No, but I thought I'd lost one of them punters," answered Alcock. "I heard a noise, see, and I thought, God Almighty, one of them's in the kitchen garden, eating the early strawberries. Gave me quite a scare. So I nipped in to roust them out, but it was only Mr. Tom having a bit of a walk. So I got back, quick as I could, to the others, but they didn't seem to have done any harm." He looked around the garden suspiciously, as if he were still expecting to discover some catastrophe engineered by the tourists in his absence. "That's what I mean about needing help," he added. "If somebody was watching with me, they could have kept an eye out while I was in the kitchen garden, you see."

Bethancourt was not at all heartened to find that Tom Prendergast had left the office and been seen so near the house. He agreed that Alcock could certainly use some help in policing the gardens and asked at what time he had seen Tom.

Alcock wasn't sure, but after detailing the arrival of each of the tourists, and the clever way in which he had peeked through the hedges to keep track of those in the rose garden, the most likely time seemed to be about four thirty.

Bethancourt thanked the old man and turned back to the house. Four thirty did not make him happy. In all likelihood Camden had arrived sometime after four, found the house empty, and gone down to the billiard room where he had been murdered. If Tom had continued through the kitchen garden at four thirty, he might well have encountered Camden in the house, or even seen him through the billiard room window.

Lunch was a casual affair. Bethancourt, learning that Tom had taken his sandwiches to the estate office, made a pretense of eating and then went in search of him.

Tom Prendergast was a quiet, self-contained young man. He seemed surprised to see Bethancourt but offered him a seat and continued eating his sandwich.

"I was just wondering," Bethancourt began, "whether you had happened to notice Camden arriving. He left his car in the tourist car park, you know, and the kitchen garden's not far from there."

Tom looked faintly puzzled. "But I was here," he said.

"Well, yes, of course," said Bethancourt a little uncomfortably. "I meant later, when you went out."

"But I didn't go out."

Bethancourt affected great surprise. "I'm terribly sorry," he said. "I was talking to Alcock, and he told me that he had seen you in the kitchen garden at about four thirty. I must have misunderstood." He rose. "I'll just go down and find him again and straighten it out."

"Wait a moment," said Tom, still quite calmly. "I suppose it was me that he saw. Not," he added, "that it's any business of yours."

"No," agreed Bethancourt. "Only I've been trying to work out alibis for everyone, and it would help enormously if I knew just when Camden had arrived. So did you see him?"

"No," answered Tom flatly. "I didn't go into the car park."

"Where did you go, then?"

Understandably, Tom seemed to resent Bethancourt's questions. He hesitated and then said, "I went out for a breath of air, and then I thought I'd wolf

down a couple of surreptitious strawberries while Alcock was busy looking after the tourists. After that I
came back here. And I must say, Phillip, that it's in
very bad taste for you to go round playing detective."

Bethancourt sighed. Having one's friends as suspects
was proving to be a great handicap. With any other
witness, he would have said something polite and left,
but now he would have to spend a lot of time appeas-
ing Tom's rather understandable ire, just as he had
spent half the morning talking Carrie round. He lit a
cigarette and plunged into a conciliatory speech.

By the time he left the estate office, he was feeling
rather emotionally exhausted by the Prendergasts. On
the way back to the house, he encountered Arnold
coming in search of him. Arnold was downcast over a
spat between Beryl and Alice, normally the best of
friends. It had not amounted to much but went to prove
that everyone's nerves were on edge.

"And it's only been two days," said Arnold gloomily.

Bethancourt privately agreed that the Prendergasts
were not holding up well under the strain, but he tried
to take the optimistic view that the police would soon
have the matter cleared up. He decided that what Arnold most needed was a sounding post, so he encour-
aged him to talk while they sat on the terrace in the
early spring sunshine. Bethancourt, listening with half
an ear to his friend, was so tired that he had to stifle a
yawn. Moreover, he was hungry, not having eaten
much lunch. He wondered if Beryl and Alice had
patched up their differences enough to make tea.

"I wonder who that is," said Arnold as the sound of
a car in the drive reached them.

They rose and wandered round the side of the house
to be greeted by the sight of the police emerging from
their car.

"Good Lord," said Bethancourt, considerably surprised. "It's Jack and the superintendent."

"Who?" asked Arnold.

Bethancourt was spared from replying by Kennick, who had accompanied the Scotland Yard detectives and who now introduced them to Arnold.

"Chief Inspector Kennick and I would like to speak to your uncle first," said Carmichael. "Sergeant, you will talk to Mr. Bethancourt."

"Yes, sir," murmured Gibbons, smiling a little at his friend's surprise. He drew him to one side and asked, "Is there somewhere we can talk in private?"

"Certainly."

Bethancourt took him up to his bedroom and shut the heavy door firmly behind them.

"What," he demanded, "is going on?"

"Quite a place, this," said Gibbons, sinking into the armchair and surveying the room appreciatively.

"Jack!"

"Yes, all right. Carmichael and I are here because Len Camden was really a drug dealer named Lester Crowley."

"Great heavens," said Bethancourt, dropping heavily into the desk chair. Gibbons grinned openly at his astonishment. "Wait a minute," Bethancourt added when his wits returned to him, "wasn't that motor mechanic's name Crowley?"

"That's right," said Gibbons. "Joe is Lester's younger brother. We caught him this morning at his mother's place."

"Mother?" asked Bethancourt wildly. "But Carrie said Len's parents were dead."

"His father is," said Gibbons. "Tell me, Phillip, do you think she knew?"

"No," said Bethancourt after a moment's reflection. "No, Carrie's very young and a bit rebellious, but she would never have considered marrying a man whose income depended on the uncertainty of the drug trade. Dammit, Jack, she was looking for financial security."

Gibbons nodded. "Well, you can see how this changes

things," he said. "It's still perfectly possible, of course, that one of the family killed him. On the other hand, his business partners may have followed him up here. You see, Narcotics Division got a warrant for his arrest a week ago, based on information from some dealers they had busted. Camden was their supplier, and it's quite possible he could have identified the higher-ups. That would give them a good motive for getting him out of the way. Unfortunately, Narcotics knew nothing about the Chelsea flat and had only staked out the Kensington address. They searched it when he didn't turn up but found nothing. We've had better luck now in Chelsea."

"So you think he was using Rokeby as a hideout?" asked Bethancourt.

"It looks like it," answered Gibbons. "This is what I think happened: Crowley was a bright lad by all accounts. He knew he couldn't get away with cocaine dealing forever, and he was probably looking for a way out when he met your friend's sister."

"It must have seemed perfect," said Bethancourt. "No one would ever dream of looking for him at Rokeby, and I don't think he realized the Prendergasts have no money. He would have seen this place, and all the stuff in the public rooms, and thought he was marrying a gold mine."

"Probably," agreed Gibbons. "Anyway, he started setting up this new identity for himself. He kept very quiet about it; his brother knew nothing about the Chelsea flat or about Rokeby, although he did know about the cocaine dealing."

Bethancourt raised a skeptical eyebrow. "If he didn't know about Rokeby, how did he end up here?" he asked.

Gibbons waved a hand. "I meant Camden didn't tell him about it. Joe was getting worried about his brother, at least according to him. Les had never been a devoted family man, but he kept in touch and a telephone call usually brought a fairly prompt response from him. But in the last few months, Les had become increasingly distant and increasingly hard to get hold of. Personally, I think he never meant to see his family again after he got married and was trying to ease into it by degrees."

"Not very nice," said Bethancourt. "But it doesn't explain how Joe decided to take a tour of Rokeby last Saturday."

"I'm getting to it," said Gibbons. "Basically, Joe got worried enough a few weeks ago to try following his brother. Not much came of it until the weekend before last when Camden was indiscreet enough to drive straight from the Kensington flat to Rokeby. Joe followed him without any trouble. When Camden turned into the gates here and didn't come out, Joe hied himself off to the village pub and heard all about the Prendergasts and even about Carrie's fiancé. He also found out that Rokeby was open for tours, although he didn't dare take one for fear of running into Les. He was pretty puzzled by the whole setup, but since Les seemed to be all right, he didn't say anything. Then, a week ago, Les didn't show up for a lunch date. Joe left messages but never heard from him, so he finally decided to come up here and see if this was where Les was hiding out. He took the tour instead of knocking at the front door because he didn't want to queer whatever deal Les had going here. When he saw his brother's body, he ran off, absolutely terrified that he'd invaded a drug lord's sanctuary and that he'd be next."

"It's a good story," said Bethancourt. "Do you think it's true?"

"I think parts of it are," replied Gibbons. "I think Joe truly didn't know about Rokeby and that he found out the way he says he did. What's missing, I believe, is that Joe was dealing himself in a small way and that, for some reason, Camden didn't give him his supply. I think that's why Joe was so worried about his brother and why he had the nerve to follow him up here."

"But you don't think he killed him?"

"He could have," said Gibbons cheerfully. "But so far there's no motive for it—it would be tantamount to killing the goose that laid the golden egg for Joe. And I must say that bit about running off because he thought the Prendergasts were master criminals sounded genuine."

"I really don't think they are, Jack," said Bethancourt, alarmed.

"Oh, neither do I," agreed Gibbons. "Camden was dealing long before he ever knew the Prendergasts existed. Anyway, with this new spanner thrown into the works, what I'm supposed to get from you is every last detail you can remember about those tourists. If Camden was killed by his bosses, the murderer might well have been among them."

"But how would they have known about Rokeby?" objected Bethancourt.

"They could have followed him the same way Joe did, or they could have gotten it from Joe himself. He swears, of course, that he never told a soul, but I doubt that's true. So if you would kindly describe your tour group . . ."

"I'll try," said Bethancourt doubtfully, "but I really don't think I can add anything to what I said before."

"Begin at the beginning," suggested Gibbons helpfully. "There you are, about to give your first historic house tour—"

"Wait a minute," interrupted Bethancourt. "What about Uncle James? Why all the interest in him?"

"Because he never went to London," answered Gibbons. "He was looking like suspect number one, but now we're not so sure. Kennick found a witness who saw him at the station Saturday morning after Tom dropped him off. He was getting into a red MG driven by a woman. The witness only saw the back of the woman's head, and assumed it was Lady Beryl picking him up. But none of the Prendergasts owns an MG."

"Sounds like a spot of infidelity."

"It probably is," said Gibbons. "Still, he might have been using the lady as an alibi. Anyway, we've got to find out who she is, and it would be a lot easier if he would simply tell us. Now, let's get back to the tourists."

"All right," said Bethancourt, without enthusiasm.

James, given a choice between telling all or having the police ask his daughter-in-law if she had borrowed a red MG and met him at the station on Saturday, decided to tell all. In a few minutes, he had given them the lady's name, address, and telephone number, and completely accounted for his time. He was dismissed, still pleading for discretion, which the detectives had already promised. Kennick departed to check on this statement, while Carmichael settled down with Carrie Prendergast. He broke the news of her fiancé's duplicity as gently as he could, and then, for the next two and a half hours, proceeded to elicit every detail she could remember about anyone she had ever met with Camden or that he had even mentioned. The superintendent was relentless and only let her go when it became clear that she was exhausted and becoming faintly hysterical. He and Gibbons then broke for supper but returned after an hour to interview Tom Prendergast about his walk in the kitchen garden.

The tension that had presided over the Rokeby meals for the last two days was somewhat alleviated at dinner that night, replaced by shock at the revelation of Len Camden's true identity. Since Carrie was having a tray in her room, everyone felt free to discuss the subject. They all reiterated how they had never liked him, Emily in particular priding herself on the intuition that had led her to forbid her daughter's marrying him. Everyone considerately refrained from pointing out just how much effect this edict had had. Eric shook his head over Carrie's gullibility and was becoming rather unbearable on the subject until Arnold pointed out that they had all spent a good bit of time with Len without ever suspecting there was anything seriously wrong with him. All in all, Bethancourt thought, they seemed relieved; they appeared to have little doubt that drugs led to murder and that therefore they were all in the clear.

"Damn!" said Bethancourt, hearing Gibbons' voice on his answering machine. Feeling there was little more he could do at Rokeby and that he had probably outstayed his welcome in any case, he had returned to town the next morning, just missing Gibbons at Scotland Yard. He had debated with himself but had finally decided to keep a lunch date rather than just sit around the flat waiting for Gibbons' call. And, of course, it was during lunch that Gibbons had looked for him.

"I've got a bit of a lead," Gibbons' voice was saying cautiously on the machine. "It seems the Morrises— those honeymooners on the tour—aren't married at all. I thought you might like to check it out with me. I'll ring you later to let you know how it comes out."

Bethancourt cursed again and flicked the machine off. As if in answer, the phone rang and Bethancourt snatched it up, but it was only Arnold Prendergast.

"Just calling to see if there's any news your end," he said in a thoroughly depressed tone of voice.

"Nothing solid yet," answered Bethancourt. "What's happening at Rokeby?"

"Tom's had a horrible row with his father," said Arnold. "Of course we'd all like to know why the police seem so interested in Uncle James, but I'm afraid Tom went a bit too far. On the other hand, you can't help but feel there's something suspicious in the way Uncle James refuses to say anything."

"Oh," said Bethancourt, feeling this placed him in a moral dilemma. "Actually," he said, "the police are satisfied with James's explanation now. He has an alibi."

"I see," said Arnold. He paused for a moment. "And the fact that you haven't told me what it is means there's a woman involved."

"Oh, hell," said Bethancourt.

"I thought it must be that, if it wasn't anything to do with the murder. Are the police quite sure?"

"Quite," said Bethancourt. "Look here, you might as well have the whole story, since you've figured out the worst part of it. James never went to London at all. His lady friend picked him up at the station after Tom dropped him off, and they spent the day together. Not only has she confirmed that, but they stopped at a pub before she took him back to the station to meet you. The people at the pub remember them, and that covered most of the relevant time."

"Well, that's good at least," said Arnold. "I don't think I'd better tell the others all that, but I'll manage somehow to vouch for Uncle James's innocence."

"Your mother's clear, too," added Bethancourt for good measure, although no one had ever really suspected her. "Kennick found that cafe she stopped at. They remembered her quite well."

There was a smile in Arnold's voice. "People always do remember Mother," he said. "Well, at least that's two of us off the hook. I don't suppose the police are making any headway with people outside the family?"

"Jack says he's got a lead," answered Bethancourt, "but I don't know much about it yet. Just that those newlyweds on the tour I gave aren't married at all. It's rather encouraging that they lied about their reason for being at Rokeby, but that doesn't get us very far."

Arnold was immeasurably cheered by this piece of news, however. "Superintendent Carmichael spent all morning with Carrie," he confided. "The poor girl's exhausted and, well, I was rather afraid that he'd found out she'd done it after all."

"Not yet," replied Bethancourt. "Try to hold on, Arnold. I'm sure the police will have it all cleared up shortly. Jack is going to ring me later about the Morrises, and I'll pass it on to you."

"Thanks, Phillip," said Arnold gratefully. "I can't tell you what a help you've been. I don't know how we'd have got through without you."

"I've done hardly anything," said Bethancourt. "Save your thanks. I'll ring you later."

He put down the receiver, wishing more than ever that he had skipped lunch and waited for Gibbons.

Gibbons did not appear until after seven that evening. He looked pale and tired as he dropped into one of Bethancourt's armchairs and shook his head at his friend's questions.

"It was no good," he said.

"Oh dear," said Bethancourt, handing him a drink. "It sounded so hopeful. What happened?"

Gibbons took a long drink from his glass. "Rick Morris is in the throes of a very nasty divorce case. Barbara Morris, who is really still Miss Banks, comes from a very staunch Roman Catholic family. They would not, it seems, look favorably on her living in sin with Morris, nor, for that matter, do they approve of divorce. So Barbara and Rick pretended to elope. To lend verisimilitude to an otherwise unconvincing story, they got dressed up and took snapshots of themselves down at the registrar's office, and then they took their vacations together so they could take pictures of their supposed honeymoon. They haven't much money, so a trip to Norfolk was the best they could do."

"It doesn't sound very likely," said Bethancourt.

"It's unlikely enough to be true," responded Gibbons. "I've spent the day looking into it. The Bankses are indeed Roman Catholics. Both Barbara and Rick have held their present jobs for years, and neither their bank accounts nor their lifestyle shows them to have any money in excess of their salaries. I've checked with their friends, who all tell the same story. I've checked with their neighbors at their old addresses, who never noticed anything untoward in their habits. If they had ever met Len Camden, I can find no trace of it."

Bethancourt sighed. "It does sound like a washout," he admitted.

"I'm sorry, Phillip," said Gibbons, "but I'm not certain this case will ever be solved."

"Oh God, don't say that," begged Bethancourt. "I've been cheering Arnold up by assuring him you'll have it solved at any minute."

"Then you've been lying," said Gibbons flatly. "Look here, Phillip, there's no evidence. Forensics didn't pick up an atom of anything that didn't belong in that billiard room, not fibers, not fingerprints. That's been a problem all along, but if we could show motive and opportunity, we might have tied it together. Unfortunately, no one seems to have more of a motive than anyone else, and everybody had the opportunity."

"Details, details." Bethancourt waved a hand. "You're just feeling discouraged because you've had a long day. Have some more whisky."

"Cheers," said Gibbons, who always appreciated Bethancourt's stock of single malt scotch. "Don't misunderstand me," he went on. "We're still working on it, and we may yet turn something up. But at the moment, if I had to guess, I would say one of the Prendergasts did it on the spur of the moment. Carmichael's been talking to Tom for most of the afternoon and thinks he could be hiding something. Tom doesn't usually work in the estate office on Saturdays, you know, and for all we know he may only have decided to go there after he ran into Crowley and killed him."

"What does Tom say?"

"That he was working Saturday because he left the

office early on Friday to go out with some friends, and that he went into the kitchen garden when he realized Alcock was otherwise occupied and he, Tom, could therefore steal some strawberries. It may be true. Or he may have been quietly killing Crowley. And if that's the truth, I don't see how we can ever prove it."

"Don't be so pessimistic," retorted Bethancourt, in whom Gibbons' attitude was provoking uneasiness nevertheless. "And I don't particularly care if you can prove it in court, so long as I can tell Arnold who did it. It's awful to think one of your nearest and dearest has committed murder and not know which of them it is. No family could stand the strain."

"I know," said Gibbons, sighing. "But they may have to."

Bethancourt eyed his friend. "You've been over-working," he said. "What you need to put you back in spirits is a nice raveup."

"No, I don't," said Gibbons hastily, alarmed by the determined glint in Bethancourt's hazel eyes. The glint nearly always meant he would soon be persuaded into doing whatever Bethancourt had in mind, whether he wanted to or not. He had no desire and was really too tired to go running off on a tour of West End night-clubs, which was Bethancourt's usual diversion. "What I need is sleep."

"Nothing too energetic," mused Bethancourt, ignoring him. "I've got it—there's a very funny film playing not far from here. It's not too long, and I'll take you for dinner afterwards."

"I really don't thin—"

"Indian food at that restaurant round the corner. You like Indian food."

"So does everybody," grumbled Gibbons ungratefully, although secretly he was relieved that nightclubs had not been mentioned. "And I'll probably fall asleep in the film."

"Nonsense. It's far too funny to sleep through. Drink up—it starts in twenty minutes."

Gibbons drank up.

The next afternoon, as Bethancourt turned in to Fortnum and Mason's, he encountered the American wife, Mrs. MacDonald, coming out. For an instant he could not place her, but then it came back to him and he hailed her pleasantly. She smiled, but her look was blank, so he reintroduced himself.

"Oh yes, of course!" she exclaimed. "Mr. Bethancourt. I hadn't really forgotten you, you know," she confided. "Or that dreadful day." She sighed.

"I hope the rest of your vacation has been pleasanter," he said politely.

"Oh yes," she said. "We've been to Canterbury and Winchester and Bath. And lots of other historic houses. But do you know—and I really mean this—none of the tours has been as much fun as the one you gave. Either the other tour guides don't know as much or else they don't tell everything. I'm going to recommend Rokeby House to everyone back home."

"Er, thank you," said Bethancourt guiltily, remembering the stupendous lies of which his tour had consisted. "Very kind of you."

He offered her tea, motioning to one of Fortnum and Mason's famous tea shops, but she declined, saying her husband was waiting. They bade each other goodbye, and Bethancourt watched her leave, vaguely uneasy for no reason he could name.

It was not until they were weighing out his order of pâté that he remembered Gibbons had told him the MacDonalds had returned to America on Monday.

"Nonsense," said Gibbons when Bethancourt finally tracked him down at the Yard. "Kennick talked to them less than an hour before they left for the airport. You must have been mistaken, Phillip."

"Jack," said Bethancourt, pushing his glasses back up on the bridge of his nose, "I *spoke* to her. She recognized me. She told me how much she liked the tour of Rokeby."

Gibbons was startled. "It doesn't seem possible," he protested, but he was flipping through the case file as he spoke. "I'll ring their hotel."

The desk clerk remembered the MacDonalds very well, but he regretted that they had checked out on Monday. No, he did not think they were still in England; he understood they were returning to America.

"Well, they didn't," said Bethancourt flatly after Gibbons had rung off.

"All right, all right," said Gibbons, turning back to the file. "Don't get your knickers in a twist. What time is it in America?"

"What part of America?" demanded Bethancourt. "Be a bit more specific, can't you?"

"New York," answered Gibbons, who was already dialing. "The state, not the city."

"Ten—no, eleven in the morning," said Bethancourt, but Gibbons was no longer listening. His attention was now on the phone, but in a moment he made a face.

"Answering machine," he said. "Well, nothing ventured . . ."

He broke off to leave a message asking the MacDonalds to contact Scotland Yard.

"Let's try the relatives," he said.

"Relatives?" asked Bethancourt.

"Yes, there's a married daughter. Kennick checked with her to make certain her parents really were in England and not sitting at home having had their passports stolen. Here's the number."

This time he got an answer. When he identified himself, Jeanine Reid gasped. "Have you found them?" she demanded.

Gibbons was taken aback. "I'm trying to get in

touch with your parents, Mrs. Reid," he said. "Are they missing?"

"Of course they are!" she said, hysteria edging her voice. "Oh God, you didn't even know, did you?"

"We thought something must be wrong," answered Gibbons, motioning Bethancourt to move to a nearby desk and pick up the receiver.

Mrs. Reid was only too willing to repeat her story. She and her husband had driven to the airport on Monday to pick up her parents. The Reids had arrived early and had gotten a good place at the barrier, with a clear view of the doors through which international passengers would emerge from Customs. Eventually, they had noticed some people whose luggage bore her parents' flight number coming through, and they had scanned the travelers eagerly, thinking it could not be long now. But the MacDonalds had never appeared. The Reids had waited a long while until at last Mr. Reid had gone off to see what he could find out, leaving his wife still waiting. The airline had confirmed that the MacDonalds had been on the flight, and a little further investigation by an airport official determined that all the luggage from that flight had been claimed. Further, no one from the flight had been stopped at Customs, nor had anyone collapsed with a medical emergency between airplane and baggage claim.

The Reids had been at a loss. They had returned home, hoping for a message, but there had been none. They had rung the MacDonalds' hotel in London, only to be told that the MacDonalds had left for America. They had contacted the police, who, in the next day or two, confirmed what the Reids had already discovered at the airport. They postulated that the Reids had missed seeing the MacDonalds and that someone, probably posing as a taxi driver, had spirited them away.

Mrs. Reid was absolutely certain this was not what had occurred. It had not been a particularly crowded time at the airport, and people had been coming out of Customs in dribs and drabs. It was simply not possible that both she and her husband had failed to see her parents coming out of doors in full view not twenty feet away. Mrs. Reid was convinced that something had prevented her parents from boarding the flight after they had checked in. The airlines maintained that this was impossible—the MacDonald's boarding passes had been handed in, and the police were taking their word for it. So yesterday the Reids had employed a private investigator in London. They had faxed him photographs of the MacDonalds, a copy of their itinerary, and the numbers of their credit cards.

Gibbons took down the investigator's name and address and then brought the conversation to a close, assuring Mrs. Reid he would do everything he could to clear the matter up.

But from the moment he had heard that the MacDonalds were missing, he had a sinking feeling that he knew what had happened to them.

He and Bethancourt looked silently at each other for a moment after they had rung off. Then Gibbons stirred.

"I've heard of this detective, David Martindale," he said. "He has a good reputation."

"We'd better try to get hold of him and have a look at those photographs," answered Bethancourt. "That is, if you're thinking what I am."

"Yes," sighed Gibbons, reaching once again for the phone. "I'm afraid I am."

David Martindale was not at his office, but his secretary said she would beep him. In ten minutes or so he rang back and agreed to come round to the Yard with the photographs.

"I hope you know what's become of the MacDonalds, sergeant," he said, "because I don't. I didn't get anything at all at the airport, or from their credit cards, and all I can tell you is that they didn't keep to their itinerary."

"We'll see," said Gibbons without much enthusiasm. "The photographs should show us, one way or the other." He hung up the phone and rose. "I should see if Carmichael's back yet," he told Bethancourt. "You had better come, too. If he's there, we'll no doubt see Martindale in his office."

"Very well," said Bethancourt, stubbing out a cigarette and rising. "God, I hope we're wrong, Jack."

"Maybe we are," replied Gibbons, but Bethancourt shook his head and the look in Gibbons' eyes showed that he thought the hope vain as well.

David Martindale was a tall, thin man in his forties, neatly dressed in a sports jacket and khakis. He must have been surprised and curious to be introduced to Detective Superintendent Carmichael rather than just Sergeant Gibbons, but he hid it well. He shook hands politely and then said, "I have the photographs and all the other information right here. I hope it matches up with whatever you're working on."

He produced several folded sheets of paper from his breast pocket and handed them to Carmichael, who thanked him and immediately passed them to Bethancourt. He smoothed out the pictures on the edge of the desk and leaned over them while the others watched him.

"No," he said, after only a moment's study. "These are not the people on the tour at Rokeby."

Martindale shifted in his chair, betraying his curiosity, but he said nothing while Carmichael took the photos back and compared them to others laid out on his desk. Gibbons peered over Carmichael's shoulder, but Bethancourt wandered away to the window and lit a cigarette.

"It's hard to tell, of course," said Carmichael. "But I think they match." Gibbons grunted an affirmative, and Carmichael looked up, beckoning to Martindale to join them. "These," he explained, "are the pictures we took of two murder victims we pulled out of the Thames on Sunday."

Martindale frowned, peering intently from one set of pictures to the other. "I can't be sure," he said at last. "The faces are too bloated, but it looks very much like it."

"Dental records will give us proof," said Carmichael.

Martindale sighed and straightened. "So they're dead. I feel sorry for Mrs. Reid," he said. Then his expression changed. "Wait a minute," he said. "You said you found them on Sunday?"

"That's right," said Carmichael evenly. "They'd been dead for some time. In fact, if they are the MacDonalds, I think they were murdered very shortly after they arrived here."

Bethancourt was allowed to go home to feed and collect his dog. On his return, a police artist awaited him, and over the next two hours they produced fairly good representations of the couple who had impersonated the MacDonalds at Rokeby. Afterwards, he was settled at a desk with endless books of mug shots to look through. He was not by nature a patient person, and thus far in the pursuit of his detective hobby, he had always been able to leave the plodding, routine work to Gibbons. But his friend could be of no help in this instance; only Bethancourt and Chief Inspector Kennick had ever seen the bogus MacDonalds. Sighing mightily, and growing increasingly fractious, he sat chained to his duty, turning over page after page of police photographs as the night wore on. He was resolved that, if he had to do it, he would get it over with quickly, that night, and not have to wake up in the morning with the prospect of coming back to the job.

It was nearly two in the morning before he found one of the pictures he had been searching for.

It was another perfect spring day. Bethancourt and Arnold paced slowly through the Rokeby park along a path dappled green and gold with sunshine. Cerberus and Henry, Arnold's favorite dog, gamboled around them, inspecting the bases of trees and chasing squirrels. Bethancourt paused to light a cigarette, and Arnold stood beside him, watching the dogs as they circled back toward their owners.

"When did they find them?" asked Arnold.

"Yesterday," answered Bethancourt. "And Kennick and I picked them out of a lineup without any trouble," he added, rather boastfully. "In any case, they were foolish enough to keep some of the MacDonalds' things, including the passports. The police think they have a pretty good case." He hesitated. "But I don't know if they'll be prosecuted for Camden's murder."

"What?" Arthur turned to him, startled.

"There's no real evidence," explained Bethancourt. "We know they killed him because there's no other reason for them to have been here or to have killed the MacDonalds in the first place, but that's circumstantial. Anyway, it hasn't been decided yet."

Arnold sighed. "I suppose it doesn't really matter," he said. "So long as we know who it was. Were they Camden's bosses in the cocaine business, by the way?"

"Lord no," answered Bethancourt. "They were just hired thugs, and I gather it's driving the police crazy that they won't identify their employers. They apparently have no doubt that their own lives would be brief if they spoke."

"But if execution is the regular punishment for naming names, why would these bosses think that Len would betray them? He wasn't a stupid man."

"Because they had found out he had a secret identity," replied Bethancourt. "And to them that signaled

a betrayal. The police think his bosses probably first
became aware that Crowley was up to something soon
after he rented the Chelsea flat. Suddenly he wasn't to
be found a lot of the time, and he'd abandoned all his
favorite haunts. So before they had him killed as an example, they put a watch on him to find out how much
he might already have revealed—it would never occur
to them that he was just trying to retire."

"I suppose not," agreed Arnold. "I don't expect
many people try to retire from that crowd."

"We don't know how they found out about Rokeby,"
continued Bethancourt. "Either someone saw Crowley
with Carrie and traced her here, or else his brother Joe
was persuaded to talk. In any case, they never found
the Chelsea flat and they couldn't have found out about
Rokeby much before the crisis."

"What crisis?" asked Arnold.

"Narcotics Division arrested one of the dealers Crowley
was supplying," answered Bethancourt, "and he talked.
When the head of the drug operation heard about that, he
realized that whatever game Crowley had been playing it
hadn't been with the police. If it had been, they would
hardly have shown their hand by arresting a relative
small-fry. It then became crucial to get rid of Crowley before the police found him.

"I don't think Crowley ever realized his bosses were
suspicious of him, but he knew the dealer would give
his name to the police and that therefore the time had
come to quit. He immediately decamped to the Chelsea
flat, taking the rest of the last cocaine shipment with
him. We may never know why he decided to come to
Rokeby, but I think in their last phone conversation
Carrie communicated more of her change of heart to
him than she meant to. Since from his point of view it
was now vital that she go through with their plans, he
came down to inject a little romance into the situation."

"Probably," said Arnold. "Carrie's not very good at

hiding her feelings. I take it the drug lords had already sent this chap Weldon and his girlfriend up here to kill him?"

"That's right. But really, Arnold, this place isn't very easy to get into."

"Nonsense," scoffed Arnold. "There are a dozen places one can get over the wall, and we leave the gates open half the time anyway."

"Yes," said Bethancourt, "but what then? You've got half a dozen dogs roaming the place, Alcock in the garden, and family members bouncing all over. Except on the days you're open to the public, an intruder doesn't have a chance. At least that's how Weldon saw it, and I think he was right. He heard about the tours and decided to pose as a tourist as the easiest way of getting into the place. He also realized that if he could pass himself off as someone else, the police might never suspect him. He sent his girlfriend to keep a lookout for Camden up here while he haunted Heathrow. We're not sure how he picked the MacDonalds up—probably by offering them a ride—but they were perfect for his purposes. They knew no one in England, had never been here before, and were about Weldon's age. With his criminal connections, it was easy to get the passport pictures altered, and then he joined his girlfriend up here to await Camden's arrival—they must have had a fit when he took a week to show up. They were probably watching the entrance to Rokeby and followed him in, hoping to catch him in the car park. But they missed him there, so they wandered into the gardens with the rest of the tourists and from there to the back of the house. They probably looked in the windows, saw Camden in the billiard room, and crept in by that back door."

"I'm surprised Alcock didn't notice they'd disappeared," said Arnold. "He keeps a fierce eye on people in the gardens."

"Yes, but he can't be everywhere at once," answered

Bethancourt. "He said when he heard Tom in the kitchen garden he thought it might be some of the tourists, so clearly he knew he didn't have them all under his eye. He just made sure the absent ones weren't in fact still in the gardens, digging up the plants, and left it at that. And Weldon was clever. He knew it might look odd—if any of the other tourists had noticed that he and his girlfriend were gone—for them to reappear in the gardens, so they came back through the car park and were waiting on the terrace for the house tour when the others came up, just a couple not very interested in flowers. Then all they had to do was sit back and pretend they were the MacDonalds. As hapless American tourists who had only been in the country a week, Kennick never suspected them. It would have worked beautifully if I hadn't chanced to run into 'Mrs. MacDonald' after they had supposedly left England."

"Yes," said Arnold, "I didn't understand that bit. I thought you said earlier that they *did* leave. So how did they end up back in London?"

"Oh, that part of the plan was very clever," said Bethancourt almost enthusiastically. "In order to assure that no one would look for the MacDonalds over here, Weldon and his girlfriend actually flew to the States with the MacDonalds' passports and on their flight. Then they turned around and flew to Paris on a different airline, still using the MacDonalds' passports. Once they were in France, they brought out their own passports and came back to England."

Arnold sighed and shook his head, but otherwise declined to comment on these machinations. "Well, I can't say I'm unhappy that Len died," he said. "Carrie's well out of it. But I do feel pretty dreadful about the Americans."

"It *is* dreadful," Bethancourt agreed. "Weldon's a brutal character. Funny, he doesn't look it at all. I actually thought he and his girlfriend were rather pleasant on the tour. I never suspected a thing."

They walked on in silence for a bit while the dogs chased each other up and down the lane.

"How's Carrie doing?" asked Bethancourt.

Arnold smiled. "She's terribly grateful to be let off and also horribly guilty about having taken up with Len in the first place. But she's resilient. She'll get over it. Everyone else is just relieved that it's all over. We're being especially nice to each other to make up for previous bad behavior."

"That's nice," said Bethancourt. "I'm glad it's worked out in the end."

"It wouldn't have if it hadn't been for you," said Arnold. "Thank you, Phillip."

Bethancourt shrugged the thanks away. "I didn't have much to do with this case beyond being a reliable witness. But I'll tell you what I did enjoy: I enjoyed being a suspect and being grilled by Kennick. It was quite an experience, that."

Arnold laughed at him. "You have strange tastes," he said. "Come on, we'd best turn back if we're to be in time for lunch."

They whistled for the dogs and began to make their way back to Rokeby House.

The Borgia Heirloom
by Julian Symons

"And now," Lady X said, "you may ask your questions."

The young man repeated, perhaps for the sixth time, that it was very good of her to receive him, and give him lunch, and talk to him. At that, she merely inclined her head, told the maid that they would take coffee in the drawing room, and led the way there. She was very old, her skin the color of parchment, her hands liver-spotted, thickly veined, the nails yellow and horny. Several rings—a large diamond, a sapphire-and-ruby cluster, a huge emerald—looked incongruous on them.

"It's not exactly questions." The young man was American, his fair hair cut close to the head, his eyes round and innocent, his manner earnest. "I'm doing this book on great unsolved British cases, they're so much subtler than our crude shootouts, and I'm trying to get accounts from people who actually knew the background and the characters. Official accounts don't really bring them to life."

"I can do that for you." Her laugh was a raven's caw, but she shook her head when, with a tentative air, he produced a notebook. "Oh, no—no. Notebooks are for reporters, my dear young man. I understand you to be a real writer."

He put away the notebook. He had, after all, a good memory.

"The place, as you know, was Gratchen Manor, where we are now—the home of my husband's family for more than a century. It is a pleasant place, one with an ambience that impresses itself on the characters of those who live in it. Do you understand me?"

The young American nodded. In truth, he was overawed by the great house, the portraits of grim-faced ancestors along the walls, the intimidating size of the dining room in which the two of them had eaten at one end of the long table, and of this drawing room with its grand piano, alcoves containing what was no doubt immensely valuable porcelain, great windows looking onto a terrace from which steps led down to what seemed acres of lawn. It seemed to him wrong that families should live in such large houses—and now not even a family, but one old woman and her housekeeper, plus a servant or two.

"This house and this English countryside formed the character of my husband, Tom, and our son Charlie. You would have had to know them to understand them. Tom—Sir Thomas—went to London two or three days each week, he was a director of this company and vice chairman of that, but his heart was here at Gratchen. He took part in every local event, thought of himself as the squire, as his father and grandfather had been before him, employed half the people in the village, felt responsible for their moral welfare. A strange thing that, in this modern world, but it was so."

The young man nodded. He had heard different tales in the village, where Sir Thomas was resented as a man who poked his nose into matters that did not concern him.

"And Charlie, Charlie was perfect. Everybody loved him." She indicated a portrait, head and shoulders, of a weakly handsome young man in officer's uniform. "I prayed for him to come through the war unharmed, and my prayers were answered. Then all I wanted was for him to marry the right girl and make this house their home. That will sound old-fashioned, too, I'm sure."

Charlie's fellow officers had said he was pleasant enough, but thick as two blocks. Feeling that he should speak, the young American said, "That was in nineteen forty-eight."

"I believe so." Lady X's small eyes were sharp within their folds of skin. "I hope you do not expect dates and hours. This is a mystery without a solution. I am telling you what happened, no more.

"In the autumn, Charlie became engaged to Susan Baybridge. They had known each other from childhood, her father was a barrister, it was a suitable match in every way." Lady X rose arthritically, took a silver-framed photograph from the top of the grand piano, and showed it to the young man. "That was Susan at the time."

The photograph showed a rather plain, heavy-featured girl with a determined chin. "Charlie was involved in some kind of commercial activity in London, which his father seemed to think necessary. He came back here, of course, at weekends. You may imagine my incredulity when he arrived one weekend in company with a young woman and told us he intended to break his engagement with Susan and marry this—this woman. Her name was Deirdre O'Connor and she was alleged to be a fashion model. It was obvious to me at once that she was out for what she could get and had no feeling for Charlie. It was found later that she had granted her favors to half a dozen young men.

"I thought her an entirely unsuitable wife for Charlie, and told him so, and I told him also that his treatment of Susan was disgraceful. I was not surprised that when at last he told her that he wished to break off their engagement, there was a violent quarrel. In front of the servants."

In front of the servants, he thought. It was certainly a different world. As if reading his thoughts, she said, "It was another world we lived in here at Gratchen. And a better one.

"In the New Year, we gave a dinner party. Of course we invited Susan. She did some job in a scientific laboratory and we invited the director of the place, a tiresome man named Cleggit. There were other friends, including our local medical man, Dr. MacFarlane—a dozen altogether. Then, quite unexpectedly, Charlie came down, the woman with him. Susan had to meet the woman—it was most unpleasant for her."

"Your son said he told you he was coming down and you must have forgotten."

"I forget nothing." Her gaze was withering. "May I continue? Thank you.—We ate simple English food, which, even in those days of rationing, was not denied to us at Gratchen. A clear soup made with stock, roast beef accompanied by the usual vegetables, an apple charlotte. It was not a happy meal. Tom was already sick with the kidney disease from which he died six months later, Susan hardly spoke, the dreadful Deirdre talked too much and too loudly, and Charlie was obviously besotted by her. After dinner we came in here, and it was then that Deirdre behaved as if drunk or drugged. She staggered about, almost fell over when sitting down in a chair, a disgusting exhibition. Then she collapsed and was taken to lie down, Dr. MacFarlane attending her. He agreed with me that she had taken an overdose of drugs, and when we questioned Charlie he admitted that she used both cocaine and heroin. She was taken ill at nine-thirty. Just after midnight, she died."

"But drugs didn't cause her death."

"Dr. MacFarlane thought so at the time."

"But Cleggit knew better. His pharmaceutical knowledge led him to suspect an alkaloid poison. He made sure that the wine glasses and coffee cups were preserved, not washed up."

"Cleggit was a busybody, a troublemaker."

"And you know what was found in one coffee cup. Coniine, the drug derived from *conium maculatum,* the spotted hemlock. The poison Socrates took, the drug Keats said induced a drowsy numbness, the drug of which even a few drops may be a fatal dose. But how was it administered? That was what the police could never establish. It must have been from some kind of phial, but none was found. Your son poured the coffee, you added sugar, but none of the guests noticed anything unusual, and in any case Deirdre O'Connor took no sugar."

The maid came in with a tray containing a coffee pot, two cups, a milk jug, and a bowl of sugar cubes. The young man continued. "Of course, there were suspects. Susan had reason enough to hate Deirdre. Your son might have found out about her other men friends. It was even suggested that your husband, knowing himself under sentence of death, might have been responsible."

"That was ridiculous. If Cleggit had not been such a busybody, Dr. MacFarlane would have signed a death certificate. As it was, the affair broke up the family. Charlie went out to Australia, married a girl there, died five years ago without an heir. I am quite alone now."

The young man's eyes were bright. He lowered his voice, almost whispered, as he said, "You arranged the dinner party, you knew your son was coming, you invited Dr. MacFarlane. I think you did it."

She seemed not to have heard him, poured the coffee into the two cups. "It was all so long ago. Do you take milk?"

"What? Oh, no, thank you."

"Sugar?"

"No sugar." He leaned forward. "Won't you tell me,

now that it can do no harm, just for my satisfaction as an amateur criminologist, how you did it?"

The little eyes in the wrinkled face were amused, contemptuous. "You are an impertinent young man. I said I was telling you a story to which there is no solution." She passed him the coffee cup, then held up her veined, spotted hand with the bright rings on it. "Would you believe that my hands were once admired? Nowadays people only look at the rings. The emerald is an heirloom, said to have belonged to a Borgia."

What followed was so quick that if she had not drawn attention to her hand he would not have seen it. From the center of the great emerald ring a tiny stream of liquid shot into her cup. She gave her raven caw at his shocked, startled face and said, "Liquid saccharin."

Dr. Hyde, Detective,
and the White Pillars Murder
by G. K. Chesterton

Those who have discussed the secret of the success of the great detective, Dr. Adrian Hyde, could find no finer example of his remarkable methods than the affair which came to be called "The White Pillars Mystery." But that extraordinary man left no personal notes and we owe our record of it to his two young assistants, John Brandon and Walter Weir. Indeed, as will be seen, it was they who could best describe the first investigations in detail, from the outside; and that for a rather remarkable reason.

They were both men of exceptional ability; they had fought bravely and even brilliantly in the Great War; they were cultivated, they were capable, they were trustworthy, and they were starving. For such was the reward which England in the hour of victory accorded to the deliverers of the world. It was a long time before they consented in desperation to consider anything so remote from their instincts as employment in a private detective agency. Jack Brandon, who was a dark, compact, resolute, restless youth, with a boyish appetite for detective tales and talk, regarded the notion with a half-fascinated apprehension, but his friend Weir, who was long and fair and languid, a lover of music and metaphysics, with a candid disgust.

"I believe it might be frightfully interesting," said Brandon. "Haven't you ever had the detective fever when you couldn't help overhearing somebody say something—'If only he knew what she did to the Archdeacon,' or 'And then the whole business about Susan and the dog will come out?' "

"Yes," replied Weir, "but you only heard snatches because you didn't mean to listen and almost immediately left off listening. If you were a detective, you'd have to crawl under the bed or hide in the dust-bin to hear the whole secret, till your dignity was as dirty as your clothes."

"Isn't it better than stealing?" asked Brandon, gloomily, "which seems to be the next step."

"Why, no; I'm not sure that it is!" answered his friend.

Then, after a pause, he added, reflectively, "Besides, it isn't as if we'd get the sort of work that's relatively decent. We can't claim to know the wretched trade. Clumsy eavesdropping must be worse than the blind spying on the blind. You've not only got to know what is said, but what is meant. There's a lot of difference between listening and hearing. I don't say I'm exactly in a position to fling away a handsome salary offered me by a great criminologist like Dr. Adrian Hyde, but, unfortunately, he isn't likely to offer it."

But Dr. Adrian Hyde was an unusual person in more ways than one, and a better judge of applicants than most modern employers. He was a very tall man with a chin so sunk on his chest as to give him, in spite of his height, almost a look of being hunch-backed; but though the face seemed thus fixed as in a frame, the eyes were as active as a bird's, shifting and darting everywhere and observing everything; his long limbs ended in large hands and feet, the former being almost always thrust into his trouser-pockets, and the latter being loaded with more than appropriately large boots. With all his awkward figure he was not without gaiety and a taste for good things, especially good wine and tobacco; his manner was grimly genial and his insight and personal judgment marvellously rapid. Which was how it came about that John Brandon and Walter Weir were established at comfortable desks in the detective's private office, when Mr. Alfred Morse was shown in, bringing with him the problem of White Pillars.

Mr. Alfred Morse was a very stolid and serious person with stiffly-brushed brown hair, a heavy brown face and a heavy black suit of mourning of a cut somewhat provincial, or perhaps colonial. His first words were accompanied with an inoffensive but dubious cough and a glance at the two assistants.

"This is rather confidential business," he said.

"Mr. Morse," said Dr. Hyde, with quiet good humour, "if you were knocked down by a cab and carried to a hospital, your life might be saved by the first surgeon in the land; but you couldn't complain if he let students learn from the operation. These are my two cleverest pupils, and if you want good detectives, you must let them be trained."

"Oh, very well," said the visitor, "perhaps it is not quite so easy to talk of the personal tragedy as if we were alone; but I think I can lay the main facts before you.

"I am the brother of Melchior Morse, whose dreadful death is so generally deplored. I need not tell you about him; he was a public man of more than average public spirit; and I suppose his benefactions and social work are known throughout the world. I had not seen so much of him as I could wish till the last few years; for I have been much abroad; I suppose some would call me the rolling stone of the family, compared with my brother, but I was deeply attached to him, and all the resources of the family estate will be open to anyone ready to avenge his death. You will understand I shall not lightly abandon that duty.

"The crime occurred, as you probably know, at his country place called 'White Pillars,' after its rather unique classical architecture; a colonnade in the shape of a crescent, like that at St. Peter's, runs half-way round an artificial lake, to which the descent is by a flight of curved stone steps. It is in the lake that my brother's body was found floating in the moonlight; but as his neck was broken, apparently with a blow, he had clearly been killed elsewhere. When the butler found the body, the moon was on the other side of the house and threw the inner crescent of the colonnade and steps into profound shadow. But the butler swears he saw the figure of the fleeing man in dark outline against the moonlight as it turned the corner of the house. He says it was a striking outline, and he would know it again."

"Those outlines are very vivid sometimes," said the detective, thoughtfully, "but of course very difficult to prove. Were there any other traces? Any footprints or fingerprints?"

"There were no fingerprints," said Morse, gravely, "and the murderer must have meant to take equal care to leave no footprints. That is why the crime was probably committed on the great flight of stone steps. But they say the cleverest murderer forgets something; and when he threw the body in the lake there must have been a splash, which was not quite dry when it was discovered; and it showed the edge of a pretty clear footprint. I have a copy of the thing here, the original is at home." He passed a brown slip across to Hyde, who looked at it and nodded. "The only other thing on the stone steps that might be a clue was a cigar-stump. My brother did not smoke."

"Well, we will look into those clues more closely in due course," said Dr. Hyde. "Now tell me something about the house and the people in it."

Mr. Morse shrugged his shoulders, as if the family in question did not impress him.

"There were not many people in it," he replied, "putting aside a fairly large staff of servants, headed by the butler, Barton, who has been devoted to my brother for years. The servants all bear a good character; but of course you will consider all that. The other occupants of the house at the time were my brother's wife, a rather silent elderly woman, devoted almost entirely to religion and good works; a niece, of whose prolonged visits the old lady did not perhaps altogether approve, for Miss Barbara Butler is half Irish and rather flighty and excitable; my brother's secretary, Mr. Graves, a very silent young man (I confess I could never make out whether he was shy or sly), and my brother's solicitor, Mr. Caxton, who is an ordinary snuffy lawyer, and happened to be down there on legal business. They might all be guilty in theory, I suppose, but I'm a practical man and I don't imagine such things in practice."

"Yes, I realized you were a practical man when you first came in," said Dr. Hyde, rather dryly. "I realized a few other details as well. Is that all you have to tell me?"

"Yes," replied Morse, "I hope I have made myself clear."

"It is well not to forget anything," went on Adrian Hyde, gazing at him calmly. "It is still better not to suppress anything, when confiding in a professional man. You may have heard, perhaps, of a knack I have of noticing things about people. I knew some of the things you told me before you opened your mouth; as that you long lived abroad and had just come up from the country. And it was easy to infer from your own words that you are the heir of your brother's considerable fortune."

"Well, yes, I am," replied Alfred Morse, stolidly.

"When you said you were a rolling stone," went on

Adrian Hyde, with the same placid politeness, "I fear some might say you were a stone which the builders were justified in rejecting. Your adventures abroad have not all been happy. I perceive that you deserted from some foreign navy, and that you were once in prison for robbing a bank. If it comes to an inquiry into your brother's death and your present inheritance—"

"Are you trying to suggest," cried the other fiercely, "that appearances are against me?"

"My dear sir," said Dr. Adrian Hyde blandly, "appearances are most damnably against you. But I don't always go by appearances. It all depends. Good-day."

When the visitor had withdrawn, looking rather black, the impetuous Brandon broke out into admiration of the Master's methods and besieged him with questions.

"Look here," said the great man, good-humouredly, "you've no business to be asking how I guessed right. You ought to be guessing at the guesses yourselves. Think it out."

"The desertion from a foreign navy," said Weir, slowly, "might be something to do with those bluish marks on his wrist. Perhaps they were some special tattooing and he'd tried to rub them out."

"That's better," said Dr. Hyde, "you're getting on."

"I know!" cried Brandon, more excitedly, "I know about the prison! They always say, if you once shave your moustache it never grows the same; perhaps there's something like that about hair that's been cropped in gaol. Yes, I thought so. The only thing I can't imagine, is why you should guess he had robbed a bank."

"Well, you think that out too," said Adrian Hyde, "I think you'll find it's the key to the whole of this riddle. And now I'm going to leave this case to you. I'm going to have a half-holiday." As a signal that his own working hours were over, he lit a large and sumptuous cigar, and began pishing and poohing over the newspapers.

"Lord, what rubbish!" he cried. "My God, what headlines! Look at this about White Pillars: 'Whose Was the Hand?' They've murdered even murder with clichés like clubs of wood. Look here, you two fellows had better go down to White Pillars and try to put some sense into them. I'll come down later and clear up the mess."

The two young detectives had originally intended to hire a car, but by the end of their journey they were very glad they had decided to travel by train with the common herd. Even as they were in the act of leaving the train, they had a stroke of luck in the matter of that collecting of stray words and whispers which Weir found the least congenial, but Brandon desperately clung to as the most practicable, of all forms of detective inquiry. The steady stream of a steam-whistle, which was covering all the shouted conversation, stopped suddenly in the fashion that makes a shout shrivel into a whisper. But there was one whisper caught in the silence and sounding clear as a bell; a voice that said, "There were excellent reasons for killing him. I know them, if nobody else does."

Brandon managed to trace the voice to its origin; a sallow face with a long shaven chin and a rather scornful lower lip. He saw the same face more than once on the remainder of his journey, passing the ticket collector, appearing in a car behind them on the road, haunting him so significantly, that he was not surprised to meet the man eventually in the garden of White Pillars, and to have him presented as Mr. Caxton, the solicitor.

"That man evidently knows more than he's told the authorities," said Brandon to his friend, "but I can't get anything more out of him."

"My dear fellow," cried Weir, "that's just what they're all like. Don't you feel by this time that it's the atmosphere of the whole place? It's not a bit like those delightful detective stories. In a detective story all the people in the house are gaping imbeciles, who can't understand anything, and in the midst stands the brilliant sleuth who understands everything. Here am I standing in the midst, a brilliant sleuth, and I believe, on my soul, I'm the only person in the house who doesn't know all about the crime."

"There's one other anyhow," said Brandon, with gloom, "two brilliant sleuths."

"Everybody else knows except the detective," went on Weir, "everybody knows something, anyhow, if it isn't everything. There's something odd even about old Mrs. Morse; she's devoted to charity, yet she doesn't seem to have agreed with her husband's philanthropy. It's as if they'd quarrelled about it. Then there's the secretary, the quiet, good-looking young man, with a square face like Napoleon. He looks as if he would get what he wants, and I've very little doubt that what he wants is that red-haired Irish girl they call Barbara. I think she wants the same thing; but if so there's really no reason for them to hide it. And they are hiding it, or hiding something. Even the butler is secretive. They can't all have been in a conspiracy to kill the old man."

"Anyhow, it all comes back to what I said first," observed Brandon. "If they're in a conspiracy, we can only hope to overhear their talk. It's the only way."

"It's an excessively beastly way," said Weir, calmly, "and we will proceed to follow it."

They were walking slowly round the great semicircle of colonnade that looked inwards upon the lake, that shone like a silver mirror to the moon. It was of the same stretch of clear moonlit nights as that recent one, on which old Morse had died mysteriously in the same spot. They could imagine him as he was in many portraits, a little figure in a skull cap with a white beard thrust forward, standing on those steps, till a dreadful figure that had no face in their dreams descended the stairway and struck him down. They were standing at one end of the colonnade, full of these visions, when Brandon said suddenly:

"Did you speak?"

"I? No," replied his friend staring.

"Somebody spoke," said Brandon, in a low voice, "yet we seem to be quite alone."

Then their blood ran cold for an instant. For the wall behind them spoke; and it seemed to say quite plainly, in a rather harsh voice:

"Do you remember exactly what you said?"

Weir stared at the wall for an instant; then he slapped it with his hand with a shaky laugh.

"My God," he cried, "what a miracle! And what a satire! We've sold ourselves to the devil as a couple of damned eavesdroppers; and he's put us in the very chamber of eavesdropping—into the ear of Dionysius, the Tyrant. Don't you see this is a whispering gallery, and people at the other end of it are whispering?"

"No, they're talking too loud to hear us, I think," whispered Brandon, "but we'd better lower our voices. It's Caxton the lawyer, and the young secretary."

The secretary's unmistakable and vigorous voice sounded along the wall saying:

"I told him I was sick of the whole business; and if I'd known he was such a tyrant, I'd never have had to do with him. I think I told him he ought to be shot. I was sorry enough for it afterwards."

Then they heard the lawyer's more croaking tones saying, "Oh, you said that, did you? Well, there seems no more to be said now. We had better go in," which was followed by echoing feet and then silence.

The next day Weir attached himself to the lawyer with a peculiar pertinacity and made a new effort to get something more out of that oyster. He was pondering deeply on the very little that he had got, when Brandon rushed up to him with hardly-restrained excitement.

"I've been at that place again," he cried, "I suppose

you'll say I've sunk lower in the pit of slime, and perhaps I have, but it's got to be done. I've been listening to the young people this time, and I believe I begin to see something; though heaven knows, it's not what I want to see. The secretary and the girl are in love all right, or have been; and when love is loose pretty dreadful things can happen. They were talking about getting married, of course, at least she was, and what do you think she said? 'He made an excuse of my being under age.' So it's pretty clear the old man opposed the match. No doubt that was what the secretary meant by talking about his tyranny."

"And what did the secretary say when the girl said that?"

"That's the queer thing," answered Brandon, "rather an ugly thing, I begin to fancy. The young man only answered, rather sulkily, I thought: 'Well, he was within his rights there; and perhaps it was for the best.' She broke out in protest: 'How can you say such a thing'; and certainly it was a strange thing for a lover to say."

"What are you driving at?" asked his friend.

"Do you know anything about women?" asked Brandon. "Suppose the old man was not only trying to break off the engagement but *succeeding* in breaking it off. Suppose the young man was weakening and beginning to wonder whether she was worth losing his job for. The woman might have waited any time or eloped any time. But if she thought she was in danger of losing him altogether, don't you think she might have turned on the tempter with the fury of despair? I fear we have got a glimpse of a very heartrending tragedy. Don't you believe it, too?"

Walter Weir unfolded his long limbs and got slowly to his feet, filling a pipe and looking at his friend with a sort of quizzical melancholy.

"No, I don't believe it," he said, "but that's because I'm such an unbeliever. You see, I don't believe in all this eavesdropping business; I don't think we shine at it. Or, rather, I think you shine too much at it and dazzle yourself blind. I don't believe in all this detective romance about deducing everything from a trifle. I don't believe in your little glimpse of a great tragedy. It would be a great tragedy no doubt, and does you credit as literature or a symbol of life; you can build imaginative things of that sort on a trifle. You can build everything on the trifle except the truth. But in the present practical issue, I don't believe there's a word of truth in it. I don't believe the old man was opposed to the engagement; I don't believe the young man was backing out of it; I believe the young people are perfectly happy and ready to be married tomorrow. I don't believe anybody in this house had any motive to kill Morse or has any notion of how he was killed. In spite of what I said, the poor shabby old sleuth enjoys his own again. I believe I am the only person who knows the truth; and it only came to me in a flash a few minutes ago."

"Why, how do you mean?" asked the other.

"It came to me in a final flash," said Weir, "when you repeated those words of the girl: 'He made the excuse that I was under age.' "

After a few puffs of his pipe, he resumed reflectively: "One queer thing is, that the error of the eavesdropper often comes from a thing being too clear. We're so sure that people mean what we mean, that we can't believe they mean what they say. Didn't I once tell you that it's one thing to listen and another to hear? And sometimes the voice talks too plain. For instance, when young Graves, the secretary, said that he was sick of the business, he meant it literally, and not metaphorically. He meant he was sick of Morse's trade, because it was tyrannical."

"Morse's trade? What trade?" asked Brandon, staring.

"Our saintly old philanthropist was a moneylender,"

replied Weir, "and as great a rascal as his rascally brother. That is the great central fact that explains everything. That is what the girl meant by talking about being under age. She wasn't talking about her love-affair at all, but about some small loan she'd tried to get from the old man and which he refused because she was a minor. Her fiancé made the very sensible comment that perhaps it was all for the best; meaning that she had escaped the net of a usurer. And her momentary protest was only a spirited young lady's lawful privilege of insisting on her lover agreeing with all the silly things she says. That is an example of the error of the eavesdropper, or the fallacy of detection by trifles. But, as I say, it's the money-lending business that's the clue to everything in this house. That's what all of them, even the secretary and solicitor, out of a sort of family pride, are trying to hush up and hide from detectives and newspapers. But the old man's murder was much more likely to get it into the newspapers. They had no motive to murder him, and they didn't murder him."

"Then who did?" demanded Brandon.

"Ah," replied his friend, but with less than his usual languor in the ejaculation and something a little like a hissing intake of the breath. He had seated himself once more, with his elbows on his knees, but the other was surprised to realize something rigid about his new attitude; almost like a creature crouching for a spring. He still spoke quite dryly, however, and merely said:

"In order to answer that, I fancy we must go back to the first talk that we overheard, before we came to the house; the very first of all."

"Oh, I see," said Brandon, a light dawning on his face. "You mean what we heard the solicitor say in the train."

"No," replied Weir, in the same motionless manner, "that was only another illustration touching the secret trade. Of course his solicitor knew he was a moneylender; and knew that any such moneylender has a crowd of victims, who might kill him. It's quite true he was killed by one of those victims. But it wasn't the lawyer's remark in the train that I was talking about, for a very simple reason."

"And why not?" inquired his companion.

"Because that was not the first conversation we overheard."

Walter Weir clutched his knees with his long bony hands, and seemed to stiffen still more as if in a trance, but he went on talking steadily.

"I have told you the moral and the burden of all these things; that it is one thing to hear what men say and another to hear what they mean. And it was at the very first talk that we heard all the words and missed all the meaning. We did not overhear that first talk slinking about in moonlit gardens and whispering galleries. We overheard that first talk sitting openly at our regular desks in broad daylight, in a bright and businesslike office. But we no more made sense of that talk than if it had been half a whisper, heard in a black forest or a cave."

He sprang to his feet as if a stiff spring were released and began striding up and down, with what was for him an unnatural animation.

"That was the talk we really misunderstood," he cried. "That was the conversation that we heard word for word, and yet missed entirely! Fools that we were! Deaf and dumb and imbecile, sitting there like dummies and being stuffed with a stage play! We were actually allowed to be eavesdroppers, tolerated, ticketed, given special permits to be eavesdroppers; and still we could not eavesdrop! I never even guessed till ten minutes ago the meaning of that conversation in the office. That terrible conversation! That terrible meaning! Hate and hateful fear and shameless wickedness and mortal peril—death and hell wrestled naked before our eyes in that office, and we never saw them. A man accused another man of murder across a table, and we never heard it."

"Oh," gasped Brandon at last, "you mean that the Master accused the brother of murder?"

"No!" retorted Weir, in a voice like a volley, "I mean that the brother accused the Master of murder."

"The Master!"

"Yes," answered Weir, and his high voice fell suddenly, "and the accusation was true. The man who murdered old Morse was our employer, Dr. Adrian Hyde."

"What can it all mean?" asked Brandon, and thrust his hand through his thick brown hair.

"That was our mistake at the beginning," went on the other calmly, "that we did not think what it could all mean. Why was the brother so careful to say the reproduction of the footprint was a proof and not the original? Why did Dr. Hyde say the outline of the fugitive would be difficult to prove? Why did he tell us, with that sardonic grin, that the brother having robbed a bank was the key of the riddle? Because the whole of that consultation of the client and the specialist was a fiction for our benefit. The whole course of events was determined by that first thing that happened; that the young and innocent detectives were allowed to remain in the room. Didn't you think yourself the interview was a little too like that at the beginning of every damned detective story? Go over it speech by speech, and you will see that every speech was a thrust or parry under a cloak. That blackmailing blackguard Alfred hunted out Doctor Hyde simply to accuse and squeeze him. Seeing us there, he said, 'This is confidential,' meaning, 'You don't want to be accused before them.' Dr. Hyde answered. 'They're my favourite pupils,' meaning, 'I'm less likely to be blackmailed before them; they shall stay.' Alfred answered, 'Well, I can state my business, if not quite so personally,' meaning, 'I can accuse you so that you understand, if they don't.' And he did. He presented his proofs like pistols across the table; things that sounded rather thin, but, in Hyde's case, happened to be pretty thick. His boots, for instance, happened to be very thick. His huge footprint would be unique enough to be a clue. So would the cigar-end; for very few people can afford to smoke his cigars. Of course, that's what got him tangled up with the money-lender—extravagance. You see how much money you get through if you smoke those cigars all day and never drink anything but the best post-war champagne. And though a black silhouette against the moon sounds as vague as moonshine, Hyde's huge figure and hunched shoulders would be rather marked. Well, you know how the blackmailed man hit back: 'I perceive by your left eyebrow that you are a deserter; I deduce from the pimple on your nose that you were once in gaol,' meaning, 'I know you, and you're as much a crook as I am; expose me and I'll expose you.' Then he said he had deduced in the Sherlock Holmes manner that Alfred had robbed a bank, and that was where he went too far. He presumed on the incredible credulity, which is the mark of the modern mind when anyone has uttered the magic word 'science.' He presumed on the priestcraft of our time; but he presumed the least little bit too much, so far as I was concerned. It was then I first began to doubt. A man might possibly deduce by scientific detection that another man had been in a certain navy or prison, but by no possibility could he deduce from a man's appearance that what he had once robbed was a bank. It was simply impossible. Dr. Hyde knew it was his biggest bluff; that was why he told you in mockery, that it was the key to the riddle. It was; and I managed to get hold of the key."

He chuckled in a hollow fashion as he laid down his pipe. "That jibe at his own bluff was like him; he really is a remarkable man or a remarkable devil. He has a sort of horrible sense of humour. Do you know, I've got a notion that sounds rather a nightmare, about what happened on that great slope of steps that night. I believe Hyde jeered at the journalistic catchword, 'Whose Was the Hand?' partly because he, himself, had managed it without hands. I believe he managed to commit a murder entirely with his feet. I believe he tripped up the poor old usurer and stamped on him on the stone steps with those monstrous boots. An idyllic moonlight scene, isn't it? But there's something that seems to make it worse. I think he had the habit anyhow, partly to avoid leaving his fingerprints, which may be known to the police. Anyhow, I believe he did the whole murder with his hands in his trouserpockets."

Brandon shuddered suddenly; then collected himself and said, rather weakly:

"Then you don't think the science of observation—"

"Science of observation be damned!" cried Weir. "Do you still think private detectives get to know about criminals by smelling their hair-oil, or counting their buttons? They do it, a whole gang of them do it just as Hyde did. They get to know about criminals by being half criminals themselves, by being of the same rotten world, by belonging to it and by betraying it, by setting a thief to catch a thief, and proving there is no honour among thieves. I don't say there are no honest private detectives, but if there are, you don't get into their service as easily as you and I got into the office of the distinguished Dr. Adrian Hyde. You ask what all this means, and I tell you one thing it means. It means that you and I are going to sweep crossings or scrub out drains. I feel as if I should like a clean job."

Policeman's Holiday
by Michael Innes

A motor tour in the West Country makes it possible to visit any number of historic houses. Having done Montacute that morning, and being pledged to do Barrington Court in the afternoon, Sir John Appleby rather hoped to slip past Roydon Abbey without stopping. But his wife would have nothing of this.

"There's a famous El Greco," she said. "Turn in."

So they turned in.

Lord Roydon's country seat was imposing but not exactly flourishing. The house could have done with a lick of paint, and the grounds with a few more gardeners. Perhaps his lordship was something of an absentee owner. Certainly there was no flag flying, so presumably he wasn't lurking on the premises.

But this made it only the more certain that the Applebys would be allowed to look around. Sir John foresaw another long tramp through a succession of chilly splendors. But Lady Appleby was adamant as she closed the guidebook she had been consulting.

"There's nothing about its being open to the public," she said. "So you'd better get out a ten-bob note."

"Quite so." Appleby was resigned. "You said an El Greco?"

"Yes. The *Beggar With Skull*."

"Good Lord!" Appleby was impressed. "I'll certainly put down ten bob to see that."

They were received by the housekeeper, a myopic old woman who appeared well used to the job. She stood them in the middle of a vast paneled hall and began her lecture.

"The family is of great antiquity," she said. "Doutremeres have lived on this spot for more than nine hundred years. But his lordship is not in residence at present."

Appleby reflected that this break with tradition was a pity. But Judith Appleby seemed possessed of some relevant information.

"Isn't Lord Roydon a great yachtsman?" she prompted.

The old housekeeper beamed. The present Marquis was certainly much distinguished in that line. The Abbey, of course, was only a few miles from the sea, and he had been brought up to sailing from boyhood.

His yachting was of an adventuresome and often lonely kind. He would go off with a one-man crew, or with no crew at all, for weeks on end. That was what he was doing now.

"Of course," the housekeeper purred, "his lordship has the magnificent physique of all the Doutremeres. It's in the blood, I say. And here is his portrait, presented by the tenantry on the occasion of his lordship's giving up active command."

Appleby and Judith looked with due respect at the portrait. Lord Roydon had a red face and a red beard, and he had been painted against a red sky in what appeared to be the uniform of a Vice-Admiral of the Fleet. As the artist had somehow contrived to indicate that his subject wasn't much short of seven feet tall, the effect was altogether impressive.

"And next to him is his brother, Lord Charles Doutremere."

With suitably modified awe the Applebys looked at
this portrait too. Lord Charles was another giant. He
was depicted in profile as clean-shaven, florid, and in
garments appropriate to shooting things. He looked, indeed, quite as if he would shoot anything on sight. A
red setter was eyeing him apprehensively from the bottom left-hand corner.

"His lordship—" the housekeeper began, and then
broke off. "But here he is," she added in a lower voice,
and in some confusion. "He's come back."

It was certainly true. Lord Roydon, in untidy nauti-
cal kit, had strode past the screen at the bottom of the
hall. Seeing the Applebys, he gave a brisk bow, barked
out a "Good morning," and marched on, civilly
enough. But suddenly Lord Roydon stopped dead in
his tracks and pointed at an empty space on the wall.

"Mrs. Cumpsty," he snapped, "what's become of the
El Greco?"

"The El Greco, my lord? Why, it hasn't come back
since you took it away."

"Since I took it away! What the devil are you talking about?"

Mrs. Cumpsty stared. "Why, three weeks ago, my
lord—the last time you were here. You had a word
with me here in the hall, my lord. And then you took
away the picture—" Mrs. Cumpsty faltered, as she
well might in face of the enraged appearance of her
employer. "And then you took away the picture, saying
you were going to have it cleaned in London."

"Absolute nonsense! You're mad, Mrs. Cumpsty—or
in a league with some scoundrel of a thief. I haven't
been near the Abbey for six weeks."

Mrs. Cumpsty—very naturally—began to weep. And
Sir John Appleby stepped forward and introduced himself. It was clearly going to be a case for the police.

The housekeeper stuck to her story. She was quite
certain that it had been Lord Roydon himself who had

taken away El Greco's *Beggar With Skull*. His lordship had been most affable and had chatted about various Abbey affairs in a manner that no impostor could have managed. If there had been the slightest cause for suspicion she certainly wouldn't have let the picture be taken out of the house. Didn't she know that it was worth far more than everything else in the house put together?

Appleby inquired whether anyone else had been aware of Lord Roydon's—or the supposed Lord Roydon's—visit. The whole household had of course heard of it. But only one of the Abbey's two footmen had actually set eyes on him—having admitted him in the first place and then been sent to summon Mrs. Cumpsty. This young man also was certain that it had been Lord Roydon. It was impressive corroboration—even though this footman, it developed, had not been long in his place.

Appleby persevered, vigorously backed by Lord Roydon himself who was now in a state of near-frenzy. All the indoor servants were interrogated, and then all the outdoor ones. None of them had been aware of the visit until it was over. Lord Roydon admitted that there was nothing surprising about this. He did from time to time come and go in an unobtrusive way. In fact, he was something of a recluse. All the Doutremeres were.

This last was a statement to which Appleby appeared to give some thought. And then he asked a question. "Anybody else? Can you think, sir, of anybody else we ought to question?"

Lord Roydon considered for a moment. "The children," he barked. "Half a dozen about the place—gardeners' kids, and so forth. Sharp nippers."

It was an astute suggestion—and it bore astonishing fruit. The fourth child questioned was a small boy called Alf who confessed, amid tears and surprising terror, that he had indeed seen Lord Roydon. He had seen him while playing near a little frequented cart-track through the park. His lordship had been preparing to drive away in an unfamiliar car. Alf appeared to brace himself at this point in his narrative.

"But first, sir, 'e stopped and took 'is beard off."

"Dear me!" Appleby said mildly. "Did you ever see his lordship do that before, Alf?"

"No, sir." Alf gulped. "But then 'e saw me a-watching, sir. And 'e come after me and said 'e'd break me jaw if ever I told on 'im."

"And you're sure that you've never seen this man with the false beard before?"

Alf shook his head. "No, sir. But I'd know 'im again. I'd know 'im by the big scar on 'is chin."

"That will do!" Surprisingly, Lord Roydon seized the small boy and ran him out of the hall. Then he turned to Appleby. "The matter is not to be pursued," he said curtly. "Be good enough to consider it closed."

But Appleby had turned to the portrait of Lord Roydon's brother, Lord Charles Doutremere—the portrait painted in profile. "I think not," he said grimly.

Lord Charles was indeed a more than typical Doutremere recluse. He lived in a remote cottage some twenty miles away, attended by only a single manservant. And the man, although respectful to Lord Roydon, was reluctant to admit them.

"Lord Charles's condition is still critical," he said. "The doctor says there should be no visitors, my lord."

Lord Roydon's eyes became worried. "Critical? What the devil do you mean?"

"A hunting accident a month ago, my lord. Lord Charles insisted you shouldn't be told. He spoke"—the man hesitated—"he spoke of the bad blood between you, my lord."

Appleby gave Lord Roydon a single glance, and turned again to the man. "Just what sort of hunting accident?"

"To the spine, sir. Lord Charles hasn't been able to stir from his bed for over a month."

* * *

It was a couple of hours later and the Appleby's were now on their way to inspect Barrington Court—much as if nothing had happened.

"I still don't really understand," Judith Appleby said.

"Lord Roydon planned to sell his El Greco secretly—and at the same time collect insurance on it. He shaved. He painted a scar on his jaw. He put on a false beard and spoke to Mrs. Cumpsty. It's not surprising the short-sighted old soul was so sure it *was* Lord Roydon, since a beard would only be a beard to her, whether false or authentic. Then, having made off with the painting, his lordship went through that pantomime with poor young Alf. No wonder he had that inspiration about my questioning the children."

"You mean—"

"Yes, he intended to plant the theft very ingeniously on his brother. The plan broke down only because of that hunting accident, which gave the unfortunate Charles an ironclad alibi. Only Lord Roydon, as we heard, knew nothing about it, since the brothers very seldom talked to each other."

"But if Lord Roydon *shaved* his beard—"

"He simply went off in his yacht and waited for it to grow back. And then he turned up at the Abbey again—a few minutes after we did."

Appleby paused, and when he spoke again there was a note of professional admiration and respect in his voice.

"Really quite a remarkable criminal formula. Unique, I think. *X* disguised as *Y* disguised as *X*. Think it out like that."

Appleby glanced at his watch and accelerated. Then he laughed uproariously.

"Or call it," he said, "a notably bare-faced fraud."

The Ministering Angel
by E. C. Bentley

"Whatever the meaning of it may be, it's a devilish unpleasant business," Arthur Selby said as he and Philip Trent established themselves on a sofa in the smoking room of the Lansdowne Club. "We see enough of that sort of business in the law—even firms like ours, that don't have much to do with crime, have plenty of unpleasantness to deal with, and I don't know that some of it isn't worse than the general run of crime. You know what I mean. Crazy spite, that's one thing. You wouldn't believe what some people—people of position and education and all that—you wouldn't believe what they are capable of when they want to do somebody a mischief. Usually it's a blood relation. And then there's constitutional viciousness. We had one client—he died soon after Snow took me into partnership—whose whole life had been one lascivious debauch."

Trent laughed. "That phrase doesn't sound like your own, Arthur. It belongs to an earlier generation."

"Quite true," Selby admitted. "It was Snow told me that about old Sir William Never-mind-who, and it stuck in my memory. But come now—I'm wandering.

A good lunch—by the way, I hope it *was* a good lunch."

"One of the very best," Trent said. "You know it was, too. Ordering lunches is one of the best things you do, and you're proud of it. That hock was a poem—a villanelle, for choice. What were you going to say about good lunches?"

"Why, I was going to say that a good lunch usually makes me inclined to prattle a bit; because, you see, all I allow myself most days is a couple of apples and a glass of milk in the office. That's the way to appreciate a thing: don't have it too often, and take a hell of a lot of trouble about it when you do. But that isn't what I wanted to talk to you about, Phil. I was saying just now that we get a lot of unpleasantness in our job. We can usually understand it when we get it, but the affair I want to tell you about is a puzzle to me; and of course you are well known to be good at puzzles. If I tell you the story, will you give me a spot of advice if you can?"

"Of course."

Well, it's about a client of ours who died a fortnight ago, named Gregory Landell. You wouldn't have heard of him, I dare say; he never did anything much outside his private hobbies, having always had money and never any desire to distinguish himself. He could have done, for he had plenty of brains—a brilliant scholar, always reading Greek. He and my partner had been friends from boyhood; at school and Cambridge together; had tastes in common; both rock garden enthusiasts, for one thing. Landell's was a famous rock garden. Other amateurs used to come from all parts to visit it, and of course he loved that. Then they were both Lewis Carroll fans—when they got together, bits from the *Alice* books and the *Snark* were always coming into the conversation—both chess players, both keen cricketers when they were young enough, and never tired of watching first-class games. Snow used often to stay for weekends at Landell's place at Cholsey Wood, in Berkshire.

"When Landell was over fifty, he married for the first time. The lady was a Miss Mary Archer, daughter of a naval officer, and about twenty years younger than Landell, at a guess. He was infatuated with her, and she seemed to make a great fuss of him, though she didn't strike me as being the warm-hearted type. She was a goodlooking wench with plenty of style, and gave you the idea of being fond of her own way. We made his will for him, leaving everything to her if there were no children. Snow and I were both appointed executors. In his previous will he had left all his property to a nephew; and we were sorry the nephew wasn't mentioned in this later will, for he is a very useful citizen—some kind of medical research worker—and he has barely enough to live on."

"Why did he make both of you executors?" Trent wondered.

"Oh, in case anything happened to one of us. And it was just as well, because early this year poor old Snow managed to fracture his thigh, and he's been laid up ever since. But that's getting ahead of the story. After the marriage, Snow still went down to Landell's place from time to time, as before; but after a year or so he began to notice a great change in the couple. Landell seemed to get more and more under his wife's thumb. Couldn't call his soul his own."

Trent nodded. "After what you told me about the impression she made on you, that isn't surprising."

"No: Snow and I had been expecting it to happen. But the worst of it was, Landell didn't take it easily, as some husbands in that position do. He was obviously very unhappy, though he never said anything about it to Snow. She had quite given up pretending to be affectionate, or to consider him in any way, and Snow got the idea that Landell hated his wife like poison, though never daring to stand up to her. Yet he used to have plenty of character, too.''

"I have seen the sort of thing," Trent said. "Unless a man is a bit of a brute himself, he can't bear to see the woman making an exhibition of herself. He'll stand anything rather than have her make a scene.''

"Just so. Well, after a time Snow got no more invitations to go there; and as you may suppose, he didn't mind that. It had got to be too uncomfortable, and though he was devilish sorry for Landell, he didn't see that he could do anything for him. For one thing, she wouldn't ever leave them alone together if she could possibly help it. If they were pottering about with the rock plants, or playing chess, or going for a walk, they always had her company.''

Trent made a grimace. "Jolly for the visitor! And now, what was it you didn't understand?''

"I'll tell you. About a month ago a letter for Snow came to the office. I opened it—I was dealing with all his business correspondence. It was from Mrs. Landell, saying that her husband was ill and confined to bed; that he wished to settle some business affairs, and would be most grateful if Snow could find time to come down on the following day.

"Well, Snow couldn't, of course. I got the idea from this letter, naturally, that the matter was more or less urgent. It read as if Landell was right at the end of his tether. So I rang up Mrs. Landell, explained the situation, and said I would come myself that afternoon if it suited her. She said she would be delighted if I would; she was very anxious about her husband, whose heart was in a serious state. I mentioned the train I would come by, and she said their car would meet it.

"When I got there, she took me up to Landell's bedroom at once. He was looking very bad, and seemed to have hardly strength enough to speak. There was a nurse in the room: Mrs. Landell sent her out and stayed with us all the time I was there—which I had expected, after what I had heard from Snow. Then Landell began to talk, or whisper, about what he wanted done.

"It was a scheme for the rearrangement of his investments, and a shrewd one, too—he had a wonderful flair for that sort of thing, made a study of it. In fact"—Selby leant forward and tapped his friend's knee—"there was absolutely nothing for him to discuss with me. He knew exactly what he wanted done, and he needed no advice; he knew more about such matters than I did, or Snow either. Still, he made quite a show of asking my opinion of this detail and that, and all I could do was to look wise, and hum and haw, and then say that nothing could be better. Then he said that the exertion of writing a business letter was forbidden by his doctor, and would I oblige him by doing it for him? So I took down a letter of instructions to his brokers, which he signed; and his wife had the securities he was going to sell all ready in a long envelope; and that was that. The car took me to the station, and I got back in time for dinner, after an absolutely wasted half day."

Trent had listened to all this with eager attention. "It was wasted, you say," he observed. "Do you mean he could have dictated such a letter to his wife, without troubling you at all?"

"To his wife, or to anybody who could write. And of course he knew that well enough. I tell you, all that business of consulting me was just camouflage. I knew it, and I could feel he knew I knew it. But what the devil it was intended to hide is beyond me. I don't think his wife suspected anything queer; Snow always said she was a fool about business matters. She listened intently to everything that was said, and seemed quite satisfied. His instructions were acted upon, and he signed the transfers; I know that, because when I came to making an inventory of the estate, after his death, I found it had all been done. Now then, Phil: what do you make of all that?"

Trent caressed his chin for a few moments. "You're quite sure that there *was* something unreal about the business? His wife, you say, saw nothing suspicious."

"Of course I'm sure. His wife evidently didn't know that he was cleverer about investments than either Snow or me, and that anyhow it wasn't our job. If he *had* wanted advice, he could have had his broker down."

Trent stretched his legs before him and carefully considered the end of his cigar. "No doubt you are right," he said at length. "And it does sound as if there was something unpleasant below the surface. For that matter, the surface itself was not particularly agreeable, as you describe it. Mrs. Landell, the ministering angel!" He rose to his feet. "I'll turn the thing over in my mind, Arthur, and let you know if anything strikes me."

Trent found the house in Cholsey Wood without much difficulty next morning. The place actually was a tract of woodland of large extent, cleared here and there for a few isolated modern houses and grounds, a row of cottages, an inn called the Magpie and Gate, and a Tudor manor house standing in a well-tended park. The Grove, the house of which he was in search, lay half a mile beyond the inn on the road that bisected the neighborhood. A short drive led up to it through the high hedge that bounded the property on this side, and Trent, turning his car into the opening, got out and walked to the house, admiring as he went the flower-bordered lawn on one side, the trim orchard on the other. The two-storied house, too, was a well-kept, well-built place, its porch overgrown by wisteria in full flower.

His ring was answered by a chubby maidservant, to whom he offered his card. He had been told, he said, that Mr. Landell allowed visitors who were interested in gardening to see his rock garden, of which Trent had heard so much. Would the maid take his card to Mr. Landell, and ask if it would be convenient—here he paused, as a lady stepped from an open door at the end of the hall. Trent described her to himself as a handsome, brassy blonde with a hard blue eye.

"I am Mrs. Landell," she said, as she took the card from the girl and glanced at it. "I heard what you were saying. I see, Mr. Trent, you have not heard of my bereavement. My dear husband passed away a fortnight ago." Trent began to murmur words of vague condolence and apology. "Oh no," she went on with a sad smile. "You must not think you are disturbing me. You must certainly see the rock garden now you are here. You have come a long way for the purpose, I dare say, and my husband would not have wished you to go away disappointed."

"It was a famous garden," Trent observed. "I heard of it from someone I think you know—Arthur Selby, the lawyer."

"Yes, he and his partner were my husband's solicitors," the lady said. "I will show you where the garden is, if you will come this way." She turned and went before him through the house, until they came out through a glass-panelled door into a much larger extent of grounds. "I cannot show it off to you myself," she went on, "I know absolutely nothing about that sort of gardening. My husband was very proud of it, and he was adding to the collection of plants up to the time he was taken ill last month. You see that grove of elms? The house is called after it. If you go along it you will come to a lily pond, and the rock garden is to the left of that. I fear I cannot entertain anyone just now, so I will leave you to yourself, and the parlormaid will wait to let you out when you have seen enough." She bowed her head in answer to his thanks, and retired into the house.

Trent passed down the avenue and found the object of his journey, a tall pile of roughly terraced grey rocks covered with a bewildering variety of plants rooted in the shallow soil provided for them. The lady of the house, he reflected, could hardly know less about rock gardens than himself, and it was just as well that there was to be no dangerous comparing of ignorances. He did not even know what he was looking for. He believed that the garden had something to tell, and that was all. Pacing slowly up and down, with searching eye, before the stony rampart with its dress of delicate colors, he set himself to divine its secret.

Soon he noted a detail which, as he considered it, became more curious. Here and there among the multitude of plants there was one distinguished by a flat slip of white wood stuck in the soil among the stems, or just beside the growth. There were not many: searching about, he could find no more than seven. Written on each slip in a fair, round hand was a botanical name. Such names meant nothing to Trent; he could but wonder vaguely why they were there. Why were these plants thus distinguished? Possibly they were the latest acquisitions. Possibly Landell had so marked them to draw the attention of his old friend and fellow-enthusiast Snow. Landell had been expecting Snow to come and see him, Trent remembered. Snow had been unable to come, and Arthur Selby had come instead. Another point: the business Landell had wanted done was trifling; anyone could have attended to it. Why had it been so important to Landell that Snow should come?

Had Landell been expecting to have a private talk with Snow about some business matter? No: because on previous occasions, as on this occasion, Mrs. Landell had been present throughout the interview; it was evident, according to Selby, that she did not intend to leave her husband alone with his legal adviser at any time, and Landell must have realized that. Was this the main point: that the unfortunate Landell had been planning to communicate something to Snow by some means unknown to his wife?

Trent liked the look of this idea. It fitted into the picture, at least. More than that: it gave strong confirmation to the quite indefinite notion he had formed on hearing Selby's story; the notion that had brought him to Cholsey Wood that day. Snow as a keen amateur of rock gardening. If Snow had come to visit Landell, one thing virtually certain was that Snow would not have gone away without having a look at his friend's collection of rock plants, if only to see what additions might have been recently made. And such additions—so Mrs. Landell had just been saying—had been made. Mrs. Landell knew nothing about rock gardening; even if she had wasted a glance on this garden, she would have noticed nothing. Snow would have noticed instantly anything out of the way. And what was there out of the way?

Trent began to whistle faintly.

The wooden slips had now a very interesting look. With notebook and pencil he began to write down the names traced upon them. *Armeria Hallerii*. And *Arcana Nieuwillia*. And *Saponaria Galspitosa*—good! And these delicate little blossoms, it appeared, rejoiced in the formidable name of *Acantholimon Glumaceum*. Then here was *Cartavacua Bellmannii*. Trent's mind began to run on the nonsense botany of Edward Lear: *Nastricreechia Crawluppia* and the rest. This next one was *Veronica Incana*. And here was the last of the slips: *Ludovica Caroli*, quite a pretty name for a shapeless mass of grey-green vegetation that surely was commonly called in the vulgar tongue—

At this point Trent flung his notebook violently to the ground, and followed it with his hat. What a fool he had been! What a triple ass, not to have jumped to the thing at once! He picked up the book and hurriedly scanned the list of names. . . . Yes: it was all there.

Three minutes later he was in his car on the way back to town.

In his room at the offices of Messrs. Snow and Selby the junior partner welcomed Trent on the morning after his expedition to Cholsey Wood.

Selby pushed his cigarette box across the table. "Can you tell it to me in half an hour, do you think? I'd have been glad to come to lunch with you and hear it then, but this is a very full day, and I shan't get outside the office until seven, if then. What have you been doing?"

"Paying a visit to your late client's rock garden," Trent informed him. "It made a deep impression on me. Mrs. Landell was very kind about it."

Selby stared at him. "You always had the devil's own cheek," he observed. "How on earth did you manage that? And why?"

"I won't waste time over the how," Trent said. "As to the why, it was because it seemed to me, when I thought it over, that that garden might have a serious meaning underlying all its gaiety. And I thought so all the more when I found that Mary, Mary, quite contrary, hadn't a notion how her garden grow. You see, it was your partner whom Landell had wanted to consult about those investments of his; and it was hardly likely that your rock gardening partner, once on the spot, would have missed the chance of feasting his eyes on his friend's collection of curiosities. So I went and feasted mine; and I found what I expected."

"The deuce you did!" Selby exclaimed. "And what was it?"

"Seven plants—only seven out of all the lot— marked with their botanical names, clearly written on slips of wood, á la Kew Gardens. I won't trouble you with four of the names—they were put there just to make it look more natural, I suppose; they were genuine names; I've looked them up. But you will find the

other three interesting—choice Latin, picked phrase, if
not exactly Tully's every word."

Trent, as he said this, produced a card and handed it
to his friend, who studied the words written upon it
with a look of complete incomprehension.

"*Arcana Nieuwillia,*" he read aloud. "I can't say that
thrills me to the core, anyhow. What's an *Arcana*? Of
course, I know no more about botany than a cow. It
looks as if it was named after some Dutchman."

"Well, try the next," Trent advised him.

"*Cartavacua Bellmannii.* No, that too fails to move
me. Then what about the rest of the nosegay? *Ludovica
Caroli.* No, it's no good, Phil. What *is* it all about?"

Trent pointed to the last name. "That one was what
gave it away to me. The slip with *Ludovica Caroli* on
it was stuck into a clump of saxifrage. I know saxifrage when I see it; and I seemed to remember that the
right scientific name for it was practically the same—
Saxifraga. And then I suddenly remembered another
thing: that Ludovicus is the Latin form of the name
Louis, which some people choose to spell L-E-W-I-S."

"What!" Selby jumped to his feet. "Lewis—and
Caroli! Lewis Carroll! Oh Lord! The man whose books
Snow and Landell both knew by heart. Then it *is* a
cryptogram." He referred eagerly to the card. "Well
then—*Cartavacua Bellmannii.* Hm! Would that be the
Bellman in *The Hunting of the Snark*? And *Cartavacua*?"

"Translate it," Trent suggested.

Selby frowned. "Let's see. In law, *carta* used to be
a charter and *vacua* means empty. The Bellman's
empty charter—"

"Or chart. Don't you remember?

He had bought a large map representing the sea,
Without the least vestige of land:
And the crew were much pleased when they found it
to be A map they could all understand.

And in the poem, one of the pages is devoted to the Bellman's empty map."

"Oh! And that tells us—?"

"Why, I believe it tells us to refer to Landell's own copy of the book and to that blank page."

"Yes, but what for?"

"*Arcana Nieuwillia,* I expect."

"I told you I don't know what *Arcana* means. It isn't law Latin, and I've forgotten most of the other kind."

"This isn't law Latin, as you say. It's the real thing, and it means 'hidden,' Arthur, 'hidden.' "

"Hidden what?" Selby stared at the card again; then suddenly dropped into this chair and turned a pale face to his friend. "My God, Phil! So that's it!"

"It can't be anything else, can it?"

Selby turned to his desk telephone and spoke into the receiver. "I am not to be disturbed on any account till I ring." He turned again to Trent. . . .

"I asked Mr. Trent to drive me down," Selby explained, "because I wanted his help in a matter concerning your husband's estate. He has met you before informally, he tells me."

Mrs. Landell smiled at Trent graciously. "Only the other day he called to see the rock garden. He mentioned that he was a friend of yours."

She had received them in the morning room at the Grove, and Trent, who on the occasion of his earlier visit had seen nothing but the hallway running from front to back, was confirmed in his impression that strict discipline ruled in that household. The room was orderly and speckless, the few pictures hung mathematically level, the flowers in a bowl on the table were fresh and well displayed.

"And what is the business that brings you and Mr. Trent down so unexpectedly?" Mrs. Landell inquired. "Is it some new point about the valuation of the property, perhaps?" She looked from one to the other of them with round blue eyes.

Selby looked at her with an expression that was new in Trent's experience of that genial, rather sybaritic man of law. He was now serious, cool, and hard.

"No, Mrs. Landell; nothing to do with that," Selby said. "I am sorry to tell you I have reason to believe that your husband made another will not long ago, and that it is in this house. If there is such a will, and if it is in order legally, it will of course supersede the will made shortly after your marriage."

Mrs. Landell's first emotion on hearing this statement was to be seen in a look of obviously genuine amazement. Her eyes and mouth opened together, and her hands fell on the arms of her chair. The feeling that succeeded, which she did her best to control, was as plainly one of anger and incredulity.

"I don't believe a word of it," she said sharply. "It is quite impossible. My husband certainly did not see his solicitor, or any other lawyer, for a long time before his death. When he did see Mr. Snow, I was always present. If he made another will, I must have known about it. The idea is absurd. Why should he have wanted to make another will?"

Selby shrugged. "That I cannot say, Mrs. Landell. The question does not arise. But if he had wanted to, he could make a will without a lawyer's assistance, and if it complied with the requirements of the law it would be a valid will. The position is that, as his legal adviser and executor of the will of which we know, I am bound to satisfy myself that there is no later will, if I have grounds for thinking that there is one. And I have grounds for thinking so."

Mrs. Landell made a derisive sound. "Have you really? And grounds for thinking it is in this house, too? Well, I can tell you that it isn't. I have been through every single paper in this place, I have looked carefully everywhere, and there is no such thing."

"There was nothing locked up then?" Selby suggested.

"Of course not," Mrs. Landell snapped. "My husband had no secrets from me."

Selby coughed. "It may be so. All the same, Mrs. Landell, I shall have to satisfy myself on the point. The law is very strict about matters of this kind, and I must make a search on my own account."

"And suppose I say I will not allow it? This is all my property now, and I am not obliged to let anyone come rummaging about for something that isn't there."

Again Selby coughed. "That is not exactly the position, Mrs. Landell. When a person dies, having made a will appointing an executor, his property vests at once in that executor, and it remains entirely in his control until the estate has been distributed as the will directs. The will on which you are relying, and which is the only one at present positively known to exist, appointed my partner and myself executors. We must act in that capacity, unless and until a later will comes to light. I hope that is quite clear."

This information appeared, as Selby put it later, to take the wind completely out of Mrs. Landell's sails. She sat in frowning silence, mastering her feelings, for a few moments, then rose to her feet.

"Very well," she said. "If what you tell me is correct, it seems you can do as you like, and I cannot prevent you wasting your time. Where will you begin your search?"

"I think," Selby said, "the best place to make a start would be the room where he spent most of his time when by himself. There is such a room, I suppose?"

She went to the door. "I will show you the study," she said, not looking at either of them. "Your friend had better come, too, as you say you want him to assist you."

She led the way across the hall to another room,

with a french window opening on the lawn behind the house. Before this stood a large writing table, old-fashioned and solid like the rest of the furniture, which included three bookcases of bird's-eye maple. Not wasting time, Selby and Trent went each to one of the bookcases, while Mrs. Landell looked on implacably from the doorway.

"*Annales Thucydidei et Xenophontei,*" read Selby in an undertone, glancing up and down the shelves. "*Miscellanea Critica,* by Cobet—give me the *Rural Rides,* for choice. I say, Phil, I seem to have come to the wrong shop. *Palaographia Graeca,* by Montfaucon—I had an idea that was a place where they used to break chaps on the wheel in Paris. Greek plays—row and rows of them. How are you getting on?"

"I am on the trail, I believe," Trent answered. "This is all English poetry—but not arranged in any order. Aha! What do I see?" He pulled out a thin red volume. "One of the best-looking books that was ever printed and bound." He was turning the pages rapidly. "Here we are—The Ocean Chart. But no longer 'a perfect and absolute blank.' "

He handed the book to Selby, who scanned attentively the page at which it was opened. "Beautiful writing, isn't it?" he remarked. "Not much larger than smallish print, and quite as legible. Hm! Hm!" He frowned over the minute script, nodding approval from time to time; then looked up. "Yes, this is all right. Everything clear, and the attestation clause quite in order—that's what gets 'em, very often."

Mrs. Landell, whose existence Selby appeared to have forgotten for the moment, now spoke in a strangled voice. "Do you mean to tell me that there is a will written in that book?"

"I beg your pardon," the lawyer said with studied politeness. "Yes, Mrs. Landell, this is the will for which I was looking. It is very brief, but quite clearly expressed, and properly executed and witnessed. The witnesses are

Mabel Catherine Wheeler and Ida Florence Kirkby, both domestic servants, resident in this house."

"They dared to do that behind my back!" Mrs. Landell raged. "It's a conspiracy!"

Selby shook his head. "There is no question here of an agreement to carry out some hurtful purpose," he said. "The witnesses appear to have signed their names at the request of their employer, and they were under no obligation to mention the matter to any other person. Possibly he requested them not to do so; it makes no difference. As for the provisions of the will, it begins by bequeathing the sum of ten thousand pounds, free of legacy duty, to yourself—"

"What!" screamed Mrs. Landell.

"Ten thousand pounds, free of legacy duty," Selby repeated calmly. "It gives fifty pounds each to my partner and myself, in consideration of our acting as executors—that, you may remember, was provided by the previous will. And all the rest of the testator's property goes to his nephew, Robert Spencer Landell, of 27 Longland Road, Blackheath, in the county of Kent."

The last vestige of self control departed from Mrs. Landell as the words were spoken. Choking with fury and trembling violently, she snatched the book from Selby's hand, ripped out the inscribed page, and tore it across again and again "Now what are you going to do?" she gasped.

"The question is, what are you going to do," Selby returned with perfect coolness. "If you destroy that will beyond repair, you commit a felony which is punishable by penal servitude. Besides that, the will could still be proved; I am acquainted with its contents, and can swear to them. The witnesses can swear that it was executed. Mr. Trent and I can swear to what has just taken place. If you will take my advice, Mrs. Landell, you will give me back those bits of paper. If they can be pieced together into a legible document, the court will not refuse to recognize it, and I may be able to save you from being prosecuted—I shall do my best. And there is another thing. As matters stand now, I must ask you to consider your arrangements for the future. There is no hurry, naturally; I shall not press you in any way; but you realize that while you continue living here you do so on sufferance, and that the place must be taken over by Mr. Robert Landell in due course."

Mrs. Landell was sobered at last. Very pale, and staring fixedly at Selby, she flung the pieces of the will on the writing table and walked rapidly from the room.

"I had no idea you could be such a brute, Arthur," Trent remarked as he drove the car Londonwards through the Berkshire levels.

Selby said nothing.

"The accused made no reply," Trent observed. "Perhaps you didn't notice that you were being brutal, with those icy little legal lectures of yours, and your drawing out the agony in that study until you had her almost at screaming point even before the blow fell."

Selby glanced at him. "Yes, I noticed all that. I don't think I am a vindictive man, Phil, but she made me see red. In spite of what she said, it's clear to me that she suspected he might have made another will at some time. She looked for it high and low. If she had found it she would undoubtedly have suppressed it. And her husband had no secrets from her! And whenever Snow was there she was always present! Can you imagine what it was like being dominated and bullied by a harpy like that?"

"Ghastly," Trent agreed. "But look here, Arthur; if he could get the two maids to witness the will, and keep quiet about it, why couldn't he have made it on an ordinary sheet of paper and enclosed it in a letter to your firm, and got either Mabel Catherine or Ida Florence to post it secretly?"

Selby shook his head. "I thought of that. Probably

he didn't dare take the risk of the girl being caught with the letter by her mistress. If that had happened, the fat *would* have been in the fire. Besides, we should have acknowledged the letter, and she would have opened our reply and read it. Reading all his correspondence would have been part of the treatment, you may be sure. No, Phil: I liked old Landell, and I meant to hurt. Sorry; but there it is."

"I wasn't objecting to your being brutal," Trent said. "I felt just like you, and you had my unstinted moral support all the time. I particularly liked that passage when you reminded her that she could be slung out on her ear whenever you chose."

"She's devilish lucky, really," Selby said. "She can live fairly comfortably on the income from her legacy if she likes. And she can marry again, God help us all! Landell got back on her in the end; but he did it like a gentleman."

"So did you," Trent said. "A very nice little job of torturing, I should call it."

Selby's smile was bitter. "It only lasted minutes," he said. "Not years."

Home Is Where the Heart Is
by Nell Lamburn

"The hearth," Godfrey Mannington would say, "the hearth is the very *heart* of the home. The bedroom may be the womb, but without warmth, without food, life itself cannot be sustained. The ancients knew that, of course. And revered them accordingly." He would smooth his fine narrow hand along the rough oak lintel: let it linger over the curved flank of the seventeenth-century bread oven, while his clients nodded and agreed and admired. How they admired! For to own a Mannington cottage was to own a living masterpiece indeed.

"How can you *bear* to sell!" they would murmur. "How can you *bear* to leave such an idyllic place!"

Then Godfrey Mannington would lay his arm, yoke-like, about his wife's stolid shoulders and shake his head just sufficiently for one lock of grey-fair hair to fall across his forehead and say,

"How can any artist bear to sell? We create to *share*—to give other people pleasures and—of course—" and here he would smile, deprecatingly, "to be admired."

"But it's your *home*!" they would protest, and he would sigh. "You know what they say—home is where the heart is—" And the yoke of his arm would press down a little more heavily. "Isn't that so, my dear?"

And obediently, Marjorie Mannington would smile and nod, like a windup doll, her tinkling laugh as ill-fitting to her broad frame as windbells to a carriage clock.

"We're just gypsies at heart! We travel light!" Her lying words conjured caravan and skewbald and lurcher where the white Range Rover was parked. A Mannington cottage did not come cheap, after all.

Why should it? With the cottage stripped and restored, furnished and decorated in a taste that clients were instantly persuaded was their own, the Manningtons would frequently abandon their own furniture as heartlessly as this year's moult. Then they would require only the slimmest of pantechnicons, just the essentials that would see them through the coming months: two beds, a few chairs, a table—mundane essentials. And it would all begin again: the discomfort and toil; the temper and tension; the knowledge that the perfection created would never be theirs.

"Of *course* we'll settle down!" Godfrey Mannington would, in answer to her query, dangle once more the bright reassuring promise, like a fruit that concealed the rottenness of the lie within. "One day."

Then, that night, in the discomfort of whatever solitary room he had assigned her to, she would take out the small rosewood casket, cradle it close against her breast, her expectation raised once more.

"One day!" she'd echo. "One day I'll bring you home! I promise!" And she'd close her eyes and let her lips linger across the burnished surface. Just once or twice a year she might lift the lid, but then pain ran through her like molten fire so that she could barely breathe for it. But she must always look again. To be sure.

And the next morning Godfrey Mannington would note the telltale signs of his wife's emotional disarray as a good stockman notes the well-being of his charges. For Marjorie was his livelihood as much as he was hers. Her skill with needle and fabric and design was as vital to their business as his with restoration, and she must perform—for just as long as he needed.

"We're a team!" He would smile at the Features girls from the London glossies, confidingly, as if sharing a secret. "So *fortunate,* don't you think?" And their commercial superiority would splinter at his practised simplicity. It was only afterwards they discovered that the only suitable photographs contained just one member of that team.

Marjorie Mannington did not mind. With her stout body and heavy face, the camera would never be her friend. Her mother had always made that quite clear. Though her dark eyes, if they had not protruded just a fraction too far, would have been remarkable. As remarkable as the rich chestnut of the thick glossy hair her mother had vociferously refused to let her cut, so that even now, with her mother long dead, she wore it in a chignon so plump and heavy that it seemed to bow her head beneath its weight.

Godfrey Mannington loathed her hair. Sometimes he would wake, sweating, at the memory of their wedding night: the terrible expectancy glowing on her moon face, the thick suffocating dark curtain that had choked his eyes, his mouth, as he'd gone about his business. For business it had been. Passport to his inheritance. To Mannington House.

"Get yourself a son! Get yourself a wife and get yourself a son!" His father's snarl had curled the edges of his voice as viciously as it curled his lip. "Three hundred years we've been here—I'll not let it die with you."

"But it's my *home!*" he'd half screamed: his birthright, his passion from his earliest years, caressed, cossetted, every corner of it beloved, yearned for to own. While other boys might climb trees or strike balls of all shapes and sizes or dream of Grand Prix victories, he'd studied their Dresden and Chelsea, learned the intimate dissimilarities of Beluchi and Kashan, tended the glowing flanks of hautboy and bureau: all to be his one day.

His mother had turned, frightened, away from his frantic gaze, and the brigadier had sneered, venomous:

"She'll not help you, you fool! Not with this. And it's not *your* home—or mine—it's the Manningtons'—dead and unborn. Get yourself a son—or it goes to Gerald!"

Cousin Gerald. Cousin Gerald with his four sons. Smug. Anticipating.

So he'd married Marjorie. With her wide, childbearing hips; her uncomplicated emotional gratitude; her convenient cottage in the Woodford Valley; and her commercial skill with her needle. In thanks for her immediate pregnancy he'd selected, as their furniture expert, the choicest items from the Salisbury auction rooms and, in complement, she had stitched and tucked, quilted and upholstered. A gem. The first Mannington cottage. A cradle for his son. For of course it would be a son.

Francis Godfrey Heyward Mannington lived two days and extracted such a vengeance on his mother for being cheated of his rightful life, that she would never bear another child. The nurses, concerned and kind, packaged up the soft grey ashes and she kept them close by her in the impersonal, pretty room while, in disbelieving grief, she murmured the nursery rhymes she'd learned and whispered of sandcastles and rockpools, flying kites and cricket bats: of a future that was only make-believe, for just the two of them.

Godfrey Mannington did not visit.

"You've had your chance!" his father sneered. "No switching mares—the house is Gerald's!"

Molten, agonised rage had crept through him until,

solidifying his emotions to a grey, cold larva of revenge, he could look on his wife again. But only just.

Perhaps she should have left him. When she came home to find the cottage all but sold, perhaps she should have refused her signature, resuscitated her business, and let him go on his way. But it never occurred to her, and exhausted, empty of child and future, she stayed, clasping about her the illusion of his wedding vows: that their need was mutual. And with that first sale, the Mannington legend was born.

But he did not know about the casket. No one knew about the casket. It was her secret, her treasure. Until she could bring him home.

And now she *was* home. On that early spring afternoon, stout legs awash with daffodils, the wicked, now familiar runnels of pain fluting her thumbs, Marjorie Mannington knew that she had, indeed, come home. Why, she did not understand. Thatched, beamed, walled in flint and brick, it could have been any one of half a dozen cottages they had viewed. Yet instantly she knew that this was where she must live. To remain here—never to move again! Never to stitch another curtain! Her hands wouldn't matter then.

Perhaps it was the setting, for it lay down an unpaved lane, set back from the shallow, silky brown water of the chalk stream, sheltered by still-naked beech and a great white ash. Private. Peaceful. Keeper's Cottage. Only now the water bailiff lived in a smart new bungalow in the village a mile away.

"You like 'n?"

Marjorie turned, her heart jumping at the boy's unexpected closeness. Only this time, seeing him so near, she saw that he wasn't really a boy. There were faint lines about his black, heavy-lidded eyes, a little looseness beneath his heavy jaw: a slight coarsening of the skin that betrayed more years than she'd thought at their earlier meeting.

"You like 'n?" His long head, sealed with dark hair

that tendrilled about his ears, bent just a little in a gesture that was curiously intimate.

Marjorie Mannington looked away quickly, oddly discomforted by his unnoticed approach.

"Yes. Yes, of course. It's—it's delightful!"

" 'Tis Bobbie's." He smiled, confidingly. " 'Tis my 'ome."

"And such a pretty one! So quiet, too." She humoured him. "My husband always insists on peace—he hates noise, you know, loathes it. It quite upsets him—"

As one, they looked back through the window. Godfrey Mannington stood before the fireplace, head bowed, arms straight by his side as a priest stands before an altar to seek divine guidance. Nearby, Mr. Austin, estate agent, waited respectfully, clipboard clasped in commercial reverence.

" 'Tis Bobbie's." The soft voice came again. "I mun stay. Mr. Austin says."

She was startled. "Oh, I think not! Vendors can't lay down conditions like that, you know!" She tried to soften her voice, to make amends for any sharpness, her hand touching his arm. "I know it's difficult to see your home sold, but I *understand*! I've moved mine so *many* times, you see!"

He seemed not to hear her. He was gazing at her hand against his heavy, dark cloth jacket: solid, square-tipped fingers, coarsened from the predations of needle and upholstery. Then, gently, with infinite delicacy, he touched her thumb.

"Poor 'and," he said softly. "Poor sick l'le 'and."

He knew! But he *could* not know! It was just a ridiculous inspired guess! For no one knew: except Dr. Farley, and he was fifteen miles away. Shock stung her, pumping her heart unpleasantly. And no one *must* know. Certainly not Godfrey. Otherwise—The thought of what Godfrey might do sent her ducking through the low doorway into the cottage again to hear Mr. Austin declare, half defiant, half apologetic:

"I'm sorry, Mr. Mannington, but there's nowhere else for him to go, you see. Those are the terms of his mother's will."

"Then his mother died crazy!" Godfrey Mannington's voice slid sharply up in bitter frustration, for he knew that the hearth, behind its ugly disguise, was the finest he had ever found. And he wanted it. Lusted for it. "Who in their right mind would take on a condition of sale like that?"

"He's an *excellent* gardener—you've only to look about you! He'll work the river hatches for you, too. And he's *most* handy about the house." Mr. Austin bared his teeth, ingratiatingly. "Not to mention a first-class cook—top marks at the village fete!"

"My wife cooks!" Godfrey Mannington cried angrily. "And does the garden."

But for how much longer? The pain shifted sharply from thumb to wrist and lingered now. The boy Bobbie watched through the window, unblinking.

Bobbie. With the suddenness of a hare breaking cover, the idea leapt from the troubled thicket of her mind. Bobbie would shield her! With Bobbie here she could manage. Godfrey need not know. Not yet. It would give her time to prepare him, to persuade him that this must be their home. Her heart fluttered in agonised anxiety.

Mr. Austin whined, "It's not often you get a resident handyman for nothing, these days. He could have his own quarter—the little brewhouse would be perfect. Most people would *welcome* the idea!"

"Bullshit." Godfrey Mannington's coarse contempt flushed Mr. Austin's cheeks as red as his tie. "It's a buyer's market. You can't lay down conditions like that. *You* should know that."

She thought Mr. Austin would cry. "I'm only doing my job," he said with a poor attempt at dignity. But

Godfrey Mannington had forgotten him. The fireplace dominated him, daring rejection, its perfections taunting him from beneath the plasterboard and disfiguring stone. He trembled, inwardly, as before a veiled mistress. Ah, what pleasure, what satisfaction he would have in restoring it! In revealing this seventeenth-century treasure to the world! *His* triumph! All at once he knew the boy was irrelevant. The boy could be dealt with.

And watching him, as she had watched him for so many years, Marjorie Mannington knew, with trembling exultation, that he would buy.

Bobbie was indeed a help. He laboured for their builders who, following them from cottage to cottage, melted away when the structural alterations were done. He cooked and gardened and never intruded. So much so that his retention became Godfrey Mannington's own idea.

"You see how much more time you have for your work! With Bobbie we'll be ready to sell in half the time!" And he knew then, by the panic that trembled his wife's long upper lip, that this time her desire to remain was as fundamental as his had been with Mannington House. It pleased him, therefore, that she should suffer: as he must for the loss of his own inheritance, his home. An eye for an eye. . . .

And Marjorie saw then how terrible a mistake she had made and scrambled up the tightly curled elm-treaded stairs to sit, trembling, on her bed. Pain licked her shoulders and ceased. That's how it would be, Dr. Farley had said. It would come and go until the coming was more than the going, and if she did not face that now and submit to treatment, then the coming would be sooner than later. And that included mucking about with old damp cottages, kneeling in wet gardens, and straining her joints in upholstering, sewing heavy cloth, and clambering up and down ladders. Cottages

were no substitutes for children and it was about time
she realised it.

Dr. Farley lived in a neo-Georgian house with
underfloor heating and double-glazing and not an uneven floorboard in the place. Dr. Farley abhorred the
old. It frightened his patients into an agility they didn't
know they possessed. But nevertheless, Dr. Farley,
grumbling, gave her pills and injections and kept her
secret. He was not Godfrey's doctor.

It was, though, only a question of time. Yesterday
she had dropped a dish and he'd cried out from the sitting room, angrily, at the sudden noise and Bobbie had
called through, his voice soft, placatory.

" 'Tis my fault, sir. 'Tis I dropped it, not Missus. Be
angry we' Bobbie—not Missus." And winked and
grinned, and Marjorie, by her gratitude, betrayed her
disability.

"Ah'll bring wax," he whispered. 'Wax from Vicar's
bees. Wax draws out soreness. 'Twill be our secret."

So, on the occasions Godfrey Mannington was away
searching for those genuine effects that were slowly
transforming Keeper's Cottage, she sat while he
spooned the hot wax over her hands until she was help-
less in the hardening fragrant armour. Then Bobbie
made tea and held the mug to her lips as if she were a
child, no matter how she protested.

"Ah done it for Ma," he confided, his long face so
close to hers that she could see the rainbow lights in
the tiny globule of spittle that lodged permanently in
the fleshy angle of his lips. "Ah done everything for
her, right t'end. Bobbie knows things, woman's things.
Missus mustn't worry. Bobbie's here."

I should be grateful, she thought. Grateful someone
cares. But she wasn't. She shrank inwardly from his
touch. He wasn't her son. Her son lay upstairs. Waiting
to come home. Her son would have been slim and
bright, a flame to illuminate their lives. Clean and

sweet. Not with the mustiness of old wool and dried sweat that filmed this boy's skin.

Grateful too that he did not mind when Godfrey used him so curtly and thus spared her the sharp impatience that never failed to cut as viciously as the tools he used. Bobbie would only smile and nod and watch Godfrey's deft hands with those brightly dark eyes, his head a little on one side, and move so quietly that Godfrey Mannington sneered.

"He's good, you know. Damn good. Knows just what I'm going to do next—never have to tell him. Worth two of you, d'you know that? We'll be finished in no time at all." And rejoiced in the terror that turned her gaze so quickly from him.

The idea, when it came to her, was so simple that she could not understand how it had evaded her. *Home is where the heart is.* That was what Godfrey always said. Her child's heart. If he were here— permanently—if she laid him to rest at Keeper's Cottage—then surely this would indeed be her home? His presence would somehow permeate his father's soul, bind him to this place too. They would be a true family. He would not know why—oh no, it would be her secret, hers and the child's. Therefore it must be a secret place. A sacred place. Inviolable.

The hearth.

Marjorie Mannington was a patient woman. It seemed that her whole life had been spent waiting: for her mother's approval; a husband; a home; to find a resting place for her son. A month or so more would make little difference. But anticipation pearled up like the first tiny jewels of sweet spring water as she watched the fireplace emerge from its despoilation. The honeyed oak lintel, ancient even when first laid; the comforting swell of the bread oven; the dark rich brick walling with its small deep cupboard; the narrow-bricked floor, smooth, pale, original. It would, she knew triumphantly, be a fitting tomb. He would be

where he should always have been: in the true heart of
the house.

On the first Wednesday of each month, Godfrey
Mannington drove to Bath. Bills must be paid on time,
craftsmen visited and consulted. And if his wife had no
need to match and choose material, he would take
Bobbie, much as he would take a dog, and leave him
with his grandmother at the Home in Chippenham
where the old people clucked and cossetted and fed
him the cakes their relatives had baked to ease their
consciences. He would make his own way back, very
late, walking cat-eyed from the late bus along the back
road as those old people had in their youth.

Bobbie loved the Range Rover. He would sit up very
straight, looking neither to right nor left, only his rigid
smile betraying his acute pleasure. Then, when the engine had faded into the dominance of water and wind-
brushed leaves, Marjorie Mannington would fetch the
casket and carry it from room to half-finished room.

"Our home!" she'd murmur. "This is our home, my
darling—we shall never leave—ever! Just you see!"

But not today. Today the hearth was completed. Today she fetched the chisel and hammer and edged the
black iron fire basket a little to one side, prised loose,
with infinite care, two narrow bricks. She did not feel,
with Dr. Farley's pills, the pain in her thumbs or
wrists, but worked with a speed and delicacy she had
thought gone forever. She hollowed out the earth and
laid in the casket. So small, so vulnerable. Never to be
seen again. Trembling, she took from her neck the
small gold cross her godmother had given her at her
confirmation and laid it beside the box.

"There!" she whispered. "There, my darling—rest in
peace."

When it was finished, when she had mixed and col-
oured the cement with the skill of long practice and
there was only its damp freshness to show what she
had done, the pain overflowed from her heart so that

she clasped her wrists and rocked in agony, letting the tears fall unchecked. But she had done right. She would never leave now. *Could* never leave. This would be her guarantee.

He knew! Even before the furious engine had died; before the slamming door, the pounding feet—the terrible realisation flash-flooded through her. He *knew*. Somehow, in some unimaginable way, Godfrey knew!

But there was no way that he could—he'd gone to Bath taken Bobbie to Chippenham. She'd been alone—all day!

"What have you done?" Godfrey Mannington wrenched aside the grate and ran his shaking fingers across the bricks. *"What have you done?"* He found the hardening cement. "Ah, desecration! That floor has lain untouched for three centuries and you—you have *despoiled it*!"

He fetched hammer and chisel and she flung herself on him.

"No! No—leave him! Let him rest in peace—ah, *please*!"

But his thrust sprawled her, crumpling her against the wall, and even as she struggled up, he was lifting the casket from its brief tomb.

"No!" Half scream, half moan. "Give him to me!"

"Him?" He prised up the lid, lifting out the little transparent bag. *"Him?"* Understanding whitened his narrow, livid face. "You have carried—*this* for all these years?" Revulsion caused his body to shudder, drew back his lips. "You're sick—sick—"

She lunged, but he was too quick. He was at the door.

"There is only one place for this!"

The compost heap, rich, moist, lay tucked behind the low wattle fence. Marjorie Mannington reached it as the ashes, fragile, ephemerous, drifted free of the bag to settle and dissolve like pale grey snowflakes in the fermenting mass.

On her knees, in awful, hopeless desperation, she clawed and scooped. But they were gone. Consumed as surely and finally as by fire.

In the white ash, a blackbird's fluting song embroidered the early evening, oblivious. A coot scuttered the water abruptly and was silent.

Slowly, very slowly she eased herself upright. He had destroyed their child. Now there was nothing. Nothing left. It seemed as if her blood no longer pulsed but crawled through her, so heavy did she feel.

Godfrey Mannington had returned to the cottage, moving with a quick angry step, and when she followed, numbly, ponderously, she saw him through the open door, on his knees inside the hearth, running his hands over its floor in a silent, absorbed anguish.

She moved close behind him. And then she screamed. She hadn't planned to. She knew that, afterwards. It was as if his destruction of their son had suddenly uncapped the great wellspring of the years past.

The sound of his skull against the bricked roof was really very soft, considering the severity of the impact. He twisted and fell across the grate. He was not dead, she knew it: not yet. Little garnet beads of blood bubbled from his ears; a streamlet edged from the corner of his half-hidden mouth. But he would die. Sooner or later he would die. She knew that with equal certainty.

She fetched a chair and, laying her throbbing hands upon her lap, waited. And watched.

No, she didn't want company. No, she wanted to be alone, thank you. Yes, she would eat. As if eating would somehow compensate. As if a meal would gather up those soft grey ashes again. But when they were gone, the policeman and the doctor and the undertaker's men, the realisation that she was now alone crept in on her with the fingers of dusk. And instead of fear, to her astonishment there was only a sweet, enervating relief.

She fetched the strong scissors from the kitchen and loosened her hair, the weight of it pulling at her scalp. Then, laboriously, forcing her fingers through their painful motions, she slowly cut and cut until she stood in a pool of brown silkiness. Then she shook her head and laughed, foolishly, at the lightness of her head.

She was free of Godfrey. Free at last of her mother. And with the selling of Keepers Cottage, she would be free of Bobbie.

She heard him return, very late. Heard the wicket gate click, his step crunch the gravel, his familiar, hawking cough as he unlocked his door. He would not know, he'd pass no houses on the back road. Well, she'd tell him in the morning. Tell him, too, that she would be leaving Keeper's Cottage just as soon as probate was granted. She would move to a nice ground-floor flat in Salisbury and complete the restoration of this, the very last Mannington Cottage, as quickly as she could. There were good doctors in Salisbury, too, a brand-new hospital. And she'd never have to stitch another curtain in her life. Even if she could.

He came to her room the next morning. He stood in the doorway, frowning, holding out the thick locks of hair before him.

"Naughty," he said softly. "Naughty Missus."

She stared at him, suddenly hating him. His subservience, his assumption of his role in the cottage, his secret knowledge of her failing body.

"Go away," she said, but he did not move, did not look directly at her.

"Should have called Doctor sooner." He began to stroke the hair. "Poor Mr. Godfrey."

Marjorie Mannington lay very very still. He knew, then. Knew Godfrey was dead. But how did he know?

"Don't be stupid! It was too late—doctors can't

bring people back from the dead! Now go! Go away!"
An unknown fear slid her voice high. "I don't want
you coming in here anymore!"

" 'Tis my 'ome." He looked at her then, a stubborn
directness. "Missus needs I."

"Not anymore. I can manage quite well for myself
now." Because now she wouldn't need to pretend any
longer, it wouldn't matter if her fingers would not obey
her. "I'm leaving. I'm selling the cottage, just as soon
as it's finished."

Defensively, she closed her eyes against him and
when she opened them again, he had gone. Only her
hair lay on the old elm boards. And a sick, cold fear in
her heart.

He couldn't *know*. Then why say she should have
called the doctor sooner? Why had Godfrey gone
straight to the hearth—as if someone had told him?
How had he known, that first day, about her hands?

She struggled out of bed. Guesswork, that's what it
was. Guess-work. The pain stabbed her knees, her an-
kles, and she sat, panting with the effort, with the awful fear of how Bobbie had known.

Godfrey Mannington was buried at Mannington
Church. His mother wept. His father growled,

"Bloody stupid way to go. But he never could get
anything right, could he?"

While Cousin Gerald, secure now in his inheritance,
merely pressed Marjorie's black-gloved hand as she returned, alone, to the hired car. There wasn't, after all,
very much he could say.

Mr. Martin, of Martin, Hendicott, and Akhurst, came
the following Thursday, bumping distastefully down
the unpaved lane in his glistening black car. Marjorie
Mannington watched as Bobbie opened and closed the
door and then, with an obsequiousness she found quite
repulsive, polished the handle where he had held it.
Marjorie did not care for Mr. Martin. He never quite

looked at you straight through his steel-rimmed glasses. He knew too much and gave too little away. She liked Mr. Akhurst, but Godfrey had called him a fool. Well, now she could change to Mr. Akhurst.

After Mr. Martin had departed, long after, she sat, quite still, her hands crumpled on her lap. Just staring. She wasn't numb. The shock was too violent for that. It was as if, she thought dully, she'd been beaten almost insensible: every inch of her body ached.

Godfrey had left the cottage to Bobbie.

"He felt, you see," Mr. Martin explained, unable to meet her disbelieving gaze, seemingly not quite convinced himself, "that it was Bobbie's *home*. But of course you would stay here for your lifetime—there's money enough to see you are provided for, so long as you stay *here,* you understand. He was concerned, you see, about your increasing disability. So touched that you tried to spare him the worry of it. He knew this was where you were absolutely determined to spend the rest of your life—and that Bobbie would care for you. No need for a nursing home—no need for strangers. It's all care in the home these days, the government says. Bobbie nursed his mother, Dr. Read told him about that. Wonderfully. Mr. Mannington wanted only the best for you, you must realise that."

The financial side had been Godfrey's. She trusted him. Now she had nothing except her widow's pension. All those years of work and she had nothing. Not even her son.

She felt, rather than heard, Bobbie behind her.

"There now, doan fret." His voice was as smooth as a snake's belly. "Bobbie'll take care of thee. Thee an' I—we be *friends,* Missus. Thee and I 'ave secrets, mm?" He touched her shoulder and her breath caught on a sob. "Just doan 'ee scream, Missus. For Bobbie doan like screamers."

The Wicked Ghost
by Christianna Brand

You'd think nothing could be more romantic and exciting than to be just an ordinary, everyday, just-out-of-college American girl and then to go and marry an Earl—a real, true, English belted Earl. And a young earl at that—Edward's relatives seemed to have combined in self-immolation so that he might attain the title, piling themselves into motor cars all together and getting themselves killed off at a tremendous rate.

Not that Edward had cared two hoots about the title; all he thought of was going off exploring in horrible foreign places. Intrepid, that's what Edward was: the newspapers were always saying so. *Intrepid young Explorer Earl, Edward Fitzmerrian, as he sets out upon yet another of his perilous voyages.* Nowadays they had changed it a bit. *Wives must weep,* they said; *lovely Victoria (Vi-vi) Fitzmerrian waves goodbye to her husband, intrepid young Explorer Earl, et cetera, et cetera.*

And even that, of course, was romantic and exciting in itself: plain Victoria Morgan from Wilmington, Delaware, suddenly promoted to Lovely Vi-vi Fitzmerrian, watching her husband's departure with tear-filled eyes.

And tear-filled was the word! For romantic and exciting it may all have been with a cathedral wedding, actually in the presence of royalty, and the Great-Aunts giving her pep talks on the Responsibilities of Privilege and the Honour of the Family and all the rest of it; but to find that Edward almost immediately afterward calmly embarked on another long adventure and just as calmly took it for granted she would remain quietly at Fitzmerrian with the Aunts in control—that was another matter! Any attempt at rebellion had been quelled with a quite astonishing firmness. Lovely Victoria (Vi-vi) Fitzmerrian began to be quite sorry for these poor old savages whom Intrepid Young Explorer Earl was always going to and bossing about.

The truth was, it was deadly dull. Fitzmerrian Manor, as everyone (in England) knows, is "at the other end of the world," an exploration in itself; too far from anywhere even to be turned into a Stately Home and visited by half-crown-paying barbarians, which would at least have brought some life to the place. As it was, the only sign of life for miles around lay in the bright dark eyes of Mario—Mario who, all the way from sunny Italy, had come to look after the Aunts' carriage horses—they weren't going to risk *their* lives in nasty dangerous motor cars—and who was the terror of the village belles for miles around.

Lovely Victoria (Vi-vi) Fitzmerrian, who up to now had never known at which end of a horse what happened, and hadn't cared—Vi-vi began to spend a great deal of time in the stables.

"Oh, dear," said Great-Aunt Honoria, "I do trust she is not going the same way as all the other gels." The other gels were various young cousins and great-nieces who had recently come paying duty visits to Fitzmerrian. "I'm afraid we shall have to tell her the story of Elizabeth and Wicked Cousin William. It cured all the others." (But really—that Mario! she added in a tone of despair.)

"It seems hard on the parties concerned," said Great-Aunt Felicity. "Not here to defend themselves."

"Cousin William fell downstairs," cried Great-Aunt Adelaide, beating softly on the breakfast table with her egg spoon. Aunt Adelaide was the slightly unstable one. Batty Addie, Vi-vi called her—to herself.

So that evening they took coffee in the Long Gallery, beneath the family portraits and more especially the portrait of that *other* William of long, long ago, who had been known, even in those conspicuously wicked days, as the "Wicked Earl." And a wicked gleam indeed he'd had in his eye, thought Vi-vi; *he* wouldn't go off exploring after savages—with something a lot better to explore here at home. Got up regardless, he was, in a coat, hugely flared, of plum-colored silk over a velvet waistcoat inappropriately embroidered with little innocent lilies in thread of gold. His wig was enormous, heavily powdered, and he carried in one hand a cane, amber-headed, with two golden tassels.

"One can't help thinking," said Vi-vi to the Aunts, "that he must have been quite a dish."

"A thoroughly bad man," said Great-Aunt Honoria. "And I am sorry to say that his namesake took after him."

"Your cousin William, you mean? The one who fell down the stairs and broke his neck?"

Veils drew down over wrinkled faces, and bright old eyes grew shadowed. "Why, by golly, I'm *sorry*!" said Vi-vi, abashed by this unlooked-for show of emotion. "But if he was so wicked—? And only your cousin, and once removed at that? And surely it must have happened a long time ago?"

"Well, yes—it's a long time. Thirty-forty years?" said Aunt Honoria consulting Felicity. "Just one year after dear Hubert brought Elizabeth here as the new Countess."

"Such a pretty girl she was," said Aunt Adelaide, musing over it, rapping gently with the egg-spoon.

"Handsome is as handsome does," said Aunt Honoria.

"And just what did Elizabeth do?" (Left all alone here with the Aunts—younger then, but no chickens even so—as she, Vi-vi, was left now. The Fitzmerrian men, it appeared, were great ones for going off on business or adventure and leaving their ladies in chastity belts at home; for Fitzmerrian Manor, away here in the back of beyond, was a chastity belt in itself.)

More veils. And what went on behind the veils? Vi vi wondered—what went on in their heads, the three funny old things? All this big talk about Honour and The Family and the rest of it—it couldn't have been difficult for them, poor dears, to safeguard their share of it; poor little crumpled-up Addie who looked as if a good huff and a puff (especially from a man) would blow her away; and Felicity lugubrious, her long thin nose oddly white against her pinched pink face; and Honoria—still solid as the house itself, and dear God! that was solid enough—rolling along, full of energy despite her eighty years, pushing around the gardeners and the dairymen and the ancient butler and the crones who still worked in the house.

(Not Mario, though— one cross word to Mario and didn't Vi-vi know it herself?—a look came into those velvety brown eyes that presaged an outburst of sulks and sudden nostalgic yearnings for Italian skies. "They no send away Mario," he had boasted to her when she confided certain breakfast-table grumblings of the Aunts about his shortcomings. "Very hard to get good man for carriage; and Mario he like an angel with the horses—Signora Honoria, she say this word herself, like an angel.")

"So," said Vi-vi, "what did Elizabeth *do*?"

And Honoria and Felicity exchanged glances and suddenly it was time for Addie's beddy-bye. An old witch known as Nanny, so ancient as to appear to have been in fact Nanny to he Aunts themselves, was summoned and led the protesting old lady away. "It would upset her," said Honoria firmly.

"You understand, Victoria, it is never to be spoken of outside the family?" said Felicity.

"Indeed no! Never to anyone at all, in fact," said Honoria. "And above all, not to dear Edward. But now that you are the wife of the head of the Family, my dear—"

"—and after all, this is between the women of the family," added Felicity.

"If you will give your solemn word—"

"Well, my goodness, of *course*!" promised Vi-vi, much intrigued.

So with many interruptions from Great-Aunt Felicity, Great-Aunt Honoria embarked on the story of Cousin William and Elizabeth—all those long years ago. A pretty girl, it was true, but—well, mettlesome. Like a young foal, like the Starlight filly that Mario was breaking in at this moment—("Such a tiresome young man, by the way; I learned today, Felicity, that there is more trouble about that Betty James in the village," said Aunt Honoria in an aside; and watched two young hands clench tight and the knuckles whiten.)

Well—and like any other young foal, longing to kick up her heels and scamper about in any meadow where the grass grew green. But of course young ladies, especially when they married into responsible positions, couldn't behave like young fillies. So the Aunts had Spoken to Elizabeth, and after that things had seemed to simmer down.

Until one morning Adelaide had come down to breakfast and announced complacently, "I saw one of the ghosts last night. I told you there were ghosts and I saw one of them last night."

"Of course there are ghosts," Honoria had said severely. Such a family would hardly be respectable, her tone suggested, without a decent ghost or two. "What did you see?"

"A shadow gliding across the upper hallway ... Ah, there is Elizabeth," said Addie, catching sight of her standing in the doorway to the breakfast room. "You saw it too, Elizabeth, didn't you?—for I caught sight of your face at your bedroom door."

But Elizabeth, it seemed, could not take the fact of a ghost quite so calmly. "A ghost? Yes, I ... Well, I did see something, Aunt Adelaide. I heard a noise and I got up and looked out."

"On the whole," said Cousin William, who just happened to be staying in the house—a compliment he seldom paid his three spinster cousins, let alone for so lengthy a visit—"on the whole isn't it usual for ghosts to make noise?" And he had leaned back and twiddled his thumbs and looked up at Elizabeth, still standing uncertainly in the doorway, with an oddly mischievous and teasing air.

"What else could it have been but a ghost?" Felicity had persisted.

"Of course it was a ghost," said Elizabeth hastily. "Aunt Adelaide saw it too, didn't you, Aunt Addie? A woman—I think it was a woman—"

"No, no, dear, positively a man. I saw his—his nether limbs, you know."

"I expect the wig deceived you," suggested William, with another of those teasing looks at Elizabeth. In those days the men wore powdered wigs."

"In which days?" said Honoria.

"Well, but wasn't it an Eighteenth Century ghost? We haven't any later ones, have we?"

"Yes, that's right," said Elizabeth eagerly. She came into the room and poured herself coffee. "An Eighteenth Century ghost. A big white wig and a long reddish-colored coat—that's why I thought it was a woman. I just saw the back of the wig and the long red silk coat."

"Not even a glimpse of the nether limbs?"

"William, if you *please*!" Aunt Honoria had exclaimed, looking horrified. She bent a somewhat anxious look on Elizabeth. "Are you telling us it was the Fifth Earl that you saw? *He* wore a plum-colored silk coat—his portrait is in the Long Gallery."

"Yes, yes, the Wicked Earl," cried Adelaide, delighted. "I saw him distinctly. A plum-colored coat."

"Gold embroidery down the front?" prompted Cousin William. "And the tasseled cane. And on his nether limbs—"

"That will do," said Honoria. "If he wore a gold-embroidered plum-colored coat and carried a cane—that is your namesake, William, certainly." And she looked at him piercingly. "Who was called the *Wicked Earl,*" she added.

"Golly!" interrupted Vi-vi, listening starry-eyed to an outline of these events. "A real ghost?" (And real was the word, she thought. That clever little Elizabeth, so quick on the uptake!) "And then?"

Well, and then, it seemed, there had been no more visitations from the ghost at least for a little while. Cousin William had betaken himself back to London; but, not at all to the Aunts' delight, he had returned—with armloads of boxes and parcels to be sure, full of presents for everyone; silly shawls for the Aunts—who put them back in their boxes and never looked at them again—and a pearl necklace for Elizabeth (not real pearls, he said)—and even, apparently, a new dressing gown for himself, to replace his old red one; a simply huge box the dressing gown had occupied.

And perhaps it was his uneasy presence in the house, perhaps it was the attraction of their identical names and not dissimilar reputations, of a certain family likeness—but soon the Wicked Earl, William, began to walk again. Aunt Felicity saw him this time—she couldn't sleep, she said, felt restless and somehow anxious; and for no reason that she could put a name to, at some early hour of the morning, she had opened her bedroom door and looked out across the wide landing.

And there he was—and there was no mistaking him this time—the great powdered wig, the plum-colored coat over the embroidered waistcoat, one hand beneath its ruffled lace swinging a tasseled cane. And the face—it was the face of the Fifth Earl, not a doubt of it, right down to that—well, that *look* of his. He glided, unhurried, across the landing and slowly mounted the curving stairway that led to the corridors above.

Vi-vi knew those corridors. The Family Wing, it was called, with guest rooms reserved for visiting Fitzmerrians. Her own suite—which had in those days been Elizabeth's, it seemed—was across the broad landing from the foot of those stairs. (Golly!)

But aloud she said, "Weren't you scared, Aunt Felicity?"

"Certainly not," said Honoria, trumpeting in with it before Aunt Felicity's pink face could show any reaction. "It was only a harmless ghost. I kept an eye out myself after that and several nights later I saw it too— wig, silks, satins, cane and all."

Honoria glanced up at the Wicked Earl in his great gilt frame and he gave her back look for look. "He was a bad man, a braggart, a gambler, a trifler with women. No wonder he rests so uneasily in his grave."

And she added that though one could not possibly be frightened, still it was all exceedingly disagreeable. On the occasion that she herself saw him, he had been going the other way—moving across the landing with his back to her; and, on hearing this the next morning, poor Elizabeth had confided, very white and scared, that he had actually appeared in her room and stood there for a long time, with one hand on the upright of her great fourposter bed (Vi-vi slept there now, in that very bed) and gazed at her. So even in the spirit he had been up to his old tricks!

And Elizabeth had seemed so nervous that Cousin William had even suggested that she move out for a while; there were lots of vacant rooms in the Family Wing.

"And did she?" asked Vi-vi.

"Certainly not. It would have been most improper, with William sleeping in the same part of the house."

"Golly, yes, of *course!*" said Vi-vi.

Nevertheless, the Aunts had grown very anxious. If poor Elizabeth were going to be upset in this way— what would dear Hubert think when he came home and heard the story? (What indeed? wondered Vi-vi.) "So we took counsel, my dear, Felicity and Adelaide and I. Felicity was for calling in the parson and having the ghost exorcised; but really one would not care to submit The Family to that sort of intrusion; and wicked or not, he *had* been a member of The Family."

"Besides, the dear Vicar—he *was* a gossip," said Felicity.

"So Felicity suggested that we do something of the sort ourselves—"

"—I had heard that Holy Water was used—"

"But then Adelaide suggested that the poor ghost would get wet, and I replied to her that one only sprinkled the water and Honoria became thoughtful—did you not, Honoria?—and said that such a man as the Fifth Earl would need something more than a sprinkling. And she went to the priest—"

"Yes, I did," said Great-Aunt Honoria firmly.

"—and in the night we each had a whole ewer of the water and stood in our bedroom doorways—"

For quite some days after that, it seemed, the house had been extraordinarily peaceful. The Holy Water apparently kept the ghost at bay; and even Cousin William was not around to talk to Elizabeth across the Aunts in that mocking, double-meaning, teasing way of his; for Cousin William, it seemed, was confined to his bed with a bad cold.

But soon the haunting began again and Elizabeth acknowledged that the apparition had come to her room once more and stood, hand on bedpost, gazing down at her. For how long she couldn't say—between waking and dreaming one really couldn't be sure. To the Aunts, sometimes catching a glimpse of him going one way, sometimes coming back—it seemed really a very long time.

Once or twice the Aunts went to Elizabeth's room in the hope of surprising him there; but Elizabeth began to keep her door locked and by the time she opened it to them, if any ghost had been there, it had vanished. The fact that the ghost apparently took no account of locks and bolts suggested that she might as well have left the door open and given the Aunts a better chance of confronting it; but no—she felt happier with the door locked, she said, and begged the Aunts most earnestly not to go to all this trouble. After all, Elizabeth said demurely, the ghost never did anything she didn't like. Cousin William choked into his cup of tea.

And then one night Nanny saw the ghost and Nanny told Cook and Cook peeked over the railing from the top story and also saw the crown of the powdered head; and soon the tongues of the neighborhood would begin to wag. And what interpretation would be put upon these events by a plebian outside world not used to the privilege of a family ghost, the Aunts did not care to think. One thing was certain: something very positive would have to be done to stop the visitations, and soon.

"We must talk to the naughty ghost and ask him not to come," said Adelaide, and the next night she called out to him as he passed her door. But he only turned his wicked white face toward her and stalked silently by and went on up the curving stairs. "If we could somehow barricade him up there?" suggested Felicity. "Put an obstruction of some kind across the stairs?"

Honoria had looked at her and once again grown thoughtful.

"If a locked door won't keep him out—" began Felicity.

But Honoria interrupted her. "The Holy Water kept him at bay for some days," she said. "Perhaps if we tied something across the stairs as Adelaide suggests—a scarf or a sash, something soft—and soaked it well with Holy Water, he would be unable to pass that. We could renew the Holy Water each day."

And she made a second excursion to the priest. "There, Addie, since it was you who thought of the idea, you shall be the one to tie it across the stairs, from banister to banister. The top of the stairs, dear." And she had sent Addie off with a soft black silk scarf well soaked in the Holy Water ..

Vi-vi's brightly enameled nails dug themselves into the palms of her hands as she listened to this recital. "Aunt Honoria—you *didn't?*"

"How was one to know that she would tie it so low down on the banisters, poor foolish creature, as to trip anyone up? And anyway, what did it matter to a *ghost* where she tied it?"

"You didn't really still believe it was a ghost?"

"Certainly," said Great-Aunt Honoria, looking back at Vi-vi with a steady eye.

"So you . . . So you sent Aunt Adelaide to tie the thing across, and that night Cousin William tripped over it and fell down those steep, curving stairs and broke his neck?"

"Such an unfortunate accident," said Felicity. "We felt very bad about it." And on the very night, she added, when he himself had made such elaborate preparations to lay the ghost.

"Preparations?"

"Why, yes, my dear. He had actually been to a costumier's, it seemed, and hired an Eighteenth Century costume, for that is what he was wearing—just like the clothes in the Wicked Earl's portrait. The plum-colored coat, you know, and the gold-embroidered waistcoat, the wig and the tasseled cane. To confront the ghost, you see, in its very own image. Or so dear Elizabeth explained to us, when she recovered sufficiently from the shock to do so. She was very much upset—so young of course in those days, and *so* impressionable. She felt it was on her account—to lay the ghost because it might be troubling her—that all these arrangements had been made and the accident had happened."

Vi-vi sat cold, frightened, filled with dread, looking into the two old faces—the heavy square old face of Great-Aunt Honoria, the pinched pink face of Great-Aunt Felicity with its prominent white nose. "You put the scarf there—tied it across at the top of the staircase—and your cousin was *killed*?" But hadn't there been a fuss, she asked. An inquiry, an inquest?

"An inquest, yes. There always has to be, it appears, in a case of sudden death—whoever the parties concerned may be. We spoke to the Chief Constable, of course—a gentleman still, my dear, in those days, whatever upstarts they may have nowadays, risen from the ranks. But he couldn't prevent an inquest, not even for us. However, he kindly arranged for a verdict of Accidental Death, with nothing to suggest what had caused the fall. We had removed the scarf of course, by his advice, and he saw to it that the fancy-dress costume was not mentioned. Indeed, we arranged a story between us that William had always been careless with the cord of his dressing gown, leaving it trailing, and that he must have been coming down to—er—the bathroom."

"You mean to say that the Chief Constable himself—he'd be the head of the police in the county, wouldn't he?—that he hushed the whole thing up?"

"There are advantages to being a Fitzmerrian, my child, as you will find. And then when we told him that it was poor Adelaide who had put the scarf there—

well, he knew her, of course, and understood that she could never be held responsible."

Vi-vi sat for a long time, silent, staring at them, and found to her amazement that her hands were actually trembling. Many months more, she had, to live with these three old women, until her husband came home; and even then, she was bound by a promise never to confide in him. But she would: she was never coming to Fitzmerrian again.

"You will remember your undertaking," said Great-Aunt Honoria, reading her thoughts, "not to mention this to anyone? Not of course that anyone would believe it. It all happened before dear Edward was even born—like everyone else he has always accepted the Coroner's verdict. But should you break your promise—" She lifted her head. "Is that the stable clock striking, Felicity? It must be ten o'clock. I hope that wretched groom is back from his evening off and not making more trouble in the village."

A hint? A threat? Could it be that they *knew*? "You could never get away with it now," said Vi-vi. "As you say, even Chief Constables have changed, these days."

"Get away with—? My dear child, you must be hysterical. You are overtired this evening—been riding too much, perhaps. I must speak to Mario about it—this unfortunate story has upset you." Honoria sat there square and stolid, her heavy hands folded in her lap. "What would there be to 'get away with'? Cousin William had so thoroughly convinced us, hadn't he?—he and Elizabeth together—that we were dealing with a ghost."

But there, repeated Great-Aunt Honoria, the young were *so* impressionable. Poor Elizabeth, for example—she had never seemed quite the same after Cousin William's accident, had she, Felicity? Never again the frisky young filly kicking up her heels where the grass grew greenest. Quite the settled little wife and Countess, she had become.

"As you will also, my dear, I'm sure. You all start off a little skittishly—some of our own dear young people have done the same, and things are even harder for you to adjust to, so far away from your home. But you all settle down. The Family—you don't quite understand it when you're young, but it's a very real thing. The sense of Family, the Honour of one's Family—there is nothing, really, one should stop at to preserve it."

"Not even murder?" said Vi-vi.

"Nothing," said Great-Aunt Honoria.

And the stable clock struck the quarter and Vi-vi got up and left them, creeping away very, very thoughtful—lovely Vi-vi Fitzmerrian, who would henceforth guard her husband's honor and play with fire no more.

Aunt Felicity watched her go. She said, "She'll tell Edward, you know."

"He'll only laugh at it, and by that time the danger will be past. Not that I think badly of the child," said Great-Aunt Honoria, "but it was best to stop it before things went too far."

"Do you think she believes it?"

"She'll never be quite *sure.*" Honoria laughed. "It does seem rather unfair, I must own, on those no longer here to defend themselves. Poor dear William! And poor dear Elizabeth!"

"And that poor dear Chief Constable!" said Felicity, laughing too.

"I don't think they'd mind. They had a great sense of Family, dear Willie, and Elizabeth too. I think they'd be more amused than—resentful?"

"I suppose it really was the dressing gown cord that caused that fall of his?" said Felicity. "How often we warned him, poor foolish fellow, 'Willie dear, you'll trip over that cord one day and break your neck.' "

Aunt Felicity rose to her feet. "I shall go to bed, Honoria. Your imagination is more fertile than mine; I do find these recitals very exhausting." In some ways, she added, wouldn't it really have been simpler to get rid of Mario once and for all?

"Oh, we couldn't do that," said Great-Aunt Honoria. "Grooms are so hard to find these days. And Mario really is an angel with the carriage horses."

The Gallowglass
by David Braly

Sergeant Brian Sullivan set the brake and cut the engine. When he turned off the headlights, everything around the small police car was enveloped in black except for small squares of yellow light from the windows of the house. Some of these yellow squares appeared to go on and off like ship blinkers because of the violent swaying of the tree limbs between them and the car.

"This is the place," Sullivan told his passenger, John McNamara.

"How do you know in this storm?" asked the locksmith. "It's too dark to tell a cottage from a castle."

"It's the only house on this part of the shore."

Sullivan forced open his door against the strong wind. The wind and heavy rain struck him like the blast from a fire hose when he stepped out. The wind's howl was so loud that Sullivan couldn't hear the car door when he slammed it shut.

Sullivan looked out toward the sea. He could not see it nor the beach. All that he could distinguish when he squinted his eyes toward the sea-bred storm were the black forms of nearby trees swaying against a black sky. Everything was black, windy, wet, and caught in the mournful howl of the storm.

Lightning flashed, followed immediately by a tremendous explosion of thunder.

Sullivan pulled up his raincoat collar, then pulled down his visor to secure his cap. He stumbled to the front of the car, then to the opposite side, pushed by the wind.

"Worst storm I've seen in my life!" shouted McNamara when Sullivan reached him.

"Aye!" shouted Sullivan.

Sullivan grabbed McNamara's arm and they hurried toward the house. Its front porch was seventy feet away at the end of an ancient stone walkway that ran past an equally ancient stone wall. From a previous visit—it was too dark to see it now—Sullivan knew that the wall was only a crumbling, moss-laden ruin.

Wind-driven into a trot, Sullivan and McNamara quickly reached the porch. Sullivan carried his lead-encased, five-battery flashlight and McNamara a small metal toolbox filled with the gadgetry of his trade. The porch wasn't shielded from the wind, and horizontal rain continued to pound them.

"I'm surprised they still have lights," said McNamara. "Winds half this strong usually bring down the wires."

Sullivan nodded, then grabbed the brass knocker and pounded.

They waited.

No one answered the door.

Sullivan knocked again. After a half minute, he did it again, as hard as he could. Still no answer.

Sullivan put his hand on the doorknob, tried it. The knob turned.

The sergeant pushed the door open, then glanced at McNamara. McNamara shrugged. Sullivan stepped inside. McNamara followed and shut the door behind him.

"I hope we don't get nabbed for housebreaking," quipped McNamara.

Sullivan ignored the remark. He looked down the narrow, dimly lit hallway that led to the stairs. No one was in sight. Nor could he hear the sounds of human presence over the now muted roar of the storm.

"Hello!" yelled Sullivan. "Is anyone home?"

Seconds later a white-haired woman appeared at the end of the corridor in front of the stairs. "Who's there?" she called.

"Sergeant Sullivan from Bandon, ma'am. Are you the woman who phoned about some trouble?"

"Yes, yes. Please come here."

Sullivan hurried down the hallway, followed closely by McNamara. The ancient oak floorboards creaked at their every step. Old candle holders were screwed into the walls, but the light came from dim overhead electric bulbs, three of which dully illuminated the sixty foot corridor. At the corridor's end, Sullivan found a stairway straight ahead, and another corridor that led away from the main one at a forty-five degree angle. The woman had come from this second corridor.

She was small, plump, and wore glasses. She looked like the sort of pleasant person who was normally happy and optimistic. She had that kind of face. Even now, when she appeared confused and frightened, Sullivan could see that normally she looked happy.

"This way, sergeant." She led them down the second corridor.

"Sorry to have walked in," said Sullivan. "We knocked hard but got no answer."

"I'm glad you came in. I don't know what I'd do if . . . I didn't hear you. . . . This wind."

She stopped abruptly in front of a door. Like the other doors in the huge house, it was tall and wide. The elaborate carving of the oaken woodwork revealed its antiquity.

"Here," she said. "George went in right after dinner.

He's been in there ever since. When I tried to enter, I found the door bolted. George never bolts the door. Never. He has no reason to. We're the only ones here."

Sullivan tried the door. It wouldn't open.

"You said he went in after dinner," said Sullivan. 'What time was that?"

"We finished about eight."

Sullivan glanced at his wristwatch: it was twelve past ten.

Thunder cracked overhead.

"Are you sure he didn't come out and go into some other part of the house without your being aware of it?" Sullivan asked her.

"Quite."

Sullivan tried the door again, and of course it still remained immobile. He nodded to McNamara and stepped back. McNamara walked to the door and knelt before the knob. He placed his toolbox on the floor and opened it.

"This is John McNamara," Sullivan explained. "He's one of the best locksmiths in County Cork—and in any case the only one we could rouse tonight."

McNamara—sifting through his tools—looked up and nodded.

"Pleased to meet both of you," she said. "Forgive my lack of manners. I'm Mrs. Harrogate."

"Quite understandable," said Sullivan. "And everybody knows that the famous Dr. George Harrogate lives here, so naturally I knew who you were."

The lights blinked twice.

"Oh, no," said McNamara. "Not now."

The wind outside continued to howl, but the lights remained on.

"Is this Dr. Harrogate's study?" asked Sullivan.

"Yes," she said. "A library and office. He usually retires here after dinner to work on his current book or his sea camera plans."

Thunder banged overhead; the huge house shook.

"We've lived here for three years," continued Elizabeth Harrogate, "and this is the worst storm we've had."

"I've lived here all of my forty-seven years," said Sullivan, "and it's the worst I've seen."

"I can top you both in years." McNamara was busy worrying a file between the door and jamb. "And I can't remember a storm this bad—ever."

The lights blinked again.

"They're going to go out for sure," said McNamara. "Keep your flashlight handy."

McNamara continued to pry at the bolt. Finally he dropped the file back into his box. He scrounged around in it for a minute and lifted out a thin chisel. He inserted it between the door and jamb near the knob.

"It isn't budging," he said.

The lights flickered four times, then went out, leaving everything as black as the inside of a coal mine.

Sullivan clicked on his flashlight and turned its beam onto McNamara's chisel.

"Trouble in threes," said Elizabeth Harrogate. "First the storm, then George not answering, and now the lights. All I need now is for the ghost to appear."

"Ghost?" said McNamara. "Is this old place haunted?"

"It's supposed to be. But we've never seen the naughty fellow in the three years we've been here. That was part of our attraction to it, too."

Sullivan knew the story of this particular ghost. Supposedly a MacSweeney gallowglass had remained in the area after being wounded at the battle of Kinsale. He had built the original house that formed the center of this building, and had lived to be almost a hundred years old. MacSweeney had taken up arms again in the 1640's despite his advanced years, and all four of his sons had been slain then, fighting under Black Hugh. The story was that MacSweeney had sworn he would kill every Englishman he saw from the day of the oath "till the crack of doom." After he died, and ever since, the house's occupants had claimed that MacSweeney's ghost walked the hallways and stairways at night.

"It isn't coming, not even by a millimeter," said McNamara. "That's one good bolt you have there, Mrs. Harrogate."

"Can you cut it?" asked Sullivan.

"I have a tool that can."

"Well?"

"It's electric."

Sullivan turned to Mrs. Harrogate. "You said that the windows are nailed down?"

"Yes."

"On the inside or the outside?"

"Oh, the outside. Whoever nailed them down didn't want to ruin those beautiful oak frames. I imagine that's why when times became bad enough to secure them they decided to nail them down on the outside instead of installing latches."

"Do you have a claw hammer in the house, Mrs. Harrogate?"

"I've got one," said McNamara. "Shine that light on my box."

Sullivan did, and McNamara rummaged around until he found a small, wooden-handled claw hammer. He handed it to Sullivan.

"Are you going through one of the windows?" asked McNamara.

"Oh, sergeant, it's wet out there."

"The only alternative is to break open the door," said Sullivan. "A door like that wouldn't give easily, and the woodwork near the bolt would be damaged."

Three minutes later, after following Elizabeth Harrogate's directions about how to reach them, a cold and wet Brian Sullivan was standing at the library's multipaned windows. There were two, and as Mrs. Harrogate had said, both were nailed down on the outside. Sullivan tried to lift each in turn, but couldn't. Five nails held down each window.

Sullivan shone his flashlight into the room. The drapes were open and he had as clear a view as the tobacco-stained glass permitted. He could not see anyone inside.

Lightning suddenly lit up everything around him, then thunder boomed.

Sullivan focused the flashlight beam on the nailheads of the one window, then on those of the other. The nailheads holding the first window looked slightly larger, which would give the claw a better grip. Sullivan decided it would be those nails he would pull out.

It took several minutes. The nailheads were flush with the wood, making it difficult to get a hold. He had to dig into the wood with the claw points to get the grip, then press hard against the body of the nail to avoid tearing off the rusty nailhead. The hammer slipped many times, scarring the wood and chewing up the nailheads.

Eventually he managed to remove all five nails.

He lifted the window, which went up surprisingly easily.

Sullivan climbed through rapidly, then lowered the window again. He did it to keep out the rain before he realized that the rain could not enter because the wind was blowing it elsewhere.

The room was warm. Not as warm as Sullivan remembered the corridor's being, but a wonderful improvement on what he'd just left.

He shone the flashlight beam around the room. He aimed it at one object, then another: the rows of books in the bookshelves, the large old wooden desk, the globe, the oil paintings, the wooden filing cabinet, the fireplace, the old wooden radio, and the door.

Sullivan did not see Dr. George Harrogate.

Lightning flashed; thunder shook the house.

In the second that the lightning illuminated the room, Sullivan had seen something odd on the floor.

He aimed his flashlight at it.

A man.

Sullivan swallowed hard.

The man was lying upon the floor, his eyes half-shut in death. He was of medium height and build, had thinning grey hair, wore brown slacks and a blue sweater, and was covered with blood. The blood had also soaked the carpet around him. The cause of the blood was evident: a battleaxe was buried in his chest.

"Sergeant?" called Mrs. Harrogate. "Are you inside yet?"

"Uh, yes. Yes, I am."

"Have you found anything?"

Sullivan turned toward the door. He examined the area near the knob to see how the bolt above it had been slid into place. The bolt itself was large, black, iron. Really solid.

Sullivan turned around, his back to the closed door, and swept the room with his flashlight beam. No one was in the room except the corpse and himself. To be sure, he slowly swept it again and again, overlooking nothing.

Sullivan stepped away from the door. He looked under the desk, up into the fireplace chimney, and around the bookcases. He examined the windows for signs of entry other than his own. There were no hidden spaces, no exits other than the door and windows, and the other window was as firmly nailed down as the one he had entered.

And yet the man who Sullivan recognized from newspaper photographs as Dr. Harrogate lay on the floor with an axe in his chest.

An impossible way to commit suicide. It had to be murder.

But the room had been locked up, sealed from the inside! Not by Dr. Harrogate because his wife had said that he never locked the door.

Lightning flashed, briefly illuminating the eerie room again, sending a chill down Sullivan's spine.

"Sergeant?" called Elizabeth Harrogate again.

"I'll be right out, ma'am."

Sullivan walked over to the corpse. He stood at its feet, quietly examining it in his flashlight beam for almost a minute. There had to be an answer to how Dr. Harrogate died. Had to be.

The battleaxe was embedded deeply. Harrogate could not have wielded the axe with such force upon himself, even if the handle had not been pointing downward. Nor would the axe have come down with enough force to penetrate deeply if Harrogate had tossed it up and let it fall on him. The low ceiling wouldn't allow that much momentum.

Sullivan bent down and rubbed his thumb over the point opposite the embedded blade.

Dull.

It would require another person swinging the axe to bury it that deeply, for surely bones had been broken. Probably it would take another man to do it.

Someone knocked on the door. "Sergeant!" called Elizabeth Harrogate.

"Coming," said Sullivan, still looking down at the body.

He turned and walked to the door. Sullivan threw back the heavy bolt, then opened the door. When he stepped out, he kept Mrs. Harrogate and McNamara back and closed the door behind him.

"What's wrong, sergeant?" asked Elizabeth Harrogate. "It's George, isn't it? Something bad has happened to him."

"Is there any other exit from that room?" asked Sullivan.

"No."

"Any way to bolt that door from out here?" Sullivan asked McNamara.

"None."

"Mrs. Harrogate, I must ask you to show me to your telephone. John, will you watch that door?"

"I'll stand here and lean against it, but I can't 'watch' it."

"That'll be adequate . . . Mrs. Harrogate?"

"Why do you want to use the phone? What's happened?"

"I need to call the station." Yes, thought Sullivan, call 41145 and let them call Dublin. Dublin because part of being a good police officer is knowing when to step aside and when your own colleagues should step aside because they too lack adequate skill to handle an investigation.

"We need a thoroughly trained, thoroughly experienced detective down here."

"Then George is—is dead?"

"I'm sorry, Mrs. Harrogate, but he is. He's been murdered."

Gardai Detective Chief Inspector Phelim Kane arrived in Bandon by motorcar late the following morning, having first flown to Cork from Dublin. Kane was pleased to find that the storm had passed out into the Atlantic and that only broken tree branches and mud puddles remained to recall it to memory.

Kane had never been to Bandon before and found its quaint architecture, its many bridges, and its rolling, very green hills a visual pleasure. He had been told before he flew down that two churches here were the oldest and second oldest Protestant churches in Ireland, and Kane was interested because he himself was a Presbyterian. He felt less of an outsider in Bandon than he normally did in Dublin.

"The house is on the coast," Sullivan was saying as he started the police car. "That's a short drive from here."

Kane settled back to enjoy the passing scenery. Soon

Sullivan began talking about the strange murder and Kane was unable to concentrate upon the view.

Sullivan was a talker.

Kane respected silent people more than habitual talkers, but Sullivan did sound knowledgeable. And he was probably rich in experience. Kane judged his age to be forty-seven. Every inch of him looked the copper: he was tall, although shorter than Kane; muscular, although not as muscular as Kane; weathered, where Kane's broad face was smooth and pale; lean, where Kane was stocky; and his steel grey hair reinforced the impression of strength, where Kane's brown hair conveyed neither strength nor weakness.

"Haunted?" Kane said suddenly.

Sullivan's narrative stopped. "Uh ... what?"

"Did I hear you say that the house is haunted?"

"Aye, that's the local legend, although McNamara, who's older than I, professes never to have heard it. The story is that there was an Irish gallowglass—you know, a mercenary soldier who fought for land grants as his pay—who bore the name of that most illustrious of all gallowglass clans, MacSweeney. He fought at Kinsale—which is just south of here—and remained in the area after the Irish and Spanish forces were defeated. Later he fought for the Stuarts and lost all his sons in the cause. The legend says that this old captain swore he would kill every Englishman he ever met until the crack of doom."

"Yet this was the English stronghold of seventeenth century Ireland," observed Kane. "I would've thought that a gentleman who felt as Mr. MacSweeney did about the English would've moved to a more Irish section of Ireland—if the legend be true."

"Aye. But they say that no Englishman ever called upon him. In any case, the Harrogates tempted fate. Mind you, sir, I don't believe in ghosts myself."

"Why was Dr. Harrogate living in Ireland?" asked Kane.

"Taxes. Not just the usual Englishman seeking a lower rate. Although Dr. Harrogate was a famous scientist and inventor, he earned most of his income by authoring textbooks and science fiction novels."

"And Ireland doesn't tax authors," said Kane.

"Exactly. . . . He should've paid. He would've been able to live in a nice English manor instead of that old hodgepodge and he wouldn't have fallen prey to a petty thief like Stritch."

"Ah, yes, Mr. Stritch. You told me at Cork that you'd arrested someone."

Kane saw a tiny smile of satisfaction form at the corner of Sullivan's lips.

"Aye," said Sullivan. "We questioned the neighbors and one told us that he saw Stritch last night. Pinned him in the beams of his headlights when returning home from Bandon. Stritch was on a bike, he was. Pedaling along the Bandon road while the rain came in a horizontal torrent. He's an old hand at thievery, is Stritch. Mostly petty stuff. Never any violence until now."

"What was taken from the Harrogate house?"

"According to Mrs. Harrogate, the doctor's plans for that new invention are missing from the library. She can't really be sure that they're stolen until she has time to search the entire house, but she says they should have been in that room. We searched it carefully, sir, and found no sign of them."

"Did you find them on Mr. Stritch?" Kane looked out the side window at the ruin of an old cottage. "Or in Stritch's domicile?"

"No. But then we wouldn't, would we? I mean, Harry's a petty thief but he's nae stupid. He would hide them someplace or give them to someone to hide for him."

"I shall look forward to meeting Mr. Stritch."

"Uh, good. . . . Of course, we've got him already.

What we really need is your help in discovering how he did it. That sealed room, I mean."

In a firm but pleasant voice, Kane replied: "I'm here to investigate *all* aspects of the case, sergeant."

"Well, yes, of course. All I meant was—ah! The house will come into view now, sir."

The motorcar came to the end of a long, elevated hedge. When it passed the end of the hedge, an enormous old two story house surrounded by the ruin of a crumbled stone wall came into view. Beyond it was what appeared to be a steep drop bordered by ancient trees, then the ocean.

"It's beautiful, that old white house near the ocean, isn't it?" Sullivan looked at Kane.

But Kane was gazing over his shoulder at the hedge.

Less than a minute later they pulled up in front of the house. Both men got out of the car.

"Looks peaceful now," said Sullivan. "But not last night during that gale."

Kane nodded. He stood beside the car a minute, studying the house. It was surrounded by the crumbling stone wall. The old central portion of the house had been built of stone and mortar, while the two wings were brick. Ivy covered most of the older wall, and the sagging middle of the second floor roof was laden with lichens.

"Where is the library?"

"You can't see it from here. It's on the east side. The house is shaped like a topless square. We are at the bottom of the square, on the south side."

"Which side of the house was hit by the gale winds?"

"The south."

Kane followed Sullivan up the stone path that led to the porch. Sullivan pounded with the brass knocker; a woman answered the door and let them in. The sergeant introduced her as Elizabeth Harrogate.

"Nobody could sneak through this house," observed Kane as the three of them walked to the library.

Every step upon the old, warped oak floor caused a creak. Sometimes even the walls along the narrow corridor creaked, their own peace upset by the movement of the floorboards upon which they rested.

"George always said that the crackling floors and creaking doors were this house's best burglar alarms," said Elizabeth Harrogate. "But you couldn't have heard a gun go off last night."

"Aye," said Sullivan. "The roar of the wind was so loud that the locksmith and I had to housebreak when we got no answer to our knock."

"Really? And you used that big brass knocker on the front door?"

"We did, sir."

Inside the library, Kane meticulously examined every piece of furniture and the bookcases. He used his fist to make soundings of the walls, the floor, and the ceiling. He could not find evidence of any secret passages into the room, and Sullivan assured him that his own measurements precluded that possibility as far as the walls were concerned. Sullivan occasionally pointed out something to Kane, but generally he observed. Mrs. Harrogate watched Kane's inspection in silence.

"What was here?" Kane pointed to hooks projecting from the wall.

"The battleaxe," said Sullivan.

"Was it genuine?"

"Aye. Mrs. Harrogate told us that it was here when her husband and she moved in, so I contacted the widow of the previous owner, Hugh O'Kennedy, and asked about it. Mrs. O'Kennedy said that her husband's father bought the weapon at an antiques auction in Dublin. She wasn't sure of the year, but it was during the Great War."

Kane walked to one of the windows. He tried to lift

it. It wouldn't budge. When he tried the other window it lifted easily, noiselessly. Then he knelt down and examined the floor beneath each window.

"No trace of moisture damage, even from your entrance," Kane said at last. "Of course, if the wind blew from the south and this window faces east, there probably wouldn't be. No rain would blow in. The killer, although perhaps as wet as you were, probably wouldn't leave any trace."

"He couldn't have used the windows," said Sullivan. "The one you opened just now was nailed down as solidly as the one you were unable to lift. I know because I tried them both."

"Yes, well . . . You say the door was bolted from the inside?" asked Kane. Sullivan nodded. "Can it be bolted from the outside?"

"No," said Sullivan. "The locksmith couldn't move the bolt at all. I had to throw it back after I was in the room."

Kane looked at the chimney.

"We examined the chimney thoroughly," volunteered Sullivan. "It's too small for even a child to come down."

"And the fireplace interior? Did you examine it for catches or panels which open or . . . You didn't?"

Kane spent the next half hour examining every potential entry or exit point, starting with the fireplace. Carefully he inspected every brick, the damper, and a blackened metal plate at the rear. He paid special attention to the damper, trying to move its handle in every direction and even pushing and pulling upon it.

Next he examined the heavy wooden door. Kane closed and opened it a score of times, attempted without success to pull its old hinges up, and tried unsuccessfully to open it after the bolt had been slammed home. It was possible only to pull back the bolt on the inside; there was no way to gain entry from the outside. Just as important, there was no way to slide the bolt home while standing outside the door.

Kane went outdoors to inspect the tall, tobacco-stained windows. He looked for footprints below them, but the ground was too stony. Kane picked up and examined the five nails that Sullivan had pulled out of the window stools and dropped onto the ground. He then examined the nailheads in the other window. The five heads were rusty; the wood was weathered, the paint having long ago peeled off. There were no holes in the frame where the other nails had been, and only the five holes in the first window. Kane tested the strength of the panes and the wooden parts. All were firm. Each window was a solid whole.

Kane climbed up an unsteady old wooden ladder to the roof. He examined the portion above the library and found that there was a boundary visible there that was not visible from inside the house. One section of the house ended and another began at the north wall of the library. It took the form of two separate roofs, one a meter higher than the other. Elevated above the newer portion was part of the original wall of stone and mortar. Decades of poor drainage had weakened it, and Kane opened up a hole in the wall simply by pulling out a large stone.

"Sullivan!" he called. "I've found the entrance. Bring up your flashlight."

Sullivan fetched the flashlight from his car and climbed up. His eyes widened when he saw the hole.

"You *have* found it," he said.

Kane clicked on the flashlight and climbed through the hole. He had anticipated encountering spiders and webs, but there were none. The space (one meter high and fifty meters across) was empty. There was no indication that any living thing had ever penetrated the area. The roof above this space, like the ceiling below it and the meter-high walls around it, was strong and solid.

Usually Phelim Kane was verbally restrained, but he left the strange crawl-space sputtering strong words.

The area beneath the library proved inaccessible. Elizabeth Harrogate's statement that the house had neither basement nor cellar was confirmed when Kane's probing proved that the old building had been erected atop a stony ledge as solid as the foundation of a castle.

"That settles it," said Sullivan after he accompanied Kane back to the library. "I don't care if Stritch was near, MacSweeney did it."

Kane smiled. He glanced around the library, hunting for anything strange, anything he had not seen before.

But now it was all familiar.

"I think it best," said Kane, "that I turn my investigation onto a different track, before *I* start thinking that old MacSweeney is guilty."

Kane looked at a nearby chair, but then he glanced down at his filthy tweed suit and remained standing.

"You said that some plans were stolen, sergeant. What plans?"

"The plans for Dr. Harrogate's latest invention. Or at least it would've become his latest invention if he'd ever got it invented. He'd been working on it for a longer period of time than he'd lived in Ireland. I think about five years. He'd given press interviews about it and mentioned it several times when speaking as a guest lecturer at universities."

"So these are not secret plans?"

"It's well known that he's been working on these plans, and from what I understand it is the subject of some amusement in less creative scientific circles on the Continent. But the details of the camera itself are secret."

"He was working on a camera?" asked Kane.

"That's what he called it: the sea camera. Actually,

sir, it's a computer. The idea—as I understand it—was to mount this contraption on an airplane or satellite and point it at large bodies of water. By some combination of photography and computer radar which Dr. Harrogate hadn't perfected, the machine would take a picture of the water and this picture would be free of particles, sand, salt, shadows, and all other obstructions. In other words, the developed photograph would show a lake or sea as being transparent. This will mostly be done by computer, much the same way NASA uses computers to sharpen images in blurred photographs."

"Remarkable. I've never heard anything about it myself, but then I don't follow scientific news very closely. We could finally learn if there is a monster in Loch Ness or if ruins of Atlantis exist in the waters near the Bahamas."

"Actually, Dr. Harrogate wanted to use it to mine ocean mineral deposits."

"Ah. . . . So the sequence of events can be summarized as follows: Last night, during a fierce gale, someone murdered Dr. Harrogate and stole the incomplete plans for an invention that potentially could be worth millions, perhaps billions, of pounds. The killer committed the crime in this room. He—or she—then bolted the door (assuming that it was not already bolted) and left. Except that the only way to leave is the door, and if the killer had used it he or she could not have bolted it. And of course there is the murder weapon. A battleaxe."

"And Harry Stritch."

"Yes, your prisoner Mr. Stritch. A thief, you say."

"Aye. A petty thief with a long record. He's never before committed violence, but obviously Dr. Harrogate walked in on him and took him by surprise."

"Being surprised would explain why he grabbed the battleaxe," said Kane.

"It would. Stritch would never carry a weapon on him. He knows it would go hard with him if we ever caught him carrying one under those or any other circumstances."

"What sort of things has Harry Stritch stolen in the past?"

"Money, jewelry, appliances, that sort."

"Never any scientific plans or other papers?"

Sullivan shook his head.

"Has Stritch ever been here before, to your knowledge?"

"I thought of that myself, especially since the handyman also has a record, as it happens, but Mrs. Harrogate said that she'd never heard of Stritch or seen a man answering his description. I also asked Mrs. O'Kennedy about him during our phone conversation. She said that she did not recall the name, and that she didn't remember ever seeing a man answering his physical description."

"I'll want to interview Harry Stritch," said Kane. "Now about this handyman?"

"Ron Pihilly. He's been the handyman and gardener here for about fifteen years. It's one of many small jobs he has. Comes out one to four times a month, depending on the season. His criminal record is for some burglaries and a confidence scheme he ran years ago. Now he's an informer."

"Steady?"

"Aye. We hear from him about three to four times a year. His information is always good."

"Hmmm. I'll want to interview Pihilly, too. First I wish to talk to Mrs. Harrogate—but not in here."

The two policemen left the library. They found Mrs. Harrogate sitting in the living room, off the corridor near the front door.

The living room was square, large, and had a higher ceiling than other rooms in the house. Its walls were painted blue, although the other walls in the house were papered. The furniture was modern here, and included a large television set.

Kane asked Elizabeth Harrogate to describe what had happened the previous night. While she talked he watched her closely, seeking any irregular eye movements, and listened for every tonal alteration.

"We finished dinner about eight," she said. "George left the dining room immediately, saying that he had work to do in the library."

"Was it normal for him to work there after dinner?" asked Kane.

"Usually he spent an hour there, then came into the living room to watch the telly.... But last night he didn't come, so I went to the library to tell him that one of his favorite programs was on. I found the library door locked. I knew instantly that something was wrong. I knocked and called his name, but he didn't answer. Thinking—hoping—that the noise of the storm had simply drowned out my efforts, I called and knocked much louder. I stood there for perhaps ten minutes pounding and shouting before deciding that it was useless. I already suspected that he was ... But I was thinking of a coronary or stroke, not murder. That's when I phoned the Bandon police. That was about nine thirty, I think."

"Did you notice anyone around the house yesterday?" asked Kane.

"No one. George and I were alone here all day. There were no visitors, and nothing out of the ordinary happened other than that dreadful storm."

"Are you usually at the house?"

"Always."

"Always?"

"Yes," said Mrs. Harrogate. "One or the other of us is always here. I don't believe that the two of us together have been absent from the house more than twice during the last year."

"That clears up one mystery," said Kane. "It explains why the thief didn't wait until you were absent to break in, especially since he would have to keep the house under constant surveillance if he wanted to enter while you were gone."

Kane rose from the sofa and thanked Mrs. Harrogate for her cooperation.

"How long were they married?" Kane asked Sullivan when they were back in the police car.

"About thirty-five years."

"She holds up well. Not a tear."

The statement hung in the air for a long time. Then Sullivan turned the ignition over. "Where to?" he asked.

"First our informer friend Pihilly, then a trip to the jail for a chat with Harry Stritch."

Ron Pihilly lived in a cottage halfway between the Harrogate estate and Bandon. It was a trim little place, painted white, with an old blue Ford motorcar parked in front of the picket fence that surrounded the house. Flowers grew along the cottage walls; the yard was kept up nicely.

Mrs. Pihilly—a short, dumpy woman with suspicious eyes—answered Sullivan's knock. She showed the officers to two armchairs in the living room, then went to fetch her husband. He'd been working out back on someone's cabinet.

Ron Pihilly flashed a broad smile when he entered the room. "Why, sergeant," he said, "what gets you out of bed before noon?"

Sullivan introduced Kane to Pihilly and informed him of Dr. Harrogate's murder.

"He was a fine man, even though English," said the handyman. "He asked only what I could do and paid me my wage promptly, and that's more than I can say for some."

Kane watched Pihilly as he spoke. Pihilly's words sounded sincere and the man looked sincere. But there was something too smooth, too glib about this weathered little man.

"Where were you last night between eight and ten o'clock?" asked Kane.

Pihilly looked surprised by the question but smiled easily. "Now where would I be but in my own home?"

"You were here the whole time?"

"I was."

"Will anyone vouch for that?"

"The wife—at least for the time after eight thirty."

"Why not before eight thirty?"

"She was at her sister's, in Bandon."

"So until eight thirty you cannot prove that you were home?" said Kane.

"That's correct."

"If you were, say, to drive off somewhere in your motorcar and not return until, say, eight twenty, no one would know. There are no neighbors close enough to see your departure or return, nor to hear it."

"That's right. . . . Are you accusing me of killing Dr. Harrogate?"

Kane smiled. "At this time, I'm accusing no one."

"Good. Because I've not killed old Harrogate or anyone else. I've done some dark deeds in my past, stupid things, but that was years ago and I've learned the error of my ways. The sergeant here can tell you that I work closely with the police now. I'm a special consultant to them, and my advice and independent investigations have led to over fifty people going to prison. Right, sergeant?"

"Aye."

"Aye! The way I figure it, inspector, is that I can use the knowledge I acquired when I was operating outside the law to help the law now. I'm a professional crime-fighter just like you. The difference is that you're paid more and your professional status is recognized, whereas I don't receive recognition."

Sullivan grinned. "Do you want recognition, Ronnie?"

Pihilly smiled. "Nae, sergeant, I do not. At least not as long as I'm a consultant instead of an officer."

"Do you hope to become an officer?" asked Kane.

"I have a record. I doubt that I could ever be accepted into the force. Still, I read a great deal of fiction about police detectives and secret agents who were once on the other side. I see no reason why reality should not copy fiction when the idea is good. It's not fair for a man with my knowledge and talent to spend his life as a handyman. I deserve better. And, considering my understanding of crime and espionage—not all of which was gathered in detective and spy novels—I think I would be worth the salary."

"I know where your first-hand knowledge of crime comes from," said Kane. "But what's this about espionage?"

"In my younger days I had my hand in. It concerned subversives here in Ireland. I can't reveal more. Perhaps Dublin can fill you in, if they're willing to declassify the files."

Kane was certain that Pihilly's talk of having been a secret agent for Dublin was nonsense, and he decided not to pursue this part of the conversation.

"When were you last at the Harrogate house?" asked Kane.

"Last week."

"Did you know about the invention Dr. Harrogate was working on? The so-called sea camera?"

"Everybody did. It was a combination camera and computer that was supposed to make water in photographs transparent. The Cork newspaper had a big article on it some months ago because of him living in the country and all. . . . What does the invention have to do with his murder?"

Kane told Pihilly that he had no further questions.

"We'll speak to Stritch after lunch," Kane told Sullivan as they drove back to Bandon. "First, I want to call Dublin."

"To find out if Pihilly ever did intelligence work?"

"Exactly."

"It would be significant if he did," observed Sullivan.

"It would be more significant if he didn't."

Kane did call Dublin and a high-placed friend at the Castle promised to call him back with information within an hour.

Kane had called from Sullivan's small office, and had only just rung off when Sullivan returned. The sergeant looked like a man who had received a shock.

"It's the autopsy," explained Sullivan. "The report isn't ready yet, but they say—unofficially—that Dr. Harrogate wasn't killed by that battleaxe."

"What!"

"They say he died from a blow with a blunt instrument on the back of his head. The axe was probably buried in his chest less than a minute later."

"What sort of blunt instrument?"

"From the impression made upon Harrogate's skull, they're positive that it was a hammer."

"A hammer. No hammer was found in the room, was there?"

"No hammer found, sir."

Kane rose from the desk chair and began pacing the floor of the small office. "A hammer," he said. "A hammer, a hammer, a hammer . . ."

"A handyman would have—"

"So would every adult male in Ireland, sergeant. No, we cannot approach this from that angle. Rather, we must ask for what purpose a thief would carry a hammer? And how would it fit in with the other elements of this case?"

Both men were silent for several minutes, deep in thought.

"We'll go to lunch now—it's already late," said Kane. "At least now we can be certain that Harrogate did not commit suicide."

"Aye, it would be a bit difficult."

"Have one of your men phone the previous owner—what was her name?"

"Mrs. Hugh O'Kennedy is the previous owner's widow."

"Have her phoned and asked if any windows in the house, especially those of the library, were ever regularly opened during the time she lived there. Perhaps to air the old place out now and again."

There was no message from Dublin Castle or from Mrs. O'Kennedy when Kane and Sullivan returned from lunch, so they had Harry Stritch brought into Sullivan's office.

Stritch was a lean dark man with stringy black hair. He walked into the office with his back slightly bent forward, head up, and long arms dangling at his sides. His smile revealed tobacco-stained teeth. Stritch nodded at Sullivan, but examined Kane with suspicion. "Have a seat, Harry," said Sullivan.

Stritch sat down in a chair facing Sullivan's desk. Sullivan was seated behind the desk, Kane beside Stritch in a narrow office chair like Stritch's.

"This is Detective Chief Inspector Kane from Dublin, Harry. He would like to ask you a few questions about last night—if you're willing to answer them without having your attorney present."

"You know I'll answer," said Stritch. "I want to get this mistaken charge dropped so I can get out of this rat-infested icehouse."

Kane looked at Sullivan.

"Cold perhaps, but no rats here," said the sergeant.

Kane turned to Stritch and asked: "Last night why were you riding a bicycle during a storm?"

"I was riding for pleasure earlier in the day. I got caught in the storm, that's all. It struck sudden, it did."

"Did it?" Kane asked Sullivan.

"Aye, but the day was no pleasant one. Cloudy, chilly, and generally uncomfortable. All in all, sir, not a day that anyone would go biking in the country, especially the likes of Harry here."

"But that's what I did," insisted Stritch.

"Do you often bike in the country?" asked Kane.

"Yes."

"No," said Sullivan. "We know Harry's habits, and biking isn't among them. Harry hates exercise. Even if he overcame that aversion for one day, I don't picture him riding down all the way to the coast through a damp chill."

"But I did."

"I don't believe you," said Kane.

"But—"

"Forget it. I don't believe a word you say. If you want to get out of here, Mr. Stritch, I recommend that you tell us the truth."

Stritch said nothing.

"Have you ever been to Harrogate estate?" asked Kane.

"No."

'Ever met Dr. Harrogate?"

"No."

"Ever hear of the invention he was working on, this strange camera-computer?"

"Of course. Everybody around here has."

"You realize that even the incomplete plans for such a device would be worth millions of pounds?"

"I hadn't really thought about it."

"Hadn't you?"

"Why would I? It's none of my business. I mean, well, sure I've got a record. We all know that. But tell me what I would do with a bunch of papers. I mean, well, I know where to fence most property and I sure do know what to do with any cash that might find its way into my hands, but papers . . . I wouldn't know what man or company would be interested in them. And I don't kill people. And if I tried to swing one of them old battleaxes, I would probably end up chopping my own foot off."

There was a sharp knock on the door.

"Come in," said Sullivan.

A constable entered and handed two sheets of paper to the sergeant. "You said that you wanted to know when these messages arrived and they were both just now phoned in, one right after the other," said the constable.

After the constable left, Sullivan read the messages and handed them across his desk to Kane.

The first read: DUBLIN SAYS NO RECORD RONALD PIHILLY EVER EMPLOYED IN ESPIONAGE OR COUNTER-ESPIONAGE WORK BY GARDAI OR ANY OTHER IRISH DEPT.

The second read: MRS. O'KENNEDY SAYS SEVERAL WINDOWS OPENED IN SUMMER TO AIR HOUSE, INCLUDING ONE IN ROOM CURRENTLY USED AS LIBRARY.

Kane stood and handed the messages back to Sullivan.

"Mr. Stritch," said Kane, "I must leave now, so you have only one last chance: why were you riding a bicycle near the Harrogate estate late in the evening during a storm that ranks with the worst in County Cork's history?"

"I told you," snapped Stritch. "I was just caught in the storm during a pleasure ride."

"And would you be willing to take a polygraph test on that question?"

Stritch paled. "I want my attorney," he said.

A constable was called to accompany Stritch back to his cell.

"See what I meant?" Sullivan said to Kane.

"Yes, but I still doubt that Harry Stritch is our man."

"Why?"

"For one thing, I can't believe that he would go all the way on a bicycle to commit a burglary. Especially for papers. He's probably telling the truth when he claims he wouldn't know where to sell them. True,

someone could have hired him to pull the job but . . .
Another thing: the entry—or perhaps the exit—showed
ingenuity on the killer's part. Harry Stritch doesn't impress me as ingenious."

"Then why won't he tell us why he was out riding a
bike during a gale?"

"Probably because he was doing something else ille-
gal or immoral, sergeant. I suggest you release him."

"Release him?" Sullivan stared at Kane incredu-
lously. "Not unless you show me better reason than
you've given, sir!"

Kane smiled. "I think I can, sergeant."

"Until you do, sir, Mr. Harry Stritch remains in our
jail."

"It will necessitate another trip to the Harrogate
house, but I was about to suggest that anyway. We will
need to take along a claw hammer and a very sharp
knife."

Sullivan got the tools, then drove Kane back to the
Harrogate estate.

"We have three suspects," Kane said after they
parked the car and began walking toward the house.
"All three are suspicious."

"Granted," said Sullivan. "Say, aren't we going to
the front porch?"

"No. To the library windows."

"Shouldn't we inform Mrs. Harro—never mind. I
see her watching us from the living room window."

Sullivan and Kane waved at Mrs. Harrogate, and she
nodded back at them.

Kane resumed his explanation: "Harry Stritch is suspicious to us because he is a known thief who was seen
nearby riding a bike during a torrential storm. But that
fact itself casts doubt on his guilt. Would he ride out
here on a bike in order to commit a burglary? He
wouldn't know that Dr. Harrogate would interrupt him.
The burglary could have gone easily, but be discovered
rapidly. That would lead to the early arrival of the po-

lice down the Bandon road—the very road Stritch had
to pedal down in order to return home. Also, he allowed himself to be seen. Notice that I say 'allowed.'
In a storm like last night's he would have seen those
approaching motorcar headlights long before the vehicle's occupants saw him. He had ample time to ride off
the road and lie in the grass or even on the flat earth.
He would never have been spotted at night in such a
storm had he done so."

"Then why didn't he?"

"Obviously because he had nothing to fear—or
thought he had nothing to fear. That means not only that
he had no hammer or stolen papers on him, but that he
had no knowledge of any crime's having been committed. I think it's a safe bet that with Stritch's record he
would have hidden from everyone if he'd known of any
crime hereabouts, whether he had a hand in it or not."

They rounded the corner of the house. The library
windows came into view.

"And Mrs. Harrogate?" said Sullivan.

"My only reason for suspecting her at all was her
lack of emotion when discussing her husband's brutal
murder. There may be many psychological reasons for
that. The most important fact about Mrs. Harrogate is
that she is obviously not strong enough to plant that
heavy battleaxe so deeply into her husband's chest—
even when the man was flat on his back dead at the
time."

They reached the nearer window. "And Pihilly?"
asked Sullivan.

"He has a motorcar and lives nearby. He could have
easily murdered Dr. Harrogate sometime past eight and
driven home before eight thirty with nobody the wiser.
That hedge along the road that prevented me from seeing this house until we approached it could have concealed his motorcar from the Harrogates. Pihilly could
have parked the vehicle on the other side of the hedge
as a precaution, come here on foot, and then hurried

back to the motorcar after he murdered Dr. Harrogate.
Mrs. Harrogate couldn't have heard the motorcar's engine because of the storm. She apparently didn't hear
your motorcar's engine that same night when you
drove it up to the front of her house."

"But if Pihilly did do it, *how* did he do it?"

Kane used the knife to dig around the head of one of
the nails holding down the window. When he had exposed enough of the head, he used the claw hammer to
extract it. The nail was three inches long, bent, and
old.

Kane walked to the next window, followed by Sullivan.

"The central problem in this case has been how the
murderer left the room," said Kane. "He couldn't have
gone out the door, nor up the chimney, and both windows were nailed down."

"Right."

"But then we learned that the battleaxe was used
only to make sure Dr. Harrogate was dead, not to strike
him down. A hammer had been used for that purpose.
And I kept asking myself, why would a burglar bring
a hammer to a house he intended to rob?"

Kane pulled a plastic bag from his pocket containing
the five nails Sullivan had extracted from the window.

"Then," continued Kane, "I remembered that although each of these windows was held down with five
nails, the size of the nailheads had been different. Did
you notice that?"

"Why, yes. The larger size of the nailheads was why
I extracted nails from this window instead of the other.
Firmer hold, you know."

Kane withdrew a nail from the small bag. It was four
inches long, bent, and old.

He held the nail he'd just extracted from the other
window beside it.

"It's longer," observed Sullivan. "But just as old."

"You can draw old nails out of any fence or building
and reuse them. Remember what Mrs. O'Kennedy

said? One library window used to be opened occasionally to air out the room. That means that one of these windows should have slid up easily—and without the nails' being extracted. An old nailhole is always larger than the old nail that fits into it if the nail has been lifted out several times when the board it was driven through was raised."

"But I tried both windows that night. Neither one would budge."

"One should have. Obviously when the window was raised to air the room in former times, the nails were left inside the frame and raised from the ledge at the same time as the window. Then, when the window was lowered again, the nails fitted back into the nailholes of the ledge. It would've ruined the window frame to renail it every time."

"You're saying that someone extracted the five nails in this window the night of the murder and replaced them with five longer nails?" said Sullivan. "Why would he bother?"

"The burglar knew that if the police realized that the window of entry could be opened easily they would suspect someone familiar with the house—someone aware that it would open easily. He therefore wanted the window shut again, and he wanted it shut firmly in such a way that the police would never realize it could have been easily opened before. He decided to renail it. And he decided to use longer nails because the old nails would not hold it down if someone tried to lift it. The longer nails would enter fresh wood, stick solid, and the police would never suspect that they were not the nails that had been there all along."

"An interesting theory."

"More than a theory, I think." Kane turned to the window ledge. He began cutting away at the portion that covered the hole of one of the nails Sullivan had extracted. For several minutes he cut and sliced, until at last he reached the hole itself. He cut away one side of the hole, leaving what looked like a cross-section. "There," he said when he finished. "Examine it carefully."

Sullivan did.

"What do you see?" asked Kane.

"A half section of a nailhole."

"And you see where the metal of the old nail has discolored the wood?"

"Yes. . . . Yes! For about two inches but not for the last inch."

"Precisely. After deducting the one inch of nail that was in the window, there should have been three inches of discoloration in the three inch hole, but instead we have only two inches. The three inch nails that were originally there were pulled out the night of the murder and replaced by four inch nails, but the killer overlooked the fact that metals leave residue on wood when contact exists for many years. The longer nails had no time to leave a trace. Or, if Pihilly did think of it, he was unable to do anything about it and just trusted that we wouldn't catch on."

Sullivan shook his head and chuckled.

"He may have even put cloth over the heads while he was driving them in," continued Kane. "That would muffle the noise and prevent chipping through the rust into a fresh part of the nail, which would've then shone through."

"But that you can't be sure of because I damaged the heads so badly when I extracted the nails," said Sullivan.

"Right."

Kane dropped the two nails into his plastic bag.

"So it's all clear now," said Kane. "Pihilly parked beyond the hedge, walked up to this window, and lifted it. I don't know whether he pulled out the old nails before he entered the house or after he left, but I think it was after he left. That's probably why he bolted the door: so that if Mrs. Harrogate *did* hear the hammering, she wouldn't be able to enter the library and discover what had happened. He may have planned this long ago and waited for a loud storm to arrive before implementing his scheme. In any case, he got in and stole the papers. But Dr. Harrogate came in, perhaps catching him in the act or perhaps not realizing that Pihilly was there. Pihilly hit him with the hammer, then took the battleaxe and used it to make sure that Harrogate was really dead. That indicates to me that Harrogate had seen him. Pihilly went out the window, nailed it down with the longer nails that were also wider and that held the window fast. Of course, Pihilly knew that this particular window could be raised easily because he had often seen it open when he worked here for the O'Kennedys."

"You keep saying Pihilly. But how do you know it was Pihilly?"

"The facts I've mentioned. That and the hammer. The hammer shows planning. I read Pihilly as a much better planner than Stritch."

"Surely there are other reasons?"

"Don't worry about insufficient evidence, sergeant. We'll nab him with the plans when he goes to Dublin. We could get a warrant and search his house, but considering Pihilly's experience and his love of intrigue, I think it's safe to assume that he's found an enormously clever place to hide those papers."

"Why would Pihilly go to Dublin?"

Kane smiled. "That's where the foreign embassies are. I spotted that part of the scheme the moment I heard about the camera and before I knew of Pihilly's involvement. Pihilly's character fitted that part of my conception of events perfectly."

Pihilly paid the taxi driver and walked toward the Soviet embassy.

"May I have a word with you, Mr. Pihilly?"

Pihilly turned and found himself facing Kane.

"Well, well. I haven't seen you in three weeks, detective chief inspector." There was sarcasm in the words.

Two sergeants walked up. "Take Mr. Pihilly down to the station," said Kane. "Search him well."

"What!"

"We have a warrant." To the sergeants: "If the papers aren't on him, search every inch of his hotel room."

The papers weren't on Pihilly.

Nor were they in his hotel room.

Kane was surprised—and embarrassed.

Then he remembered the old Ford that Pihilly had driven up in and had it torn apart.

The papers were there.

Phelim Kane was in his office later that afternoon reviewing a gun smuggling case in Donegal when the call came in from Sergeant Brian Sullivan.

"The espionage angle was really the simplest factor of all," explained Kane. "Consider Pihilly's personality, his character,"

"You mean his love of spy fiction?"

"More than that. He was financially ambitious, yet strapped for cash. He wanted to be a professional, claimed to be a 'police consultant' instead of an informer with a criminal record. Pihilly even claimed that he had once been involved in intelligence work when in fact he had not."

"In other words," said Sullivan, "he wanted to be a cop or a spy."

"And obviously he could never become a cop. Not with a criminal record. But anyone with access to information that a foreign government considers valuable can become a spy."

"And the valuable material was the incomplete plans for a combination camera-computer to make water appear transparent in photographs? Why would the Russians care about the Loch Ness monster or Atlantis? I admit, mineral deposits would—"

"None of the above, sergeant. Such a device would be valuable for another purpose. An obvious use that Dr. Harrogate may never have thought of but that our espionage-loving friend recognized immediately."

There followed a long silence while Sullivan thought. Finally he gave up. "What was it?" he asked.

"Tracking American nuclear submarines."

Fen Hall
by Ruth Rendell

When children paint a picture of a tree they always do the trunk brown. But trees seldom have brown trunks. Birches are silver, beeches pewter color, planes grey and yellow, walnuts black, and the bark of oaks, chestnuts, and sycamores green with lichen. Pringle had never noticed any of this until he came to Fen Hall. After that, once his eyes had been opened and he had seen what things were really like he would have painted trees with bark in different colors, but next term he stopped doing art. It was just as well—he had never been very good at it and perhaps by then he wouldn't have felt like painting trees anyway. Or even looking at them much.

Mr. Liddon met them at the station in an old Volvo estate car. They were loaded down with camping gear, the tent and sleeping bags and cooking pots, and a calor gas burner in case it was too windy to keep a fire going. It had been very windy lately, the summer cool and sunless. Mr. Liddon was Pringle's father's friend and Pringle had met him once before, years ago when he was a little kid, but still it was up to him to introduce the others. He spoke with wary politeness.

"This is John and this is Roger. They're brothers."

Pringle didn't say anything about Roger always being called Hodge. He sensed that Mr. Liddon wouldn't call him Hodge any more than he would call *him* Pringle. He was right.

"Parents well, are they, Peregrine?"

Pringle said yes. He could see a gleam in John's eye that augured teasing to come. Hodge, who was always thinking of his stomach, said:

"Could we stop on the way, Mr. Liddon and buy some food?"

Mr. Liddon cast up his eyes. Pringle could tell he was going to be "one of those" grownups. They all got into the car with their stuff, and a mile or so out of town Mr. Liddon stopped at a self-service shop. He didn't go inside with them, which was just as well. He would only have called what they bought junk food.

Fen Hall turned out to be about seven miles away. They went through a village called Fedgford, and a little way beyond it turned down a lane that passed through a wood.

"That's where you'll have your camp," Mr. Liddon said.

Of necessity, because the lane was no more than a rough track, he was driving slowly. He pointed in among the trees. The wood had a mysterious look as if full of secrets. In the aisles between the trees the light was greenish-gold and misty. There was a muted twittering of birds and a cooing of doves. Pringle began to feel excited. It was nicer than he had expected. A little farther on, the wood petered out into a plantation of tall straight trees with green trunks growing in rows, the ground between them all overgrown with a spiky plant that had a curious prehistoric look to it.

"Those trees are poplars," Mr. Liddon said. You could tell he was a schoolteacher. "They're grown as a crop."

This was a novel idea to Pringle. "What sort of a crop?"

"Twenty-five years after they're planted, they're cut down and used for making matchsticks. If they don't fall down first. We had a couple go over in the gales last winter."

Pringle wasn't listening. He had seen the house. It was like a house in a dream, he thought, though he didn't quite know what he meant by that. Houses he saw in actual dreams were much like his own home or John and Hodge's, suburban Surrey semi-detached. This house, when all the trees were left behind and no twig or leaf or festoon of wild clematis obscured it, stood basking in the sunshine with the confidence of something alive, as if secure in its own perfection. Dark mulberry color, of small Tudor bricks, it had a roof of many irregular planes and gables and a cluster of chimneys like candles. The windows with the sun on them were plates of gold between the mullions. Under the eaves swallows had built their lumpy, sagging nests.

"Leave your stuff in the car. I'll be taking you back up to the wood in ten minutes. Just thought you'd like to get your bearings, see where everything is first. There's the outside tap over there, which you'll use of course. And you'll find a shovel and an axe in there which I rely on you to replace."

It was going to be the biggest house Pringle had ever set foot in—not counting places like Hampton Court and Woburn. Fen Hall. It looked and the name sounded like a house in a book, not real at all. The front door was of oak, studded with iron and set back under a porch that was dark and carved with roses. Mr. Liddon took them in the back way. He took them into a kitchen that was exactly Pringle's idea of the lowest sort of slum.

He was shocked. At first he couldn't see much because it had been bright outside, but he could smell something dank and frowsty. When his vision adjusted, he found they were in a huge room or cavern with two small windows and about four hundred square feet of squalor between them. Islanded were a small white electric oven and a small white fridge. The floor was of brick, very uneven, the walls of irregular green-painted, peeling plaster with a bubbly kind of growth coming through it. Stacks of dirty dishes filled a stone sink of the kind his mother had bought at a sale and made a cactus garden in. The whole place was grossly untidy, with piles of washing lying about. John and Hodge, having taken it all in, were standing there with blank faces and shifting eyes.

Mr. Liddon's manner had changed slightly. He no longer kept up the hectoring tone. While explaining to them that this was where they must come if they needed anything, to the back door, he began a kind of ineffectual tidying up, cramming things into the old wooden cupboards, sweeping crumbs off the table and dropping them into the sink. John said:

"Is it all right for us to have a fire?"

"So long as you're careful. Not if the wind gets up again. I don't have to tell you where the wood is, you'll find it lying about." Mr. Liddon opened a door and called, "Flora!"

A stone-flagged passage could be seen beyond. No one came. Pringle knew Mr. Liddon had a wife, though no children. His parents had told him only that Mr. and Mrs. Liddon had bought a marvelous house in the country a year before and he and a couple of his friends could go and camp in the grounds if they wanted to. Further information he had picked up when they didn't know he was listening. Tony Liddon hadn't had two halfpennies to rub together until his aunt died and left him a bit of money. It couldn't have been much surely. Anyway, he had spent it all on Fen Hall—he had always wanted an old place like that. The upkeep was going to be a drain on him and goodness knows how he would manage.

Pringle hadn't been much interested in all this. Now

it came back to him. Mr. Liddon and his father had
been at university together, but Mr. Liddon hadn't had
a wife then. Pringle had never met the wife and nor
had his parents. Anyway, it was clear they were not to
wait for her. They got back into the car and went to
find a suitable camping site.

It was a relief when Mr. Liddon went away and left
them to it. The obvious place to camp was on the high
ground in a clearing and to make their fire in a hollow
Mr. Liddon said was probably a disused gravel pit. The
sun was low, making long shafts of light that pierced
the groves of birch and crabapple. Mistletoe hung in
the oak trees like green birds' nests. It was warm and
murmurous with flies. John was adept at putting up the
tent and gave them orders.

"Peregrine," he said. "Like a sort of mad bird."

Hodge capered about, his thumbs in his ears and his
hands flapping. "Tweet, tweet, mad bird. His master
chains him up like a dog. Tweet, tweet, birdie!"

"I'd rather be a hunting falcon than Roger the
lodger, the sod," said Pringle and he shoved Hodge and
they both fell over and rolled about grappling on the
ground until John kicked them and told them to stop it
and give a hand, he couldn't do the lot on his own.

It was good in the camp that night, not windy but
still and mild after the bad summer they'd had. They
made a fire and cooked tomato soup and fish fingers
and ate a whole packet of the biscuits called iced bears.
They were in their bags in the tent, John reading the
Observer's Book of Common Insects, Pringle a thriller
set in a Japanese prison camp his parents would have
taken away if they'd known about it, and Hodge listening to his radio, when Mr. Liddon came up with a torch
to check on them.

"Just to see if you're okay. Everything shipshape
and Bristol fashion?"

Pringle thought that an odd thing to say considering
the mess in his own house. Mr. Liddon made a fuss

about the candles they had lit and they promised to put them out, though of course they didn't. It was very silent in the night up there in the wood, the deepest silence Pringle had ever known, a quiet that was somehow heavy, as if a great dark beast had lain down on the wood and quelled every sound beneath under its dense soft fur. He didn't think of this for very long because he was asleep two minutes after they blew the candles out.

Next morning the weather wasn't so nice. It was dull and cool for August. John saw a Brimstone butterfly, which pleased him because the species was getting rarer. They all walked into Fedgford and bought sausages, and then found they hadn't a frying pan. Pringle went down to the house on his own to see if he could borrow one.

Unlike most men, Mr. Liddon would be at home because of the school holidays. Pringle expected to see him working in the garden, which even he could see was a mess. But he wasn't anywhere about. Pringle banged on the back door with his fist—there was neither bell nor knocker—but no one came. The door wasn't locked. He wondered if it would be all right to go in and then he went in.

The mess in the kitchen was rather worse. A large white and tabby cat was on the table eating something it probably shouldn't have been eating out of a paper bag. Pringle had a curious feeling that it would somehow be quite permissible for him to go on into the house. Something told him—though it was not a something based on observation or even guesswork—that Mr. Liddon wasn't in. He went into the passage he had seen the day before through the open door. This led into a large stone-flagged hall. The place was dark with heavy dark beams going up the walls and across the ceilings and it was cold. It smelled damp. The smell was like mushrooms that have been left in a paper bag at the back of the fridge and forgotten. Pringle pushed open a likely looking door, some instinct making him give a warning cough.

The room was enormous, its ceiling all carved beams and cobwebs. Even Pringle could see that the few small bits of furniture in it would have been more suitable for the living room of a bungalow. A woman was standing by the tall, diamond-paned, mullioned window, holding something blue and sparkling up to the light. She was strangely dressed in a long skirt, her hair falling loosely down her back, and she stood so still, gazing at the blue object with both arms raised, that for a moment Pringle had an uneasy feeling she wasn't a woman at all but the ghost of a woman. Then she turned around and smiled.

"Hallo," she said. "Are you one of our campers?"

She was at least as old as Mr. Liddon, but her hair hung down like one of the girls' at school. Her face was pale and not pretty, yet when she smiled it was a wonderful face. Pringle registered that, staring at her. It was a face of radiant, kind sensitivity, though it was to be some years before he could express what he had felt in those terms.

"I'm Pringle," he said, and because he sensed that she would understand, "I'm called Peregrine really, but I get people to call me Pringle."

"I don't blame you. I'd do the same in your place." She had a quiet, unaffected voice. "I'm Flora Liddon. You call me Flora."

He didn't think he could do that and knew he would end up calling her nothing. "I came to see if I could borrow a frying pan."

"Of course you can." She added. "If I can find one." She held the thing in her hand out to him and he saw it was a small glass bottle. "Do you think it's pretty?"

He looked at it doubtfully. It was just a bottle. On the window sill behind her were more bottles, mostly of clear colorless glass but among them dark-green ones with fluted sides.

"There are wonderful things to be found here. You can dig and find rubbish heaps that go back to Elizabethan times. And there was a Roman settlement down by the river. Would you like to see a Roman coin?"

It was black, misshapen, lumpy, with an ugly man's head on it. She showed him a jar of thick bubbly green glass and said it was the best piece of glass she'd found to date. They went out to the kitchen. Finding a frying pan wasn't easy but talking to her was. By the time she had washed up a pan which she had found full of congealed fat, he had told her all about the camp and their walk to Fedgford and what the butcher had said:

"I hope you're going to wash yourselves before you cook my nice clean sausages."

And she told him what a lot needed doing to the house and grounds and how they'd have to do it all themselves because they hadn't much money. She wasn't any good at painting or sewing or gardening or even housework, come to that. Pottering about and looking at things was what she liked. "What is this life, if full of care, we have no time to stand and stare?"

He knew where that came from. W. H. Davies, the Super-tramp. They had done it at school.

"I'd have been a good tramp," she said. "It would have suited me."

The smile radiated her plain face.

They cooked the sausages for lunch and went on an insect-hunting expedition with John. The dragonflies he had promised them down by the river were not to be seen but he found what he said was a caddis, though it looked like a bit of twig to Pringle. Hodge ate five Mars bars during the course of the afternoon. They came upon the white and tabby cat with a mouse in its

jaws. Undeterred by an audience, it bit the mouse in
two and the tiny heart rolled out. Hodge said faintly, "I
think I'm going to be sick," and was. They still resolved to have a cat-watch on the morrow and see how
many mice it caught in a day.

By that time the weather was better. The sun didn't
shine but it had got warmer again. They found the cat
in the poplar plantation, stalking something among the
prehistoric weeds John said were called horse tails.
The poplars had trunks almost as green as grass, and
their leafy tops, very high up there in the pale-blue sky,
made rustling, whispering sounds in the breeze. That
was when Pringle noticed about tree trunks not being
brown. The trunks of the Scotch pines were a clear
pinkish-red, as bright as flowers when for a moment
the sun shone. He pointed this out to the others but
they didn't seem interested.

"You sound like our auntie," said Hodge. "She does
flower arrangements for the church."

"And throws up when she sees a bit of blood, I expect," said Pringle. "It runs in your family."

Hodge lunged at him, and he tripped Hodge up and
they rolled about wrestling among the horse tails. By
four in the afternoon, the cat had caught six mice.
Flora came out and told them the cat's name was
Tabby, which obscurely pleased Pringle. If she had
said Snowflake or Persephone or some other daft name
people called animals he would have felt differently
about her, though he couldn't possibly have said why.
He wouldn't have liked her so much.

A man turned up in a Land Rover as they were making their way back to camp. He said he had been to the
house and knocked but no one seemed to be at home.
Would they give Mr. or Mrs. Liddon a message from
him? His name was Porter, Michael Porter, and he was
an archaeologist in an amateur sort of way—Mr.
Liddon knew all about it—and they were digging in
the lower meadow and they'd come on a dump of

Nineteenth Century stuff. He was going to dig deeper, uncover the next layer, so if Mrs. Liddon was interested in the top now was her chance to have a look.

"Can we as well?" said Pringle.

Porter said they were welcome. No one would be working there next day. He had just heard the weather forecast on his car radio and gale-force winds were promised. Was that their camp up there? Make sure the tent was well anchored down, he said, and he drove off up the lane.

Pringle checked the tent. It seemed firm enough. They got into it and fastened the flap, but they were afraid to light the candles and had John's storm lantern on instead. The wood was silent no longer. The wind made loud sirenlike howls and a rushing, rending sound like canvas being torn. When that happened, the tent flapped and bellied like a sail on a ship at sea. Sometimes the wind stopped altogether and there were a few seconds of silence and calm. Then it came back with a rush and a roar. John was reading Frohawk's *Complete Book of British Butterflies,* Pringle the Japanese prison-camp thriller, and Hodge was trying to listen to his radio. But it wasn't much use, and after a while they put the lantern out and lay in the dark.

About five minutes afterwards there came the strongest gust of wind so far, one of the canvas-tearing gusts but ten times fiercer than the last; and then, from the south of them, down towards the house, a tremendous rending crash.

John said, "I think we'll have to do something." His voice was brisk, but it wasn't quite steady and Pringle knew he was as scared as they were. "We'll have to get out of here."

Pringle put the lantern on again. It was just ten.

"The tent's going to lift off," said Hodge.

Crawling out of his sleeping bag, Pringle was wondering what they ought to do—if it would be all right, or awful, to go down to the house—when the tent flap was pulled open and Mr. Liddon put his head in. He looked cross.

"Come on, the lot of you. You can't stay here. Bring your sleeping bags and we'll find you somewhere in the house for the night."

A note in his voice made it sound as if the storm were their fault. Pringle found his shoes, stuck his feet into them, and rolled up his sleeping bag. John carried the lantern. Mr. Liddon shone his own torch to light their way. In the wood there was shelter but none in the lane and the wind buffeted them as they walked. It was all noise, you couldn't see much, but as they passed the plantation Mr. Liddon swung the light up and Pringle saw what had made the crash. One of the poplars had gone over and was lying on its side with its roots in the air.

For some reason—perhaps because it was just about on this spot that they had met Michael Porter—John remembered the message. Mr. Liddon said okay and thanks. They went into the house through the back door. A tile blew off the roof and crashed onto the path just as the door closed behind them.

There were beds up in the bedrooms but without blankets or sheets on them, and the mattresses were damp. Pringle thought them spooky bedrooms, dirty and draped with spiders' webs, and he wasn't sorry they weren't going to sleep there. There was the same smell of old mushrooms, and a smell of paint as well where Mr. Liddon had started work on a ceiling.

At the end of the passage, looking out of a window, Flora stood in a nightgown with a shawl over it. Pringle, who sometimes read ghost stories, saw her as the Grey Lady of Fen Hall. She was in the dark, the better to see the forked lightning that had begun to leap on the horizon beyond the river.

"I love to watch a storm," she said, turning and smiling at them.

Mr. Liddon had snapped a light on. "Where are these boys to sleep?"

It was as if it didn't concern her. She wasn't unkind but she wasn't involved, either. "Oh, in the drawing room, I should think."

"We have seven bedrooms."

Flora said no more. A long roll of thunder shook the house. Mr. Liddon took them downstairs and through the drawing room into a sort of study, where they helped him make up beds of cushions on the floor. The wind howled round the house and Pringle heard another tile go. He lay in the dark, listening to the storm. The others were asleep, he could tell by their steady breathing. Inside the bag it was quite warm and he felt snug and safe. After a while, he heard Mr. Liddon and Flora quarrelling on the other side of the door.

Pringle's parents quarrelled a lot and he hated it—it was the worst thing in the world, though less bad now than when he was younger. He could only just hear Mr. Liddon and Flora and only disjointed words, abusive and angry on the man's part, indifferent, amused on the woman's, until one sentence rang out clearly. Her voice was penetrating though it was so quiet:

"We want such different things!"

He wished they would stop. And suddenly they did, with the coming of the rain. The rain came, exploded rather, crashing at the windows and on the old sagging depleted roof. It was strange that a sound like that, a loud constant roar, could send you to sleep . . .

She was in the kitchen when he went out there in the morning. John and Hodge slept on, in spite of the bright watery sunshine that streamed through the dirty diamond window panes. A clean world outside, new-washed. Indoors the same chaos, the kitchen with the same smell of fungus and dirty dishcloths, though the windows were open. Flora sat at the table on which sprawled a welter of plates, indefinable garments, bits

of bread and fruit rinds, an open can of cat food. She
was drinking coffee and Tabby lay on her lap.

"There's plenty in the pot if you want some."

She was the first grownup in whose house he had
stayed who didn't ask him how he had slept. Nor was
she going to cook breakfast for him. She told him
where the eggs were and bread and butter. Pringle remembered he still hadn't returned her frying pan,
which might be the only one she had.

He made himself a pile of toast and found a jar of
marmalade. The grass and the paths, he could see
through an open window, were littered with broken bits
of twig and leaf. A cock pheasant strutted across the
shaggy lawn.

"Did the storm damage a lot of things?" he asked.

"I don't know. Tony got up early to look. There may
be more poplars down."

Pringle ate his toast. The cat had begun to purr in an
irregular throbbing way. Her hand kneaded its ears and
neck. She spoke, but not perhaps to Pringle or the cat,
or for them if they cared to hear.

"So many people are like that. The whole of life is
a preparation for life, not living."

Pringle didn't know what to say. He said nothing.
She got up and walked away, still carrying the cat, and
then after a while he heard music coming faintly from
a distant part of the house.

There were two poplars down in the plantation and
each had left a crater four or five feet deep. As they
went up the lane to check on their camp, Pringle and
John and Hodge had a good look at them, their green
trunks laid low, their tangled roots in the air. Apart
from everything having got a bit blown about up at the
camp and the stuff they had left out soaked through,
there was no real damage done. The wood itself had
afforded protection to their tent.

It seemed a good time to return the frying pan. After
that they would have to walk to Fedgford for more

food—unless one of the Liddons offered a lift. It was with an eye to this, Pringle had to admit, that he was taking the pan back.

But Mr. Liddon, never one to waste time, was already at work in the plantation. He had lugged a chain saw up there and was preparing to cut up the poplars where they lay. When he saw them in the lane he came over.

"How did you sleep?"

Pringle said, "Okay, thanks," but Hodge, who had been very resentful about not being given a hot drink or something to eat, muttered that he had been too hungry to sleep. Mr. Liddon took no notice. He seemed jumpy and nervous. He said to Pringle that if they were going to the house would they tell Mrs. Liddon—he never called her Flora to them—that there was what looked like a dump of Victorian glass in the crater where the bigger poplar had stood.

"They must have planted the trees over the top without knowing."

Pringle looked into the crater and sure enough he could see bits of colored glass and a bottleneck and a jug or tankard handle protruding from the tumbled soil. He left the others there, fascinated by the chain saw, and went to take the frying pan back. Flora was in the drawing room, playing records of tinkly piano music. She jumped up, quite excited, when he told her about the bottle dump.

They walked back to the plantation together, Tabby following, walking a little way behind them like a dog. Pringle knew he hadn't a hope of getting that lift now. Mr. Liddon had already got the crown of the big poplar sawn off. In the short time since the storm, its pale silvery-green leaves had begun to wither. John asked if they could have a go with the chain saw but Mr. Liddon said not so likely, did they think he was crazy? And if they wanted to get to the butcher before the shop closed for lunch they had better get going now.

Flora, her long skirt hitched up, had clambered down into the crater. If she had stood up in it, her head and shoulders, perhaps all of her from the waist up, would have come above its rim, for poplars have shallow roots. But she didn't stand up. She squatted down, using her trowel, extracting small glass objects from the leafmold. The chain saw whined, slicing through the top of the poplar trunk. Pringle, watching with the others, had a feeling something was wrong about the way Mr. Liddon was doing it. He didn't know what, though. He could only think of a funny film he had once seen in which a man, sitting on a branch, sawed away at the bit between him and the tree trunk, necessarily falling off himself when the branch fell. But Mr. Liddon wasn't sitting on anything. He was just sawing up a fallen tree from the crown to the bole. The saw sliced through again, making four short logs now as well as the bole.

"Cut along now, you boys," he said. "You don't want to waste the day mooning about here."

Flora looked up and winked at Pringle. It wasn't unkind, just conspiratorial, and she smiled, too, holding up a small glowing red glass bottle for him to see. He and John and Hodge moved slowly off, reluctantly, dawdling because the walk ahead would be boring and long. Through the horse tails, up the bank, looking back when the saw whined again.

But Pringle wasn't actually looking when it happened. None of them was. They had their final look and had begun to trudge up the lane. The sound made them turn, a kind of swishing lurch and then a heavy plopping, sickening, dull crash. They cried out, all three of them, but no one else did, not Flora or Mr. Liddon. Neither of them made a sound.

Mr. Liddon was standing with his arms held out, his mouth open, and his eyes staring. The pile of logs lay beside him, but the tree trunk was gone, sprung-back roots and all, when the last saw cut went through, tipped the balance, and made its base heavier than its top. Pringle put his hand over his mouth and held it there. Hodge, who was nothing more than a fat baby really, had begun to cry. Fearfully, slowly, they converged, all four of them, on the now upright tree under whose roots she lay.

The police came, and a farmer and his son and some men from round about. Between them they got the tree over on its side again, but by then Flora was dead. Perhaps she died as soon as the bole and the mass of roots hit her. Pringle wasn't there to see. Mr. Liddon had put the plantation out of bounds and said they were to stay in camp until someone came to drive them to the station. It was Michael Porter who turned up in the late afternoon and checked they'd got everything packed up and the camp site tidied. He told them Flora was dead. They got to the station in his Land Rover in time to catch the 5:15 for London.

On the way to the station he didn't mention the bottle dump he had told them about. Pringle wondered if Mr. Liddon had ever said anything to Flora about it. All the way home in the train he kept thinking of something odd. The first time he went up the lane to the camp that morning he was sure there hadn't been any glass in the tree crater. He would have seen the gleam of it and he hadn't. He didn't say anything to John and Hodge, though. What would have been the point?

Three years afterwards, Pringle's parents got an invitation to Mr. Liddon's wedding. He was marrying the daughter of a wealthy local builder and the reception was to be at Fen Hall, the house in the wood. Pringle didn't go, being too old now to tag about after his parents. He had gone off trees, anyway.

MYSTERY ANTHOLOGIES

☐ **MURDER ON TRIAL** *13 Courtroom Mysteries By the Masters of Detection*. Attorney and clients, judges and prosecutors, witnesses and victims all meet in this perfect locale for outstanding mystery fiction. Now, subpoenaed from the pages of *Alfred Hitchcock's Mystery Magazine* and *Ellery Queen Mystery Magazine*—with the sole motive of entertaining you—are tales brimming with courtroom drama.
(177215—$4.99)

☐ **ROYAL CRIMES, New Tales of Blue-Bloody Murder, by Robert Barnard, Sharyn McCrumb, H. R. F. Keating, Peter Lovesey, Edward Hoch and 10 others. Edited by Maxim Jakubowski and Martin H. Greenberg**. From necromancy in the reign of Richard II to amorous pussyfooting by recent prime ministers, heavy indeed is the head that wears the crown, especially when trying to figure out whodunit . . . in fifteen brand new stories of murder most royal. (181115—$4.99)

☐ **MURDER FOR MOTHER by Ruth Rendell, Barbara Collins, Billie Sue Mosiman, Bill Crider, J. Madison Davis, Wendy Hornsby, and twelve more.** These eighteen works of short fiction celebrate Mother's Day with a gift of great entertainment . . . a story collection that every mystery-loving mama won't want to miss.
(180364—$4.99)

☐ **MURDER FOR FATHER 20 Mystery Stories by Ruth Rendell, Ed Gorman, Barbara Collins, and 7 More Contemporary Writers of Detective Fiction.** Here are proud papas committing crimes, solving cases, or being role models for dark deeds of retribution, revenge, and of course, murder. (180682—$4.99)

*Prices slightly higher in Canada
